The Spring Revolution

Ondine Book 4

Ebony McKenna

Copyright

Dedication

To the generous, kind-hearted and flat-out crazy people of Brugel, for whom the Soviet Union days never really went away. Good luck with the Venzelemma 2026 Winter Olympics bid, I'm looking forward to the seeing you take the gold medal in Snow Goating.

This quartet of novels could not have been possible without the kind and generous support of my personal history tutor, Shaaron Melvedeir, whose seminal work *The Complete History of Brugel* formed the bedrock of these books. Thanks to Shaaron, these novels are as historically accurate as possible. Thanks to human frailty, any mistakes herein are completely my own.

Enormous thanks to my critique partners in The Saturday Ladies' Bridge Club for their enduring endurance of all things Brugelish.

Finally, for the fans, otherwise known as Ondine's Army of ravenous readers. You are the best.

Acknowledgements

First up, I have to give the biggest hugs and kisses to my sensational husband for reading the earlier drafts of all four Ondine novels, brainstorming ideas, offering suggestions (and hugs when I felt it was all too hard) and generally being there. Mega thanks to Mum, who is a constant source of material both factual and imaginary. She really did run a restaurant with her second husband in the 1980s, which meant that my brother and I were quickly indentured into the family business.

To my brother, who turned those early years of restaurant "slave labour" into a career in hospitality. You're still working in it, I just write about it.

To my dad and step mum, because balance. But also, because they are the classic "public broadcaster" type audience, yet they watched four nights in a row of live commercial television, with all the ads, because I was on a quiz show, and they were being supportive.

Most of all, hugest ever thanks to my fans. Ondine's Army wouldn't exist without you. These books would not exist without you. Thank you by the Brugelish bucket load. (The buckets are bigger in Brugel).

~ Part One ~

~ Chapter One ~

Astral projection. Some people are great at it; others are famous for sleeping right through it.

Take the almost-sixteen-year-old Ondine, for example. By all accounts she's a healthy teen, eats well, has her regular share of bad and good hair days. (Long, wispy and brown. What can you do?) Being our brave and clever heroine, Ondine is blessed with 'resting curious face', which means she often looks like she knows what's going on. Even if she doesn't.

At the end of a long day of working for her family in their pub, *The Duke and Ferret* in downtown Venzelemma, the capital city of Brugel, Ondine is also blessed with the ability to fall asleep three minutes and twenty-two seconds after climbing into bed. She has neither the energy nor the inclination to develop her astral projection abilities. It would involve meditating, then separating her spiritual body from the physical to then journey – along what is known in psychic circles as the astral plane – from her mind and project herself into the mind of another.

Or travel to various psychic destinations.

On the other hand, witch-in-training Melody, who is getting the colour back into her cheeks after the strain of working with the 'bad witch' Mrs Howser, is an absolute natural at astral projection. Melody and Ondine first met at Psychic Summercamp, three seasons (and three books) ago. Melody proved to be so good at astral projection, she can now travel by day or night and visit people who are either asleep or awake – sometimes without the recipient even knowing. Plus, Melody can take people with her on these journeys, visiting places or people anywhere in the city, or indeed any part of Brugel (a country in eastern Europe that has still not won the Eurovision Song Contest).

So it came as no surprise to Ondine, as she was asleep in her bedroom above the family pub, to see and hear Melody appear at the end of her bed one rainy spring evening, sitting as comfortably as you like. Even though it was the middle of the night, and, as previously stated, it was raining. Pouring down, it was. Hitting the windowpanes at a fierce angle and diluting the last of the winter snow into slurry. Exactly the kind of weather you don't want to be out in, even if you do have seriously important news you simply can't wait until morning to tell your friend. Which is again why astral is so useful, as travel along the psychic plane is not weather-dependant.

Melody looked dry and warm as she folded her travelling witch cloak over her knees and smiled her brightest smile for Ondine.

"You're totally owning astral," Ondine said.

Melody beamed with confidence. "Yeah, I am. You're still asleep, by the way."

"Am I?" Ondine made to rub her eyes, like she

normally did upon waking, but found that her arm had turned rubbery and she only mooshed her head into the pillow instead. The pillow felt as soft and squishy as pizza dough. So doughy. So drowsy.

"I have something you need to see," Melody said, holding out her hand. "Come with me."

"Do I have to wake up?" Ondine nibbled at the corner of her pizza dough pillow. Mmmm, yeasty.

"No, it's best if you stay asleep for this," Melody took her limp palm. "This is really important, so hold my hand the whole time and don't fall asleep on me, OK?"

"I thought you said I *was* asleep?"

"You know what I mean."

As Ondine's hand slipped into Melody's, she saw a third person appear in the room.

"Hey there sleepy head," Hamish said, giving her a cheeky wink.

Suddenly Ondine hoped she wasn't having one of *those* dreams where she turned up to school naked. She checked herself and noted, with a relieved sigh, she was completely decent. If you could count her nattiest flannel pyjamas with holes in the armpits decent.

For his part, Hamish was dressed in a dinner suit straight out of a classic 1920s movie. High white collar, black bow tie, tight-fitting dark grey suit and black lapels. Not to mention the creased pants and shiny black shoes. Despite his fancy appearance, Hamish's black hair refused to sit right, with a disarming lock blocking the vision from his cheeky green eyes. ('Cheeky' is so a colour.) He tugged at his neck and complained in his endearing Scottish accent, "I couldnae dream about being at a toga party, could I? That would be far too comfortable."

Curiosity ate her up as Ondine took in the lush sight of him. "What were you dreaming about?"

"My worst nightmare. Ballroom dancing."

For many, ballroom dancing would be the subject of an exciting dream, but considering Hamish's back story, where he was first cursed by Ondine's great-aunt Col to be a ferret when attending her debutante ball, that kind of setting was a source of constant upset.

"Was I in it?" Ondine asked.

Melody made an exaggerated harrumph. "Can you two stop gushing and pay attention? This is serious."

"Yes ma'am," Hamish said.

Ondine nodded.

"Good," Melody said. "Now, prepare yourselves this won't be pretty. Lord Vincent is visiting his mother at the asylum, and we need to make sure he doesn't do anything stupid."[1]

"What sort of stupid?" Ondine wondered.

" Seriously stupid," Melody said. "You know Mrs Howser is being kept at the same facility, don't you?"

"No," Ondine and Hamish said together at the mention of their nemesis and Ondine's former Psychic Summercamp teacher.

"And you know that the vacuum bag with Mrs Howser's soul in it has gone missing, don't you?"[2]

Did they have to be talking about Birgit Howser? The woman had gone from being a batty old pest to becoming Ondine's mortal enemy. Sickened by the revelation that the bag was missing, Ondine looked first to Hamish then to Melody. "I didn't know that."

----

[1] Did you think I'd forgotten about the footnotes? Not a chance! Vincent's mother was previously known as Duchess Kerala. However, now that Kerala's husband Duke Pavla is no more, mostly because Kerala fed him pastries made from poisonous rhubarb leaves, she is known as The Dowager Duchess Kerala.

[2] If none of this is making any sense, it's most likely because you've accidentally picked up the fourth book in the series instead of the first.

Melody's eyebrows shot up. "It's been all over the news! What have you two been doing?"

Something on the floor became incredibly interesting as Ondine studied the carpet at her feet.

"Fine!" Melody tisked loudly and tightened her grip on Ondine's hand. "I'll catch you up to speed on the way there."

"Eh lass? I can't go out like this."

Ondine looked up to see Hamish's spiffy suit had vanished, replaced by the more comfortable toga he'd requested. He even had a laurel wreath on his head, his dark locks brushed forward to fan his temples.

"It doesn't matter what you're wearing, they won't see us anyway, we're astraling," Melody said. "Now stop yammering and pay attention. The future of Brugel is at stake!"

"It sounds so dramatic when she says it like that," Hamish said as he gave Ondine a wink.

The bedroom melted away and they floated out into the dark sky above. It rained all around them, yet they didn't get wet. It wasn't even cold, for which Ondine was incredibly grateful.

"Are we spying on Mrs Howser?" Ondine asked.

"Only a little," Melody said, then quickly added, "I know last time didn't end well, but this will be different."

The 'last time' of which Melody referred, had ended very badly. Mrs Howser had seen straight through Melody's magic and had screamed at them for invading her memories. It was the kind of unpleasant encounter that put Ondine right off wanting any repeats. Now Melody was dragging her straight back to the old witch.

"Is it too late to go back home instead?" Ondine asked.

Melody wore a determined look. "That would be a 'yes'. We're here already."

Looking around, Ondine took in what Melody meant

by 'here'. They were in a hallway with fake wood panelling to mid-height; the rest of the walls were painted in custard-yellow, while the ceiling was half a tone lighter. Prints of cottages in impossibly pretty country settings were set along the walls. Beige linoleum covered the floors and curved the first few centimetres up the walls.

The acrid smell of cold chicken soup hung in the air.

Hamish wrinkled his face. "Are we in hell?"

"No, we're in the Duchess Yelena Memorial Asylum,"[3] Melody said, "If I've done this right . . ." she leaned sharply towards a door, nearly clonking her head on the knocker. Instead of being hurt, the top half of the young witch's body vanished right though the wood, like a ghost. Just as Ondine was about to yelp with the shock of it all and loosen her grip, Melody pulled herself back into the hallway. She gave a smile of triumph and finished the sentence she'd started so much earlier, "... Vincent and his mother are behind that door."

"And they didnae see you, lass?"

A wary look came over Melody. "Course not."

Ondine murmured, "You said that last time."

Ignoring their scepticism, Melody said, "We're going to be very quiet and float in like dust motes. Then we're going to listen in. No talking, OK?"

The instructions had Ondine wrinkling her forehead. "I thought you said they couldn't hear us?"

"They can't, but if you're nattering on I won't be able to hear *them*, got it?" Melody said.

"How about I wait out here?" Ondine asked.

Hamish gave her a lopsided smile and said, "You're not worried it's going to all end badly are ye?"

---

[3] "It's fun to stay at the DYMA," is a popular Brugelish refrain when someone starts acting loopy.

Zhoop, before Ondine could answer, they dissolved through the door and into the room. Here was Vincent sitting beside his mother, the Dowager Duchess Kerala.

At first Ondine didn't recognise the frail woman in the room, her hair thin and balding under a cotton cap. She was missing her shiny dark helmet of hair and ubiquitous glass of wine (which had turned out to be apple juice, just to throw people off the scent of her nefarious activities). The room was a far cry from the splendour of the Autumn Palace at Bellreeve. The linoleum from the hallway continued in here, as did the enforced cheer of the yellow colour scheme.

"If ye weren't crazy already, you soon would be, eh?" Hamish whispered.

Ondine nodded and murmured back, "It's giving me a headache."

Melody glared at Ondine. "Be quiet."

"How come you told me off and not him?"

"Because he's charming and you're not, now hush."

Moving closer, yet also keeping their distance (Ondine still wasn't convinced they'd be unnoticed), the trio floated towards Kerala's bed, where they found the former duchess sitting up, dressed in a mauve, velour tracksuit.

As they were floating above their targets, Hamish tilted his head to indicate a small patch on the top of Vincent's golden head with less hair than the rest. What with Vincent's glossy dark shoes, neat suit, perfect gold tie and golden cufflinks, he looked like a young man with the world at his feet. If only people didn't look too close to the scalp. Ondine snorted at the sight of the lord's future bald patch, which earned her another glare from Melody. With a waft of her hand, Melody sent a trail of glimmering dust through the air towards Vincent, repairing his tresses to their youthful lustre. Ondine threw up in her mouth a little at the sight of Melody's blatant adoration of Vincent.

Honestly, the girl really needed to get out more.

When Ondine turned back to Hamish, her breath hitched. Amongst his lustrous dark locks were three glaringly silver strands of hair. Silver! Alas, they weren't here to worry about Hamish's hair – or Vincent's – they were here to eavesdrop on a conversation. Ondine stopped her noisy internal thoughts and listened in.

"You're doing so well, I knew you would," Kerala said, softly touching Vincent's cheek in a loving gesture.

The former duchess and husband-knocker-offer had certainly changed in strength and tone from the last time Ondine had seen her. Much calmer now. Not ranting and weeping like she had over Duke Pavla's frail body, pretending to care even though she'd been the one slowly poisoning him all that time.

Vincent's voice was calm and low as he spoke. "You're being good here, aren't you? Taking your medicine?"

"I'm a good girl." Kerala became infantile and needy as she spoke. "I've always been good."

Is this it? Is this what they'd come to hear? In that case Melody could have come on her own. "Is this relevant?" Ondine asked.

With a tilt of her head, Melody indicated Vincent's satchel, which he'd left slumped on the floor. Something moved inside it, like a rolling lump of . . . something lumpy.

"I brought you a present," Vincent said, reaching into that very satchel. He withdrew a bulky present, wrapped badly with too much paper and sticky tape. He must have done it himself, in a hurry.

"Is it my birthday?" Kerala asked, her face wobbling in fright. "Did I forget it was my birthday?"

"No, course not," he said. Kerala's smile returned as Vincent pressed the gift into her hands and said, "Can't I give you a present just because?"

"Of course you can. I love presents." Her fingers dug into the paper and battled with the tape to reveal an over-stuffed teddy bear. "Oh I love it!" She squeezed it to her chest, making dust blow out.

Looking to Hamish, Ondine mouthed, "Dust?"

"I have to go now, dear Mother," Vincent said, giving her a dutiful kiss on the forehead. "Be good now and keep taking your medicine."

Kerala hugged the teddy, sending more dust into the room. The teddy's stomach bulged under the pressure.

Vincent turned, lifted his now-empty satchel from the floor and tucked it over his shoulder as he walked out. Melody began to waft after him, tugging Ondine's hand towards the door. "Was that an heirloom or something?" Ondine asked.

"Aye, I was wondering that meself, although it looked new," Hamish added.

"It is new. You haven't worked out what's inside it, have you?" Melody said as she drew them after Vincent.

"A bag of dust . . ." Ondine thought out loud. She would have slapped her forehead in realisation had she not been gripping Hamish and Melody's hands so tightly. "It's the dust bag from the vacuum cleaner. The one with Mrs Howser's soul in it."

"That's why we're such good friends, because you're so smart," Melody said, giving Ondine a wink of encouragement.

"But why would Vincent give Howser's soul to his mother? Are they going to merge or something so Kerala can use Howser's magic to escape the asylum?"

"I doubt it," Melody brought them through another closed door, where they found Vincent crouching down to speak to a woman who was kneeling in the corner of the room. She was curled up, her arms tucked tightly over her knees, rocking slowly back and forth. Her hands were covered in mittens, which were securely fastened to a solid jacket she wore.

Vincent touched the woman's shoulder, but she didn't react to him. With a tug of her hand, Melody pulled Ondine and Hamish around to get a better view, which resulted in them emerging through a connecting wall.

The woman was Mrs Howser. Her face was gaunt and grey, the lines deeper after rapid weight loss and perhaps a nervous breakdown. The shocks kept coming when Mrs Howser opened her eyes to reveal opaque irises and pupils; like dirty windowpanes in need of a good clean.

Cold fear prickled Ondine's spine. They thought they'd been safe from Mrs Howser, after her body and soul separation last month in Savo Plaza. But now only a child-woman and her teddy bear separated the most powerful witch's body from her evil essence.

Thank goodness for the mittens, so she couldn't touch anyone and transfer magic, Ondine thought.

"Now you see why I brought you here," Melody said, pulling them upwards, away from Vincent.

"He won't stop till he's Duke, will he?" Ondine asked, although she already knew the answer, so it was more like a statement.

"Exactly." Melody said. "Which is why I already have a plan. I'm going to work with Vincent and keep an eye on him. Meanwhile, you have to help Anathea any way you can. We'll meet up and share what we know, to make sure Brugel stays on the straight an narrow."

Of course Melody would volunteer to work with Vincent.

"Ma's going to kill me," Ondine said. "She doesn't want any of us having anything more to do with the royal family ever again."

"Then don't tell her," Melody said. "What she doesn't know won't hurt her."

"Aye. It'll be like old times eh lass?" Hamish gave her a wink.

Ondine's lips twisted in thought. Could she really do this? "I thought we'd have a little more time for normal things before everything turned bonkers again."

"Come on." Melody gave her hand an encouraging squeeze. "As if you could ever stay away from the crazy."

~ Chapter Two ~

A few evenings after their frightening astral projection
excursion with Melody, Ondine was doing her level best
to act as if nothing had happened.

She and her family were in their pub, *The Duke and
Ferret*, tapping their feet to music. It was the end of a long
night, and Ondine's clever and talented, and, more
importantly, *in-tune* sisters Marguerite and Cybelle were
performing a classic four-chord pop song for the
customers.

Despite finishing their meals, desserts, coffees and
nightcaps, the customers showed no signs of wanting to
leave. They did, however, show many signs of still being
infected by magic every time Ondine and Hamish showed
public displays of affection. Things like fresh flowers
appearing at the tables, people's hair-styles looking
amazing all night and matronly customers seeming to
grow younger as the hours wore on. It was probably the
reason why the restaurant was so popular, along with the
incredible food and just mentioned entertainment. Extra

money manifested in people's coat pockets as they said yes to a second dessert. Ma didn't seem to be too worried about so much wayward magic, so Ondine decided not to let it worry her either.[4]

Ondine leaned into her beloved Hamish as they watched the singing from the kitchen doorway. They'd had so many adventures and near-heartaches and real heartaches to last a lifetime, which was why moments like these were so precious. Not that Ondine could focus on the negative when her sisters sang so beautifully and her darling Hamish held her close, as he did right now.

"This is pure magic, eh lass?" Hamish murmured into her ear. Then he kissed her earlobe and her knees turned to pâté. "And yer all magic to me."

He said the sweetest things.

Margi and Cybelle finished their song to rapturous applause. In the middle of the room, Margi's husband Thomas set a camera onto a tripod to record their next performance. Since the wedding, Margi's face had taken on an almost angelic glow. Her Cupid's bow lips didn't *fix* the way they used to, as she was nearly always smiling and laughing. Cybelle was as cool and composed as ever, having radically trimmed her perfect bob of hair on one side, giving it a stylish and sharp angle.

"Thank you." Margi beamed as the applause died down. "We'd like to sing something original that we hope you'll like just as much. It's called *You Are My Star*."

Thomas blew her a kiss and pointed to the camera. "It's going straight to BrugelTube."[5]

----

[4] Considering the magic had caused so much mayhem only a season earlier, and continues to cause mayhem around the country if recent news reports are anything to go by, Ma should still be worried about this. As should Ondine and Hamish.

[5] Brugel's answer to Instagram. You thought it was going to be YouTube, but nobody in Brugel knows what that is.

The footage would also end up in Ondine's media studies portfolio for high school. Media studies had become her favourite subject, although she very nearly hadn't enrolled, thanks to her parents wanting to dole out suitable punishment after a particularly awful family altercation back in summer. But since then Ondine had proved she could be good, and the increase in the pub's income meant they could afford the camcorder fees. Now that she had a camera, everyone else loved using it too. Cybelle nodded to Margi and launched into a power ballad, filled with soaring chords that could make you fly. Ondine, battling to focus on her sisters because Hamish was nibbling at the place where her neck met her shoulders, thought the song was amazing. The chorus lifted the room as Margi sang, "*You are my star, and I'm the one who's shining in your light.*"

The room, so raucous only moments earlier, was utterly still as Margi performed. She hit every note and finished the song with tears in her eyes. The restaurant erupted into applause. Margi beamed, her gaze fixed on Thomas, who stepped forward and wrapped his wife in a loving embrace.

Behind her, Ondine heard Hamish sniff. She turned to him, tears pooling in her own eyes. "It's beautiful, isn't it?"

"Aye, the best. I wish I could write a song like that for you."

Ondine wiped his cheek with the pad of her thumb. Uh-oh, more silver strands appeared at his temples. She cupped his face in her hands and turned his face side-to-side, panic rising in her chest.

"What's wrong lass?"

"Hamish, you're turning grey!"

"I'm nawt. Am I?"

Grabbing his hand, she whisked him off to the

bathroom to show him the truth.

"Aww no! I'm getting old!"

"There aren't that many. I can pull them out for you, here." Ondine grabbed a set of tweezers and set to work.

"Awww! Stop it." He batted her away. "I can do it meself."

Out of nowhere, Old Col appeared at the bathroom doorway. "There you are. Ma's looking for you, saying you need to clear plates. What are you doing in here?"

"Getting rid of Hamish's grey hairs," Ondine said.

"Goodness, if I did that, I'd be bald," Old Col patted her head. "Wait a minute, Hamish, how old are you?"

"You tell me?" Hamish pushed the tweezers away. "You're the one that put the staying spell on me."

Old Col's face lost a shade of colour at that, her skin taking on a grey tone.

"What's wrong?" Ondine didn't like where this could be going.

The original spell that Old Col had cast on Hamish to turn him into a ferret had included the phrase, 'and you can stay like that', which was why he hadn't aged since he'd been ferretised. "Is your spell wearing off Col?"

"Maybe it is," she said, with a heavy swallow that made the wattle at her neck wobble. "Anyway, let's not dwell on that, Ma is calling for you. Come along."

As Hamish and Ondine set to clearing the plates in the dining room – Ondine's thoughts swirling over her worries about Hamish ageing – a woman approached Margi and Cybelle and gave them her business card. Ma stepped forward and hugged her daughters, then kissed them multiple times on the cheeks. Josef, their father who usually tended bar, approached with a bottle of *Busuioacă de Bohotinand* and a tray of glasses.[6]

---

[6] Fabulously sweet Romanian wine, which is hugely popular in Brugel because of its peachy overtones, which reminds them of plütz.

Her father, being friendly? *Giving away wine?* Ondine felt sure something momentous had just happened.

"Oh, by the way Hamish, " Old Col said as they returned to the kitchen with arms filled with plates. "Would you do me the honour of partnering me at my abnormal formal?"

"Your what?" Ondine and Hamish said together.

"My do-over debutante ball. We didn't get it right the first time around, so let's try again for old time's sake. It's not until May. Plenty of time to rehearse."

The old dear had such a hopeful look; Ondine didn't want to let her down.

Considering how much her great-aunt had done to help the two of them this past year, it would be a good way to return the favour. Then something zinged in her brain at how fortuitous this could be. It would give Ondine and Hamish the perfect excuse to be out of the house, which meant she could dart off and meet with Duchess Anathea and keep her informed of Vincent's nefarious endeavours. "Of course he'll do it, won't you Hamish?"

"Aye," he agreed with a nod. "It's the least I can do for ye."

"Lovely!" Old Col clapped her papery hands together. "This will be such fun. Oh, and you might want to dye your hair for the big night if the grey keeps sprouting out like that."

✶✶✶

Having spent a significant part of the past three seasons slagging off The Democratic Republic of Slaegal, it is important to note that Brugel's eastern neighbour has a great many good points.[7]

____

[7] Slagging off means saying things that are uncomplimentary. Even if they are true.

It has more beach frontage of The Black Sea than Brugel, and therefore more holiday resorts and a larger tourism industry. However, their claim to have more sunny days per year than Brugel is completely false.[8]

They have the ordinariness of a rectangular flag, although their unique selling point is that theirs is the only completely blue and red flag in the world, being mostly blue with a horizontal slash of red at the top. Their national motto, "Proudly Not Brugel", resonates with the country's longstanding animosity with their neighbour. This sets Slaegal apart from nearby Craviç, whose motto is, "We are so different to Moldova."

Slaegal has more wine production than Brugel and also produces a national car, the Slabi, which doubles in value when filled with petrol. Being further north than Brugel, Slaegal takes longer to wake up from winter. Snow is still thick on the ground in March, when only the bravest yellow crocus and snowdrops dare show their heads.[9]

On this particular not-really-spring afternoon, Lord Vincent of Brugel stood in a Norange street. Standing beside him, the young witch Melody puffed a cloudy breath onto her gloved hands.

"Thank you, for your help with this." Steam poured from his mouth as he spoke.

"Happy to," she said with a nod and another puff of steam.

It had been winter when Melody came into his life; she'd brought sunshine and possibilities with her wherever she went. When she'd offered to assist him just a few days ago, he'd accepted.

---

[8] The Slaegal Tourism Bureau never lets facts get in the way of a good marketing campaign.

[9] Fret not. This is not a Slaegal book, but somebody from Brugel – that would be Lord Vincent – is spending time in Slaegal, and we need to know what he's up to.

The house before them was a big sloppy lump of a thing, which tapered like a badly built sand castle. Behind the windowpanes were hinged timber panels, closed against the cold of winter. Heavy columns stood guard near the front door, with lavish baroque cherubs smiling down upon visitors. On closer inspection, the cherubs weren't smiling but were cracked across the face from centuries of weathering.

"Are you ready?" He asked.

"Let's do this." She answered.

Straightening his shoulders, Vincent rapped on the heavy wooden door. Footsteps echoed, somebody opened the door with a shudder and a pained creak. A butler in faded clothes greeted them, his greasy hair dragged back into a ponytail.

"Please wait here," the butler said, as they stepped into a vestibule. The umbrella stand in the corner lay empty. A panel of wood nailed to the wall would have held their coats, had there been any brass hooks on them.

The butler kept walking.

Vincent shot Melody a confused look. In turn she volleyed him an equally confused one straight back. Were they supposed to stand around or walk after the Butler? Maybe it was a Slaegal thing, where "wait here," really meant, "follow me".

They followed the butler until they came to an atrium in the centre of the house. He then nodded and walked off, leaving them there.

Right in the middle of that atrium grew an impressively huge tree with a trunk so wide it would take four people to hug it. The bark was deeply furrowed like a grandfather's forehead. Its roots twisted in and out of the soil, creating crevices and rolling hills for moss and mushrooms.

Its branches reached outwards in all directions, resting

on the balustrades and balconies of the upper floors. Some branches cut straight through the floors of the upper rooms, or, more correctly, the upper floors had been built to allow the branches to keep growing.

"That's some tree," Melody said as she gazed at the snow-covered glass ceiling. More accurately, a cracked and groaning snow-covered glass ceiling, as the top of the tree pressed hard against its bonds in an effort to break through.

On a soft breath, Vincent said, "I'm sure you're just bursting to tell me about it." Chatting about something innocuous would stop his terrible fear from taking over. The fear that reminded him that every day spent outside Brugel was another day out of the public's sight. Every day allowed his aunt, Anathea, to become entrenched as Duchess. Which was why he was here, doing everything he could to gain support for his claim. His *rightful* claim. Even if it meant going to Slaegal.

"It's a gorgeous custom," Melody beamed. "The oldest families in Norange plant the Slaegalpine trees first, then they build their houses around them. As the tree grows, they add further storeys to the houses. But never taller than the top of the tree."[10]
Vincent looked up and caught a subzero snowflake in his eye. The pine was not simply pressing against the ceiling; it had broken through in places, allowing rain and snow to fall through.

"The tree is hundreds of years old," Melody continued. "So is the house. You would have noticed the different architectural eras on the facade? I mean, of course you did. Because you're so clever."

---

[10] Norange has no height restrictions on buildings per se, but the roof of the house cannot be taller than the tree in the atrium. Therefore if you want a multi-storey house, choose a very tall tree and build your house around it.

He didn't want to dampen her enthusiasm, but there had to be a way to deal with this annoying crush of hers in a non-traumatic way. He just hadn't worked out how yet.

He puffed a warm breath into his chilled hands. If they had to wait any longer, the Zendgraf and Zendgravine would find their visitors turned into frozen ornaments.[11]

Hardly conducive to having top-level meetings if Vincent's mouth froze shut.

Changing his weight from left to right, gently stamping his feet to keep the blood flowing, Vincent exhaled with relief when the butler emerged through a set of double doors with an elderly couple behind him.

"My dear cousin." Vincent held his arms wide to embrace Nikolai, the Zendgraf of Norange. "How good it is to see you again." When they embraced, as family is wont to do, Vincent was gentle so as not to damage his frail-looking relative, who was of the same vintage as his aunt Anathea.

"And I you, cousin-mine." The Zendgraf said.[12] Being closer gave a better view of the *gin blossoms* on his cousin's aged face, no doubt the result of the cold climate breaking his capillaries.[13]

---

[11] The Zendgraf (literal translation; *Sent Lord*) is the lord ruler of Norange, dating back to the days when the Holy Roman Emperor would send his lords to keep an unruly mob in line. The wife of a Zendgraf is a Zendgravine. In modern times it has become a hereditary but purely honorary title. Like Brugel, Slaegal embraced democracy, with mixed results, after the fall of the USSR in 1991.

[12] Vincent and the Zendgraf are only cousins by marriage, and second cousins at that. It's the Zendgravine's mother, Lady Nelly, and Vincent's father, the Late Duke Pavla (may his soul rest in peace) who are first cousins. Don't stress, there won't be a test.

[13] Over many years, exposure to cold weather extremes breaks the capillaries under the skin, leaving the cheeks and nose red and blotch-ridden. The same effect can be achieved much sooner from drinking hard liquor.

The matronly Zendgravine Bohdanna extended her liver-spotted hand, indicating Vincent should bow over it and kiss it. A year ago she would have curtseyed to him. Not that he'd show signs of discomfort here. If cousin Bohdanna wanted her status, she'd get it. He didn't want her respect. Just her money.

"This is Melody, my witch," Vincent said, indicating the young woman at his side.

"I'm honoured," Melody said, making the most courteous of curtseys.

Good girl. He'd thank her later for picking up on the vibe.

"A real witch?" Bohdanna raised one eyebrow. "Or a personal assistant?"

"A little of both," Vincent said, keen to hurry them on to business matters.

"An *asswitchant*," Nikolai said.

Melody nodded but Vincent was pleased to see her keeping her opinions to herself. He opted for, "I like it." *I hate it.*

"Let us honour the tree," Nikolai said, his hand wafting towards the pine. His fingers did not straighten. The long winters must be agony on his arthritis.

Bohdanna linked her arm with her husband.

Must we? "Of course," Vincent said, having no clue what Niko was on about. "When in Norange."[14]

"Be my guest," Nikolai motioned his bent fingers to a wooden pail that sat near the edge of the tree trunk.

What was Vincent meant to do with it? If he asked, he'd be exposing his ignorance of Slaegalese customs. Doing the wrong thing would insult his hosts; a terribly bad way of beginning negotiations.

---

[14] The full idiom is, "When in Norange, do as the Noranges." In other words, when you're in a strange place, do your best to blend in.

The water in the half-full wooden bucket had iced over from the cold. Leaning against it was a long-handled wooden spoon.[15]

Silently moving beside him, Melody touched her ungloved (and cold!) fingers to his wrist. Enough to transfer magic, so he'd know what to do. With a nod to his hosts, he took the spoon by the handle, cracked through the ice and ladled a splash against the base of the tree. Then he turned and offered the spoon to Melody, who did the same. Melody passed the spoon to Bohdanna who gave a gracious nod, as if everything were in order and she was pleased. Not that she smiled, but at least she wasn't grimacing. When it was Nikolai's turn, his hands shook in the effort to hold the wooden spoon, but he managed to water the tree all the same. Then he leaned the long wooden ladle against the bucket.

No, not quite, the spoon slipped. Nikolai grabbed it and straightened it again. It slipped, so he straightened it again. Vincent didn't know where to look. The longer Nikolai took, the more Vincent wondered if he should step in and help. The water's skin began freezing over. Cold drafts clawed at Vincent's sleeves and crept inside his coat. He couldn't feel his feet. Flakes of snow fell between his neck and his collar.

At last Nikolai was satisfied the spoon wasn't going to slip away. The butler directed them to a room off to the side.

In comparison to the atrium, it was a tropical paradise in here.

----

[15] Vincent has always been a bucket-half-full kind of person. Or as they say in Brugel, "You can be sad that a goat has horns, or be grateful the horns have goats on them, and the goats give you milk."

"You honour us with your adherence to our customs," Bohdanna said as she patted the cushion beside her, inviting Vincent to sit. "I feared there was too much Brugel in you."

"I'm adaptable," Vincent said as a wave of relief fell over him. "Would you care to honour one of our customs?"

"I know the one," Nikolai said. "How I miss the taste of plütz."

Melody delved into her witchy satchel and produced a cloth-covered bottle. Then she retrieved a set of shot glasses, also wrapped in cloth to prevent breakage. With a deft flick of the wrist and a metallic crack, Melody opened the plütz and poured four shots; filling the glasses so high they spilled onto the tray below.

They each took a glass, Vincent saluted their continued good health, then they crashed their glasses together so a little of everyone's drinks slopped into the others'.[16]

They downed their drinks in one swallow. When the burn left his throat, Vincent said, "Who needs a roaring fire when you have plütz?"

Nikolai and Bohdanna exchanged glances, then Bohdanna said, "You should have mentioned you were cold. Living so much further north than you, we are quite acclimatised."

Did she have to come right out and say how soft he was? "I am very comfortable," Vincent lied so smoothly he surprised himself. "How are the children, by the way?" Not that he should call them children, when they were all older than he.

----

[16] Crashing cups or glasses together is a tradition as old as time. Less about friendship and more about self-preservation, the act helps the drinkers avoid an early grave. If one or more glasses is tainted with poison, crashing them together slops the toxin into all drinks, thus putting everyone on an equal footing.

A smile plumped Bandanna's cheeks and crinkled her eyes. "They are doing well and send their regards. It is a pity they cannot be here to receive you. Boris is at a manufactory and Kolja is giving a speech at the university."

"Given the choice, I'd much rather be busy than idle," Vincent said.

"Oh yes, we're all terribly busy," Nikolai chimed in.

"In which case." May as well push on. "Now that the formalities are out of the way, perhaps we shall get down to business?"

"Of course," Nikolai sat on the opposite sofa. In doing so, his sleeve caught the doily on the armrest, revealing threadbare stitching beneath. He laughed it off. "That's the trouble with antiques, not built for today's bodies."

"I shall not take up much more of your time," Vincent said. "I'm sure you have been following our family's fortunes, and how my dear Aunt Anathea has taken my birthright from me."

Bohdanna accepted another shot of plütz. "But she is older than you, she has more experience."

"This is true," Vincent agreed. "But she never had the training, nor the *expectation*, of leadership. And now my cousins, Ausra and Viktorija . . . and the other one . . ."

Silence hung over them.

"Electra," Melody prompted.

" . . . That's right, Electra. The three of them are getting way above their station," he said, with what he hoped sounded like concern, not distaste.

"Perhaps," Nikolai looked to Bohdanna. "They are merely showing support for their mother?"

"You are being far too kind," Vincent said, as he too had another shot of plütz.

Finally he was starting to feel warm, although his feet remained stubbornly numb.

"Let's be honest. Anathea's not up to it. We know I am; yet I lack the finances to change things back to the natural order. To draw this to its obvious conclusion, I need money."

~ Chapter Three ~

Vincent's blunt words hung in the air like a poison gas nobody dared breathe.

"I see." Nikolai said at last, taking another shot of plütz.

Vincent waited. Nobody said anything further. Nikolai and Bohdanna didn't make eye contact. Another shot of plütz ought to do it. No, he still couldn't feel his feet.

Enough of this waiting. "It is the truth. I need money from you," he said, hating that he had to state the bleeding obvious.

"Ahh," Nikolai said as he put his glass down. "That could be problematic."

"We cannot be seen to interfere with another sovereign state," Bohdanna said. "Not only would it be unconstitutional, it would be unseemly."

"I understand my request has come at short notice," Vincent said, idly playing with the doily over his armrest. Something caught his eye; the label on the reverse side came from a discount supermarket chain.

"Perhaps we should leave the Zendgraf and Zendgravine to consider your request?" Melody said as she screwed the lid on the plütz bottle and wrapped everything back into her satchel. Either Melody had seen the signs of thrift or she was very, very good at reading his mind. Maybe she'd cast some kind of exposure spell, so Vincent would see for himself why his cousins were so reluctant to help?

"That might be for the best," Nikolai said, rising from his seat.

The handshakes may have been friendly, but the atmosphere was colder than the atrium as Vincent and Melody said their goodbyes.

As they walked through the snow-slurried streets back to their rental car, a late model Slabi, Melody put on her chauffeur's cap and took the wheel.

"Thank you," he said. "For the spell."

"It's as old as dirt. Drink as much as you want and not get drunk. Helps tremendously when you're negotiating. Of course, it has the effect of making the other people drunker, but that's no bad thing."

Vincent scratched his head. "I meant the revealing spell, so I'd see the truth. They can't afford to replace the glass roof, let alone help my cause."

"I didn't cast that kind of spell. But I will at the next one, if you want me to?"

What a mess. What a miserable, cold, waste-of-time mess they were in. "Please do."

Melody negotiated the streets of Norange like a local. Vincent tapped his feet to get the circulation moving. "I guess you didn't need a spell to see how broke they were."

"The Sletto clothing was a dead giveaway."[17]

---

[17] Sletto is Slaegal's own chain of deeply discounted supermarkets, where you not only bring your own bags, you bring your own trolley.

"And the lack of heating," he said, leaning forward and flicking the car's thermostat up so his toes didn't snap off. "I bet Boris isn't visiting a '*manufactory*' or whatever they want to call it. He's probably working in one."

"Manufacturing is very important," Melody said as she negotiated a three-lane roundabout.

Vincent let out some pent-up expletives. Melody held up her palm to stop him. "Your fine words butter no parsnips!"[18]

Vincent dragged his fingers through his hair and looked out at the sleet-filled sky. "Any idea what the hell we're going to do?"

"Oh yes," Melody beamed as she wove their car into another round about streaming with traffic, "I know just the right person, I set up a meeting with him, just in case the Old Money didn't pay out."

"Not another relative without a bean to fry?"

Melody pulled out of the traffic like a rally driver. "You're going to love the next one. He's Babak Balakhan. New money. Emphasis on *money*."

"Good," Vincent felt his body warming, his circulation *circulating* again. "Should I ask where he gets his money from. Because I've never heard of his family."

"It's not *family* money, it's oil money. That's what his wiki says.[19] He also bankrolled Slaegal's last three PopEuroTube entries."[20]

"No taste in music then?"

---

[18] Merely talking about a problem doesn't solve it. You've got to take action.

[19] A user-edited database for all things Eastern European, www.cantbelieve_itsnotwikipedia.br.

[20] Several former Soviet Bloc countries, including Brugel and Slaegal, have formed their own song competition to rival Eurovision. That's not to say they are exclusive, as some countries *cough* Craviç *cough* are known to enter both.

With a rueful smile, Melody turned off the side road and onto timber-lined track that slipped and slopped in the mud. In front of them lay a field of icy brown slush. In the midst of it loomed a three-storey concrete extravaganza, shrouded in scaffolding and tradies.[21] They parked on more mud-set slabs of timber that substituted for a car park. Melody exited first and unfurled a double-width umbrella, then opened Vincent's door. More planks of wood lay in a haphazard pathway towards the door. Every step squelched as the wood sucked and slopped in the thick wet clay. By the time they reached the doorway – there wasn't a door in place yet – Vincent's hair was streaked with damp.

Babak Balakhan himself stood there, a huge smile on his cold-blotched face. "Ah! Beloved guests. Welcome, welcome!"

The man wore a black three-piece suit that only just buttoned up over his ample stomach. His hair was shaved low to disguise how fast it marched backwards. A thick twist of gold sat around his neck, while the fingers on both hands were studded with chunky jewellery. He looked more like the head of security than the head of a household.

Extending his hand in greeting, Vincent said, "Gaspado Balakhan, I am so pleased to meet you."[22]

"So formal, My Lord!" He grabbed Vincent in a bear hug, "Call me Babak. All my friends do. Come, come, let's be out of this miserable weather."

---

[21] Tradies is the non-sexist way to describe tradesmen and women. Women are highly represented amongst Slaegal bricklayers and are amongst the most sought after in the world.
[22] Gaspado is Slaegalese for 'honourable man', which is their equivalent of the western honorific of Mister. Gaspada is 'honourable woman' and is used for both 'Miss' and 'Mrs', because all women are honourable, whether married or not.

"I tell you, never build in a Slaegal winter. Build during the other three weeks of the year. Ha!" Vincent grinned but he refused to guffaw. That would be unseemly. As if to ram home his wealth, Babak's silk tie flipped over in the wind to reveal the logo of a Paris fashion house. No discount Sletto clothing for him.

"Babak, may I introduce my personal witch, Melody?"

"Oh but you are beautiful!" Taking her free hand, Babak kissed it on both the back and the palm.

It pleased Vincent to see Melody blush. If Babak charmed her enough, maybe she'd shift her romantic attentions to him instead.

"Thank you." Melody took her hand back, then fumbled as she closed the umbrella.

"I have never met a witch before," Babak said, "We don't have so many in Slaegal, Brugel is hogging them all."

Inside the construction-zone mansion, they found an atrium. It was completely open to the sky, with no tree. Good, Vincent thought, they wouldn't have to make nice around the trunk while their toes snapped off. Unlike his cousin's crumbling pile, Babak's halls and promenades were dotted with portable oil heaters, throwing a deep red heat out to anyone nearby.

"It's freezing here, you'll catch your deaths," Babak said. "Come into the . . . sitting room, I think they call it. My office is not yet finished. Ah, and we have something for your umbrella. Here, here," he gestured to a series of ornate galvanized hooks.

"But it will drip on the floor." Melody hesitated.

"And the rain won't? Ha! There is such mud and rain, with an open sky and the trucks outside. The cleaners do their best, but eh, what can you do?" He shrugged, as if damaged timber flooring was of no concern. "Come in here, out of the cold."

A servant stepped out of nowhere and opened the

triple-glazed doors that led to an airlock. The next set of doors were triple-glazed as well, and once they were closed behind them, they were warm and draft free.

"Ah! The tree!" Babak said as he looked out the window.

A heavy tray-truck backed into the yard, its fat tyres sinking into the gloop.

"So," Babak said as Melody unpacked her satchel and prepared three shot glasses of plütz. "You are here for money, yes?"

Vincent tried – and failed – to keep his expression neutral as he turned to face his host.

"Ha! I am direct. But then, being direct is a good thing." Babak held his arms wide as if to show off his luxurious house and all that it entailed. His success. From being direct.

"I guess now you've said it, I have to say you're right." Vincent felt the tension ease out of his shoulders. Being direct would save them a lot of messing about.

"Everyone wants money from me." Babak said. "How much, and what will I get in return?"

A quick glance to Melody's contrite face revealed her interference. She must have used some kind of revealing spell in here, to reveal what Babak really wanted. Laid it on a little thick, though.

Swallowing past a rock in his throat, Vincent's mind fast-forwarded through the polite chitchat and shadow boxing he'd prepared, so he could move to the end game. "I honestly don't know. Because it could take a while to –"

"Stop now. The rain may drip here with no end, but my money is no endless winter. You want to be Duke again, yes?"

The man's brain moved fast. Vincent had to adapt. "I have not yet been Duke, so I cannot be Duke *again*. But I will regain my birthright."

There was a steely gleam in Babak's eyes as took his shot glass and held it up. "I shall meet you under the table."[23] Babak downed his drink, so Vincent grabbed his and downed it too. It wouldn't do to let the man drink alone when they were supposed to be . . . what, friends?

Melody refilled their glasses, but did not serve herself.

"You. Drink too," Babak's gaze homed in on Melody. "I don't trust people who don't drink. There is no truth in them."

Melody poured a shot and drank hers, then turned her shot glass upside down for no more refills. "I love the stuff, but I'm also driving. The conditions out there are woeful and I need a clear head."

Babak laughed. "Slaegal weather. What's not to love? More booze."

This was some kind of game where Vincent didn't know the rules. Babak had said he'd give him money, which was a plus. It didn't stop a lump of dread growing in his belly. Not even the plütz could dissolve that.

Babak tilted his hand to the window, to see the tree being unloaded from the truck. "Look at my beautiful pine! Is it not the very best money can buy?"

It surely had to be. The workers wrapped thick hessian strips around the tree base, then fastened a set of hooks on the end of a crane. Slowly, securely, the crane lifted the hundred-or-so-year-old pine into an upright position. It swayed in the wind and the crane driver slowed progress to make sure it didn't crash into the building.

---

[23] The full expression is, "When the gale is blowing and the plütz is flowing, we shall meet under the table." This harks back to the days of poor building regulations, where shoddy workmanship often resulted in collapsed walls and roofs. The safest place to be was with a bottle of plütz (for its warming properties on a cold night) underneath a table (for its stability and security).

"This is a good meeting," Babak slammed his glass down and motioned with his hand for a top up. "I have plenty of money and no respect. You, Vincent, have the name and respect, but no money."

He'd summed it up perfectly.

"So, what's standing in the way of you becoming Duke, eh? Your aunt? Your cousins? That's a lot of people to push aside."

Panic burned the back of Vincent's throat. "No! Not like that." He steadied his hands on his thighs to stop them shaking. "My cousins cannot be harmed. That's not how we're going to play this."

"Play what?" Babak looked offended and pointed to his empty glass as he eyed Melody. "More booze."

Dammit, Vincent felt five times heavier now he'd insulted his host. Scrambling to get things back to where they should be, he said, "The issue is, yes, I do want to be Duke. I'm here because I'm broke. What's in my favour is my people want me to be Duke." Oh dear, was that the plütz talking? Had Melody cast a spell on him too? He was saying far more than he should.

"Good. We are near the truth. You should be in politics, not waiting for relatives to die. More booze." Babak clinked his glass to Vincent's and nodded.

The alcohol wrapped Vincent in a fuzzy blanket. How lucky he was already sitting, because his knees no longer worked.

"What is wrong with your cousins?" Babak asked, while also encouraging Melody to pour more shots.

In the edge of his vision, Vincent could see the pine flying higher outside. Yikes, the plütz had gone straight to his head. But wait, hadn't Melody put that spell on him to stop the effects of alcohol? There was no food in here to space out the drinks. No water to dilute it. He and Babak were sure to meet under the table very soon at this rate.

Wait a minute, his brain said, the tree wasn't flying, it was on the end of the crane, and the crane was lifting it up so it could lower it into the middle of the house and into the atrium.

A sigh of resignation seeped from Vincent. "There's nothing really wrong with them. They're just not . . . not suited, not trained, not sensible. Not anything."

"You should marry the oldest one," Babak said. "Then you'd be Duke."

"No I wouldn't. I'd be consort to an unsuitable Duchess. And they're all broke as well. That and the fact I'm not the cousin-marrying kind."

"I like your truth." Babak upturned his glass to show their drinking session was at an end. "Now here is mine. You have ambition and status, but no resources. I have all the resources in the world, but no respect. Let us make an alliance. My money, for your respect."

"What's the catch?"

Melody shot him a look, like he was forgetting himself. Because he was in the throes of "plütz truth", that terrible affliction that removed the social conventions of keeping your secrets.

"My daughter," Babak said. "She is very much a catch."

Vincent slumped, Melody sat up straighter. The man with all the money reached into his inside suit pocket and pulled out a phone. "Ruslana, come to the sitting room. There's someone here I'd like you to meet."

The room swayed. The woman who walked in took Vincent's breath away. In a really, *really* not-very-good-way at all. The girl had whiter than white blonde hair that sat up a good ten centimetres above her forehead, which then flicked and flailed its way down to mid torso. That wasn't the worst of her.

Despite the cold, she wore a cut-off tank top that came perilously close to showing underboob. But even that wasn't the worst of her.

The mini skirt the width of a seat belt and the platform lace-up boots did her no favours either, but they merely served to highlight the very, *very* worst of her.

Her skin. Her terribly *orange* skin.

The public would have a field day with this orange from Norange.

***

Could that be the sun peeking through the clouds? Ondine peered through her bedroom window at the finger of light hitting the neon dragon that guarded the front door of *On The Fang*, the restaurant across the road from their pub in Venzelemma.

Come on spring, where are you?

Trudging downstairs, Ondine knew a good way to keep warm would be to submerge her arms into a sink of hot soapy water, filled with breakfast's greasy dishes. Which was exactly what her family needed her to do this morning, just as it was every other morning. Yawning her way into the kitchen, she nodded her family greetings. Sure, she was tired, but she couldn't complain. Everyone else had been up a few hours earlier to cook and serve breakfast to the customers.

"Happy birthday darling," Ma said as she landed a kiss on the top of her head.

Sunshine flowed through Ondine. Today was her sixteenth birthday, and her family had remembered. Not that birthdays were as important as name days in Brugel (her parents had botched that spectacularly a couple of months ago) but it was lovely that they were making the effort.

"Thanks Ma," she said with a grin as her mother handed her a card with sixteen cupcakes on the front. Opening it, a twenty-schlip note fell out and she caught it before it could land in the sink and get wet. Then she gave Ma a hug and sat the card up on the high shelf above her.

Da poked his head around the corner. "Has Ma given you our card?"

"Sure did. Thank you very much."

Da moved in for a hug, and excellent excuse for Ondine to put off doing the dishes for a few more minutes. "You're very generous, I'm feeling well-loved."

With a soft chuckle as the hug continued, Da said, "Wouldn't even pretend to forget, not after your name day dramas."

Trust Da to bring that up. "Already forgotten."

Da planted a kiss on her forehead. "When did my baby girl grow so mature?"

It rankled that he called her a baby girl, but she pushed it down. "Don't worry Da, if it makes you feel better, at least I'll never be as old as you."

"Cheeky." He tickled her chin. "Aww come here again, my big baby."

There was no escaping this hug as Da gave her an extra squishy squish.

"Happy birthday Ondi," Cybelle said, jamming a card between their bodies.

"That's from me as well," Margi called out.

It was the excuse Ondine needed to pull back from the suffocating love. Da headed back to the dining room. A five-schlipp note fell out of the card. Seriously, five? She pocketed it all the same and put their homemade card on the shelf, away from soapy, soggy-making water. Hamish sidled up to her. He too had a hand-decorated card, but coming from Hamish it held far more meaning. It proved he'd taken the time to make something for her. As opposed to her sisters, who'd simply been cheap. And he'd put a twenty-schlipp note in there.

"Yer ma said this was all I was allowed to do."

A smile broke over her face. "You're so thoughtful."

"Aye, that's me all over." His immodest words led to utterly immodest kissing, which Ondine took part in fully. They did things to her brain, his kisses. Melted reality and warped time. Made her feel like the most important person in the world.

"All right you two, back to work." That would be Ma, interrupting them as usual.

One more kiss, then she'd stop.

"Come on," Ma said.

Reluctantly (was there any other way to end a kiss?) Ondine pulled away and promised she'd kiss him for longer next time. Hamish left her side and she faced the dishes. Before plunging her hands in, she turned the radio on to bring in some music. She nearly dropped a plate when she heard Margi and Belle's voices, singing on the radio.

"Everyone, listen to this!" she grabbed at the volume up with her sud-soaked hand.

"Turn it up!" That was Cybelle.

"I'm trying."

"Give it here." Not normally pushy, Cybelle nudged Ondine aside and turned the noise to maximum. Margi's clear voice washed over them, but Ondine could tell by the look on Belle's face that she was listening to the music more than the lyrics.

Da stepped back in to the kitchen. "Is that yours?"

"Shush! Yes!" Belle said.

Margi's eyes were huge with delight as she ran to Belle and hugged her. They jumped up and down on the spot.

Pride soared through Ondine for her sisters' success. It was a great song. The kind that would be sung at weddings, or played in the background while loved-up couples had a really good snog. Josef stood there in silence, beaming at his daughters. Then Ma joined in the three-way hug. Henrik and Thomas gave each other high-fives.

When the song finished, Margi and Belle started giggling and jumping up and down again.

"You can turn it down now," Da said, rubbing his ear as the radio played something modern, which Ondine loved but knew her parents hated.

Great-Aunt Col sauntered in to the kitchen and dished herself a plate of scrambled eggs from the stovetop. "Good morning everyone, how are we?"

"Good thanks. Um, Auntie dear," Ma said, as she took the plate away from her and handed her a bowl of stewed fruit instead, "You are welcome to stay any time, as you know, but please don't take food from the mouths of paying guests."

"Yes Young Col," Old Col said as she reached for the tongs beside the hotplate of bacon, "But I need protein this morning. Hamish and I have dance rehearsals."

Dancing lessons would provide the perfect cover for Ondine to sneak off and visit Anathea, so she could warn her about Vincent.

Grabbing a piece of bacon she declared, "I'm coming too."

***

Lord Vincent, Melody, Babak and his citrus-skinned daughter Ruslana stood in the freezing atrium of the Balakhan mansion while an army of landscapers rushed around shifting soil and securing ropes to stabilise the gargantuan pine tree into place. On the floors above, tradies worked in the swirling rain to tie the tree's multiple branches to the balconies. Each kiss of cold wind deepened Vincent's misery. If only Babak hadn't brought his daughter into the negotiations. He needed Brugelish people to like him, but with Ruslana on his arm, the predominant emotion he'd get would be ridicule.

Another worker rushed in and gave Babak a cardboard box.

"Ah! Excellent! Ruslana, you have long nails, help get this open for me."

In a moment they had it open, Babak held the bubble wrap and was popping the little bubbles, while Ruslana held a small wooden pail and matching spoon.

"What is it, Daddy?"

"New tradition. Ah! I have idea," Babak turned to Melody. "Young witch, pour the plütz in here."

"Is that good for pine trees?" Melody raised her brow.

"Eh, we'll mix it with Slaegal rainwater. Best in all of the Europe."

Somebody must have been paying attention, because yet another tradie approached with a metal bucket, filled with clear water. He poured some into the wooden pail, then stepped out of the way. Melody handed the plütz bottle to Babak.

"Excellent. New Slaegal and Brugel tradition. Wonderful combination," Babak said, pouring the plütz in. A peachy aroma floated on the swirling breeze. "Ruslana, Vincent, please do the first honours."

Sickness swirled through Vincent like sleet through the atrium. *Do I have to?* "Thank you, I'd be honoured." Together, he and Ruslana dipped the spoon in the plütz-water and splashed it on the base of the tree. Ruslana's perfume clogged his nostrils as she leaned to his ear. "You're the fourth boy he's tried to marry me off to."

This was beyond ridiculous. "Fourth time lucky then?"

"What's she saying? Eh?" Babak said as they returned the spoon to him.

"Nothing," Ruslana and Vincent said together.

"Ah!" Babak rubbed his hands with glee. "What a great

match. Talking sweet nothings already." Then he grabbed Vincent in a strong hug. "Welcome to the family. You can call me Daddy. Now, what is this on your hand, eh?" The man gripped Vincent and turned his palm back and forth. "Why is it blue? It is not so cold?"

"It's stained. Won't wash off."

"A stain? From what?"

With a shrug of his shoulders and honesty-plütz still in his veins, Vincent said, "My inheritance was . . . scattered. I was retrieving some of it from a hotel in Venzelemma when I was captured and treated to this."

"Your inheritance? So you do have money after all?"

"Accessing it proved difficult."

Babak turned Vincent's hand over again before declaring, "Stain it again, darker now. It will be your symbol. Your rallying cry. Your signature, eh?"

Vincent curled the corners of his mouth down in thought, then found himself nodding in agreement. "Good idea. A blue hand for Brugel."

"It will link you to Elmaree," Melody offered.

All three looked at her like she'd spoken in Craviçian. Melody explained. "Your ancestor, Grand Duchess Elmaree. She had a blue hand, after she broke her writing quill and refused to sign her marriage contract with . . . oh I can't remember who it was. But I remember reading about her blue hand. They called it Elmaree's Stain."

Of course, Elmaree's Stain, Vincent thought back to his history lessons and remembered it now. The *someone* Elmaree had refused to marry was a Slaegalese prince. No point mentioning that while standing here in Slaegal, getting himself shackled to this neon-Slaegalese heiress.

"Ha! Excellent," Babak grabbed Melody in a fierce hug and kissed both her cheeks. "A blue hand, it is a sign from above that Vincent is the true Duke of Brugel. And Ruslana darling will be his Duchess."

~ Chapter Four ~

Weak sunlight tried to warm the ground as Ondine, Hamish and Old Col walked several blocks towards the dance hall. The icy northern winds pinched their ears. Snow landed in Hamish's hair, making him look so much older than he should. Ondine chastised herself for being so superficial. Everyone looked older in winter, what with all the frowning at the dark clouds above.

Turning her collar up, Ondine shuddered. "Is it just me, or is spring not coming at all this year?"

"You're getting soft," Old Col said. "Plenty of winters that wouldn't let go back in my day."

On they trudged, the ballroom coming into view as they reached the next intersection. At first, Ondine thought its stately stonewalls and arched windows had been decorated in that modern 'distressed' look. On closer inspection, it really was a distressed building. Peeling paint curled along the walls and orange streaks ran from the rusty guttering above. The windowsills were no longer flat, having become lumpy and white from decades of bird droppings.

Inside offered no respite from neglect. It was a draughty place that had seen far better days. Leaky stains drizzled down the walls, bubbling the paintwork. The floorboards creaked and whined with age. As did the masses of people assembled for rehearsal.

With a shrug, Old Col said, "It will look better on the night, and you won't hear the floorboards over the music."[24]

Two young instructors wearing shiny black leggings and tank tops, with sheer, fluttery pink skirts tied around their hips swanned in. "Places everyone," one of them said.[25]

The men and women paired up. Slowly. Old Col looked like the spriteliest one there. Ondine giggled at the thought of the big night having defibrillating machines and ambulances on standby.

A tinny stereo filled the air with classical music. One of the instructors stepped forward. "Positions! *Gentlemens*, take your ladies for the Brugelish three-step. Ahhhhhhnnnd *One two three, one two three, one two three, rest! One two three, one two three, one two three, rest! Excellaimont!*" On the instructor went, counting and resting and exclaiming. The dancers, who previously moved at glacial slowness to get up from their chairs, glided around the room like youngsters. The music and movement did, as Col promised, drown most of the creaky floorboard noises out.

"*Excellaimont!*" The woman said again.

---

[24] The ballroom is a short walk from Savo Plaza, which will prove incredibly convenient later on.

[25] If we gave the instructors names, they'd take on far too much importance in the story. In reality they did have names and their parents loved them very much, but they're little more than extras in Ondine's story.

No such word. Ondine promised to look it up later.

"No, no, no!" The lady moved to Hamish and slapped her palms hard on his upper arms. "No touching your ears with your shoulders. Down. Down. That's better."

"With all due respect, it's *noat* like I'm interested in a career in dancing." Hamish shot back.

Where was the heating? Ondine wondered, because the snow from Hamish's hair hadn't thawed.

"That may be," the instructor said, "but your partner here needs her night to be special, and if you are not in the right position, arms held the right way, you will not guide her properly when she twirls."

"Oh," he said.

Watching from the sidelines, Ondine couldn't believe it when the instructor produced a twisted bar, which she slotted over Hamish's shoulders to force him in the shape of a warped scarecrow.

"Are you sure we need that?" Old Col voiced Ondine's thoughts.

The instructor tut-tutted. "He must hold himself like a gentlemans!"

From where Ondine sat, Hamish looked more like a yoked cow than a 'gentlemans'.

"The more you fight it, the deeper the bruises," the instructor said. "Now, off we go again, *one two three, one two three, one two three*, rest!"

All dancing came to a sudden stop as somebody important walked into the ballroom. Instantly everyone made a gracious bow or curtsey to acknowledge Duchess Anathea's entrance. Beside her stood a dashingly well-preserved man, his hair streaked with silver.

"Who's that?" Ondine whispered as Old Col and Hamish stood to the side of the assembly.

"I think it's an old beau," Old Col said, trying to get a better look. "Don't stare, it's rude."

Was he a former husband? Ondine recalled a conversation she'd had with Anathea many months ago, about an ex who had dumped her because they'd only produced girl children. "I thought he left her because he wanted boys?"

"Not that one," Old Col said. "This is the other one; the one her family didn't like. Don't they make a lovely couple?"

In that case, Ondine was happy for Anathea to rekindle an old flame.

"My Lordship, what an honour," the instructor said as she walked towards Brugel's ruling Duchess.

Anathea smiled to all assembled. "How are the rehearsals coming along?"

"Eh, we've jest started," Hamish said with a shrug.

Ondine winced as the bar across his back held him firmly in place.

"Carry on, pretend I am not here," Anathea said as she made her way towards Ondine.

Oh goody, now was her chance to let Anathea know about Vincent. "My Lordship, I have important news I must share with you."

Without turning her head, Duchess Anathea said, "What deeds are being done?"

Keeping her voice low, she said, "Vincent visited his mother in the asylum, giving her a teddy bear which had the bag of vacuum dust that was full of Mrs Howser's spirit. Then he went down the hall and saw the rest of Mrs Howser."

Anathea swallowed, but made no outward sign of distress. "Was the bag of dust checked by anyone first?"

"Probably not, it was inside the teddy bear."

"Oh dear me." Anathea said. "If Mrs Howser's body and soul are reunited, untold damage could be done to Brugel. How far apart are their rooms situated?"

"Not far enough," Ondine said.

From her clutch purse, Anathea produced silvery coins. "Where can the nearest payphone be found?"[26]

"This way, My Lord," Ondine said, a buzz flickering to life inside her. She had done good work today. The Duchess would order increased security at the asylum, somebody would confiscate the teddy filled with the vacuum dust bag and Mrs Howser's soul, and then life would go back to normal.[27]

When they reached the payphone, Anathea slipped her fingers into the coin return to check for loose change.

"Sorry, old habit." Then she picked up the handle, slipped the coins into the slot and dialled a number.

Silently, they waited by Anathea, the dull brrr-brrr of the ringing phone echoing from the receiver. It kept on ringing.

Finally someone picked it up. "Venzelemma Asylum, how may we help you?"

With a quick clear of her throat, Anathea spoke firmly down the line. "This is your Duchess Anathea. I would like to be told of the whereabouts of a Mrs Birgit Howser."

"Yes, of course it's the duchess, and I'm Catherine The Great. Pull the other one why don't you?"

"This is not the response due to me. I will be put through to the management."

Leaning close to Hamish, Ondine whispered, "They think it's a prank call."

---

[26] A payphone is a public telephone secured to a fixed position, which is connected to a landline. A rarity in most modern countries, Brugel's plethora of public phones is a source of national pride. And a reminder of how unreliable mobile phone coverage is.

[27] If Ondine had things her way, this latest adventure would come to a swift conclusion and she could get back to borrowing Da's eyebrow dye to fix Hamish's hair.

"Give me the phone," Old Col interrupted. Then she muttered some incantation down the line about speaking the truth and the voice down the line completely changed.

So did Old Col's expression. And her pallor. "I see. Thank you."

She hung the phone up.

Anathea slipped her fingers in the coin return to see if any change would fall.

Old Col said, "Don't let anybody see how upset we are. We must absolutely behave as if nothing is wrong."

Which meant everything was completely and utterly wrong.

"Let's have it," Hamish said.

Old Col took a breath and squared her shoulders. "Mrs Howser has escaped the asylum."

Gulp, Ondine gulped.

"Oh dear," Anathea said. "Events have quickly been escalated."

***

"What happened back there?" Vincent couldn't get enough air into his lungs as Melody drove them away from the Balakhan estate. How long had they been there? Was it late evening or early morning? He'd lost track of time and geography.

"You got engaged. That's what happened. To an Oompa loompa."

His breath fogged the side window as he leaned his head on the cool glass. "I think maybe you used too much magic and we all said things we should have kept to ourselves."

"I didn't use any." The car took a sharp turn.

Vincent reeled. "You must have."

"I read up on Babak. He is direct and blunt. Pouring

honesty magic on that would be like tipping rocket fuel on a bonfire."

"Not buying it." Residual nausea from his sudden engagement grew into full-blown dry-heaves from Melody's driving. "You used too much magic and it backfired."

"I didn't use any."

"Why not?"

"Because . . . I needed to show you how life would be without me."

A filthy curse leapt from Vincent, followed by, "You put the entire negotiations at risk!"

She gave him a sarcastic look, which meant she wasn't watching the road and fresh panic surged inside him.

Clearly not noticing his discomfort, she kept on talking. "You're such a good negotiator, I knew you'd be all right."

Eyes back on the road, she overtook a slow car and accelerated away.

"Then tell me, oh clever witch, what am I paying you for if you're not using your magic?"

"You're not paying me, you're broke." They veered sharply as she overtook another car.

"Hey! Take it easy!"

She took the next bend sideways.

Vincent's heart crashed into his ribs. "Slow down, you'll kill us both."

In a screech of gravel and slurry, Melody pulled over. She slammed the gear lever into neutral, but kept the engine ticking over.

Grateful she'd stopped, Vincent waited for his panicked pulse to climb down from the roof. "What the hell has gotten into you?"

"You!" She started slapping at him with her palms.

"Ow! Ow!" It didn't hurt so much as annoy. Vincent trapped her hands in his to make her stop. The face looking back was wild. "What is wrong with you?"

"You can't work it out?" Melody cried. "I'm in love with you, you idiot!"

Damn. "Well," not letting go of her hands, he shrugged, "I knew that much. Obviously. Why else would you bother helping me?"

Her face displayed utter puzzlement.

Vincent let out a sigh. "What I don't get is why you are so upset now."

Her cheeks turned a shade of purple and her lips thinned. "Because you're going to marry that . . . that rich *nobody* you only just met."

"Yes. I am going to marry her. Because her father is loaded and I'm broke."

"But . . . you were supposed to get money, not get engaged."

"You didn't think a rich nobody with a weddable daughter would hand over a fortune with no strings?"

In a pathetic voice she said, "You were supposed to marry me!"

He could have sworn he heard something screeching to a halt. Perhaps it was his brain. "Was I? But what could you possibly bring to the marriage?"

A gasp from Melody, then a quick recovery. "I'd bring *me*, you insufferable turd!"

***

"How was rehearsal?" Ma asked the moment they stepped through the door of the family pub. "Ondi love, the sink is full of dishes, there's a good girl."

Best get the bad news out of the way early. Taking a dramatic breath, Ondine said, "Mrs Howser has escaped the asylum."

"Oh yes?"

"I know, it's terrible!" Ondine said. "Wait, what? Why aren't you worried?"

"Should I be?" Ma said as she handed Ondine a pair of washing gloves. "It's not like we're involved in any way, are we?"

Oh, about that –

"Exactly," Ma said, as if to answer her own question. "Back to work, now, there's a good girl."

Several stacks of dishes later, Old Col came sidling up to Ondine and waggled her fingers at the water to suds it up with magic. The finger waggling produced zero results, so Ondine handed her the bottle of detergent instead.

Keeping her voice low, Old Col said, "I've been making some calls. Mrs Howser has turned up at Fort Kluff."

"Why does that sound familiar?"

Handing Ondine another dirty plate, she whispered, "It's where the late Duke Pavla sent Vincent, to drum some sense into him."

Ondine dropped the plate into the water with a sudsy splash. "There's no knowing what damage she could do at a place like that."

"Tell me about it. Especially as the magic is still spreading."

"What magic?" Ondine asked.

That earned her a stern look.

"I mean, what magic in particular?"

Uh oh, Old Col's expression told Ondine she was in for a lecture. She might not have been psychic, but she always knew when she was in trouble.

"My dear girl, do you think your ability to make people's dreams come true has simply gone away?"

"Oh, that."

"Yes that. It doesn't just end when you're not with Hamish. The people who've caught it still have it, and they're still spreading it about as well."

That horrible, plummeting feeling came over Ondine. "But I thought we stopped it when we caught Howser at the snow maze festival, and Anathea trapped her soul in the vacuum bag."

"We did, but it was only temporary. And now her body and soul are back together, and so the spell is working its mad magic all over the place."

"What are you two conspiring about?" Ma said as she arrived with more dirty dishes.

"Nothing," Ondine and Old Col said together, making them both sound incredibly guilty.

It earned a suspicious look from Ma who said, "Nothing? As in 'I have nothing to do with any of that lot any more,' right?"

Mutely, Ondine nodded assent and wished she didn't have to lie to her mother, because it felt so incredibly wrong to be doing that. At the same time, the news that Mrs Howser's horrible magic was working again, and that she was at Fort Kluff, set light to the idea that she had to do something to make it stop.

If only she knew what that *something* should be.

✳✳✳

Driving over the border from Slaegal to Brugel, the roads became bumpier and the potholes harder to avoid. After the seventh jarring thud, Vincent whined, "Someone should fix these miserable roads!"

"At least you're not giving me the silent treatment any more." Came the reply from the uptight young witch in the seat beside him. She'd spent the last forty kilometres fuming away. He could tell by the way her lips were so tightly pressed, and the huffing and the overdramatic sighs. Even her blinking was noisy.

"Take a right here."

"That's not the way to Venzelemma," Melody said.

"We're not going to Venzelemma," he said, then mentally counted down from ten, waiting for her interjection. Which never came. Instead, she kept driving, a tightly wound bundle of fuming upsettedness.

They took the curving road upwards and onwards, the dense pine trees dripping water as the last of the snow melted. The engine whined down into a lower gear as they reached a long hill, until eventually they came to a wide gravel driveway.

Still Melody said nothing. Perhaps she'd put a stewing spell on him or something, to make every tiny thing annoy the tripe out of him. Well, she'd know soon enough where they were, especially when they saw an enormous sign, fixed on a gate next to a security checkpoint.

Fort Kluff.

"What the hell are we doing here?" Melody hit the brake.

"Catching up with an old friend. Keep driving, there's a gatehouse coming up."

When they reached the gatehouse, he showed his old Fort Kluff Cadet identity card to the woman on guard, who welcomed him like an old friend. A *respected* friend. "Welcome home, Sir."

The gates opened, they drove through and Melody found a parking spot near the entrance.

"Right this way, sir," the guard surprised him by opening his door. She gestured towards a security gate near the administration entrance. Here they swiped Vincent's card through an electronic reader, which earned him smiles all round.

"Can you please sign in?" The woman said. At first Vincent thought they were referring to him, but then he noticed Melody behind him. Melody signed the book, showed her driver's licence and they allowed her through.

"She will be in the gymnasium," the guard said to Vincent, then checked her watch, "Although training won't be over for another half hour."

He nodded. "I'll get to see her in action then."

How his chest puffed at the sight of the gymnasium. Dozens of male and female cadets, their heads universally shaved short, snake crawling under a low net, running across obstacle courses, shimmying up ropes, huffing and puffing but otherwise making as little noise as possible.

In the centre of it all stood Mrs Birgit Howser, dressed in a heavy winter witch-cloak with military-style epaulettes on the shoulders. She was quietly directing the human traffic to go harder, faster, stronger. She didn't need to yell; she had them all completely under her control with hand gestures and a baton, conducting the students like an orchestra.

Melody sidled up closer to him. "Are they all . . . ?"

"Cadets, yes."

"But are they under some kind of spell?"

"No, this is normal. I'm sure we'll be treated to the cadets under a spell soon enough." If Vincent had harboured any doubts about Mrs Howser's usefulness, they evaporated as he took in the sight of her working the cadets into the fine fighting specimens he saw before him. And to think, all he'd had to do was remove Mrs Howser's ego from her soul trapped in the dust bag and she'd become so . . . what was the word he was looking for? Useful.

No, even better, she'd become *reliable*.

Mrs Howser spotted him near the doorway and made her way over. "It's an honour to see you, My Lord," She said with a Brugelish military salute. Her right hand came over her heart and formed a fist, while she nodded her head.

Outranking her, Vincent returned the right-fist-over-heart salute but without nodding his head. "You're settling in well here," he said.

"It's good to be using my talents."

Melody did not greet Mrs Howser, nor did the old witch acknowledge the younger.

Noticing they had an observer, the cadets worked harder. The room filled with the noise of their heavy breathing from lifting their knees higher and climbing faster. Vincent smiled and nodded to the class in appreciation. "I like your *talents*. When will they be ready?"

"They will be ready when you give the word, My Lord."

"And what will you be expecting in return?"

"Nothing, my lord. I live to serve."

A wry grin formed, but he fought it back as he watched one cadet fight off three others in hand-to-hand combat. "I recall a time where you demanded a great deal for your services."

"That was a lifetime ago. I find without ego to cloud judgement, one can achieve so much more." Mrs Howser turned to the battle scene playing out before them and said to the cadet under attack, "Finish them off."

The battle was quick and exacting. The cadet's defeated opponents writhed on the ground in various states of distress.

"Has she broken their bones?" Melody whispered to Vincent.

"So what if she has?" He shot back. If he wanted to be Duke, he needed warriors, not wimps.

"Very good," Mrs Howser said to the triumphant cadet. "Come here."

Puffed but steadying her breath, the cadet obeyed, doing her best to salute and show due deference to her betters, despite her exertions. Sweat trickled down the side of her face, which she wiped away with the back of her hand. This revealed her marked palm.

"What is that tattoo?" He asked Mrs Howser.

Mrs Howser smiled and turned to the cadet. "Introduce yourself and answer his Lordship."

"Raluca Pflüg, My Lord. The marks indicate I've reached level six."

She held her hand out, so Vincent could see what looked like a wheel with eight spokes. On closer inspection, he saw the spokes were not quite perfectly aligned, and some were more recently marked than others. She must have earned each stripe as she rose in the ranks.

"Very good," Mrs Howser nodded to Raluca to take her hand back. "You are ready to move to the advanced group."

"If you deem me worthy," she said.

What an obedient student, Vincent thought.

"If you will come this way, My Lord, Ms Pflüg and Melody," Mrs Howser said, indicating a door at the other end of the training hall, "We shall see how the enhanced students are developing."

Enhanced students? He already liked the ones from Raluca's group. All except the moaning trio on the ground, who were only now getting to their feet and saluting, the slackers. The enhanced students were down a hall, up a set of stairs and behind another security door, which Mrs Howser opened with a series of palm and retina scans. Vincent wasn't even aware Brugel had that kind of security.

"Bought it from the Broaku markets," Mrs Howser said, without prompting.[28]

----

[28] The Broaku markets on the Caspian Sea are clandestine traders' yards where excess munitions from government stockpiles are bought and sold. Cash only. No time wasters.

Inside this training hall were twice as many cadets as the last one. This group carried the close-cropped hairstyles of the other cadets, but that was where the similarity ended. These cadets had weapons, built into their bodies. One man who looked barely Vincent's age, had an arm that turned into a whip, slashing at his assailants and tripping them down. The fallen cadets flicked their hands into long knives, slashing chunks off the end of the whip each time it neared them.

Screams filled the air, along with gunfire.

"Is that –?" Melody started.

" –Live ammunition? Yes," Mrs Howser said. "Which is why we need to remain behind this protective glass. Raluca, come here and get a closer look." The old witch took the young cadet by the hand and held it, palm upwards. "You are level seven now. Be careful what you wish for."

Vincent's ears pricked at that last phrase. He didn't want to say anything stupid such as 'what do you mean by that?' but at the same time he couldn't help wondering exactly what Mrs Howser did mean by that.

"The mutating magic is still going, isn't it?" Melody asked. She was standing on the edge of the group, the furthest away from Mrs Howser, yet her words were directed to her former mentor.

Ignoring that they were talking over him, Vincent listened in.

"Of course it is. My separation only placed the spell in hiatus. Now that I'm whole, the magic is fully operational once again."

"But it was just to cause chaos around Ondine and Hamish," Melody said. "Wasn't it?"

"What a waste if that's all it was going to be. Don't you see? Ondine was the stone in the pond, these cadets are the ripples." Mrs Howser waved her hand out in front of her, encompassing the group of mutated cadets. "What we have here is the third wave; the magic feeds their need for obedience and order."

Raluca saluted Mrs Howser. "I am ready." A second set of arms sprouted behind her back, giving her the appearance of Kali, the Hindu goddess of destruction. "I am the end. I am the beginning." Then she charged into the *melée* of cadets and fought all who came near her.

It was impressive viewing. Whips, shields, live bullets, a flamethrower too! Vincent was in heaven. Whoever survived this kind of training would be invincible. The exact kind of soldier he wanted on his team.

The noise of battle rattled the protective glass. Melody took a step back. "We're perfectly safe," Vincent assured her.

"What makes you so sure they're on our side?" Melody didn't have to keep her voice low, not with the cacophony around them. All the same, Vincent only just heard it.

"You make a good point." He turned to Mrs Howser and asked, "Birgit, how do we know the cadets will remain loyal to me?"

"They have sworn an oath, but even so, you shall know their loyalty through their actions." Looking over the crowd, Mrs Howser singled out Raluca, battling four assailants at once, cracking skulls together with her multiple arms. "Cadets, stop now!"

All fell silent. Mrs Howser's smile widened. "Cadet Pflüg, confirm your fidelity to Vincent."

At once, Raluca fell to one knee and spoke with the deepest sincerity. "Lord Vincent is the true born Duke of Brugel. He has my lifelong allegiance, in word and deed."

Another cadet sprang forth to attack Raluca while she knelt. Raluca rolled with the attacker's weight and quickly dispatched her with a resounding thud into the mats, her four arms pinning the other woman down. The other woman's legs turned into octopus tentacles, wrapping around Raluca, ripping and whipping her face and body. With magical speed, Raluca knotted the octopus legs into pretzels.

"Show me your loyalty," Mrs Howser said. "Finish her off."

Another cadet stepped forward. "Please, no! She could be useful."

"Raluca?" Mrs Howser raised her brows.

With a slash of something sharp through the air, Raluca grabbed a sabre from the shield of a nearby cadet and stabbed it through her octopus attacker's heart.

Melody gasped and ran from the room.

Stunned by the savagery, Vincent couldn't fault the effectiveness of Mrs Howser's training.

"Clean the training area, then you may take breakfast." Mrs Howser said. Then she turned to Vincent. "I hope you never have need to question my methods, or my cadets again. They are precious to me and I would hate to lose another one."

~ Chapter Five ~

There were noises of family waking up and getting on with work in the pub, but Ondine refused to join them, pulling the covers over her head and chasing a few more minutes of sleep. She'd just had a particularly thrilling dream about spending private time with Hamish. Then Melody had to go and ruin it by astrally projecting into her space.

Wait, Melody was here. Or at least, astrally here. That meant something important must have happened.

"Ondine, I have to be quick," Melody said. "Something important has happened."

"Why isn't Hamish here?" Much to Ondine's embarrassment, this was her first thought. She quickly added. "Are you all right?"

"No, I'm not." Melody said, joining her cold hand to Ondine's warm sleepy one. "I'm at Fort Kluff. Mrs Howser is back in one piece and the mutating magic is worse than ever. I've just seen her training cadets. They're unstoppable. It's the same magic she put on you and Hamish. It didn't end when we took her soul away; it only took a rest. Now she's back and the magic is more powerful than ever."

Images of mutated army trainees filled Ondine's sleepy vision. One of them had four arms, taking on all comers and sending them flying. Then Vincent asked Mrs Howser something about loyalty and the scene played out in all its horrible detail, the four-armed cadet impaling the tentacle-legged one into the mat. "Someone's coming," Melody said. "Tell Hamish. Tell everyone. Anathea won't stand a chance against them!" The young witch pulled her hand away and blinked out of the room.

Sitting up with a jolt, sickness rocked Ondine. The cadets she'd just seen. Were they real or a figment of Melody's fevered imagination? No, they had to be real. Melody had never lied before. Sure, she might have a thing for Vincent, but she was keeping Ondine updated with events, just as she'd promised. And what horrible events they were.

Climbing out of bed and pulling on her dressing gown, Ondine headed to Hamish's room to pass on Melody's message. And to figure out what to do next. Warning Anathea would be high on the list.

"Hamish, wake up," she said, stepping into his room and closing the door behind her.

He did not wake up. The little light that seeped under the curtains made it hard to see, but the lump in the bed didn't move. Hamish must be fast asleep.

"Wake up, Melody just gave me terrible news." She pushed against the lump in the blankets and her hands felt no resistance. "What?" Pulling the covers back, she found Shambles the ferret curled up into a tight ball. Furious, she scooped the ferret up into her hand and dangled him in mid air. He still didn't wake, hanging there limp like a dead animal. Fear overtook her, was he dead? No, his little heart beat against her palm. And he was warm to the touch. And soft and floppy. He had to be alive. But why was he sleeping as a ferret? "Wake up!"

"Whoa! I am awake!" Shambles twisted and turned in her hand and flipped himself onto the bed. "I'm awake, where's the fire?"

A thousand questions fought for attention, but she kept calm and concentrated on the important things first. "Melody just appeared to me in an astral projection. Mrs Howser is training the cadets in Fort Kluff. They're all affected by mutating magic and they're unstoppable."

"I'm listening," Shambles said as he dived under the covers. The fabric bulged and stretched, he groaned a little from the pain, then a moment later, properly human Hamish poked his head out.

Ondine reached for the side lamp and had a good look at her charmingly dishevelled boyfriend. Here they were, alone in his room, and they couldn't take advantage because there was so much mayhem going on all around them.

One day, though. One day.

"Your hair," she said, running her fingers through it. "The grey is gone."

"Thank goodness for that," Hamish let out a huge breath of relief. "I wasnae sure it would work, but remember when I broke my jaw at the palace and when I changed intae meself it was all fixed? I was hoping that would be the same."

"We have bigger things to worry about than you going grey," Ondine said, remembering the bigger picture just in time.

"We must tell Auntie Col about the cadets and work out what to do."

"Between you and me, best let her sleep a little longer,

she was into the lunatic soup last night."[29]

"I was not," a voice said from the doorway. They looked up to see Auntie Col, dressed and ready for a new day. "It was a drop of plütz with dessert to calm my nerves. Now, what's this about Mrs Howser's magic?"

They quickly relayed the news, Ondine remembering more details with the second telling.

"This can't be good," Old Col said after a moment of turning things over in her mind. "It sounds like Mrs Howser's magic is stronger than ever. If she's still using the two of you to set off the mutating magic, more and more people keep catching it. Perhaps it would be best if Hamish was a ferret as much as possible, to stop you kicking off a new wave of magic?"

"It's not that bad, is it?" Ondine said.

"We need to find a way to stop it," Hamish said.

Ondine and Col said together, "Exactly."

***

Sleep-glue kept Vincent's eyes shut as he slump-rolled over in bed, wondering what vengeful deity he'd offended to feel so hideous this morning. It was the morning, right? Grey light filtered through his closed lids. There were morning-type noises funnelling down his ear, like a coffee machine and somebody stacking crockery. The chug and thrum of the traffic outside crept into the room. Somebody was walking around; their footsteps growing louder as they came closer.

A radio blasted out good cheer.

As long as he kept his eyes shut, he could pretend the world didn't exist. It wasn't that he had a hangover. He knew how to hold his plütz.

------

[29] Lunatic soup is two or more types of alcohol mixed together.

It wasn't bad food eating away the lining of his stomach either. It was that horrible, inner-nag of a conscience, kicking him from inside his head. He thought he'd stomped on that voice years ago, yet here it was, telling him how stupid he was.

Worthless.

He wasn't worthless, he reminded his brain. He was the rightful Duke of Brugel. Mrs Howser's cadets at Fort Kluff would provide the muscle; the Balakhans would provide the money.

"Good morning, *affiance*." A woman kissed him on the forehead.

His eyes snapped open. He was in a hotel room. It took a few shakes of his brain cells to remember the hotel was in Slaegal. He'd come back here after visiting Fort Kluff. He was awake now and looking around him in horror. The bed sheets were covered in orange smears, as if someone had washed half the bed in fruit juice. Memories flooded him. Last night, he'd met with the Balakhans in Norange again. Last night he'd drunk plütz again.

"Look at you!" The woman – it was Ruslana – said, "relax, you idiot, nothing happened. But you fell asleep before you could be a gentleman and offer to sleep on the sofa." She said the last thing with a shrug, which made Vincent look at the sofa and wince. Made of white leather, it would have been a vibrant citrus colour if she'd slept on that. He reached for his dressing gown and shrugged out of bed.

"I called for breakfast. It came a couple minutes ago," she said, lifting a silver lid off a plate.

Tentatively, Vincent walked to the table and sat opposite Ruslana Balakhan, his fake-tan fiancé.

"Relax." There was that word she liked to use. "You're not my type."

Spearing his bacon, he dared to ask, "What is your

type?" He shoved it into his mouth and crunched down.

She cast a meaningful look at his groin and gave a conspiratorial grin. "You. Not my type."

Vincent couldn't help smiling. Relief, yes, that was the emotion coursing through him. He only had to sleep beside an Oompa loompa, not with one. "Then we're going to get along great."

"I know what you're thinking," she said. "Why bother with the marriage if it's of no use? Yes?"

He needed more vitamin bacon. "That did cross my mind."

"Because it will please Daddy. He wants the best for me. As far as he can tell, you are the best for me. And for him. And it will not be forever. I can spare a few years to make Daddy happy."

He topped up his coffee. "Does he know about your . . . *type*?"

"Of course. But he also thinks I . . ." she made quotation marks in the air with her fingers, "Haven't met the right man yet."

Fragments from the night before came back. He, Melody, Babak and Ruslana had signed papers and agreements and sealed the deal with plütz. There had been singing at some point. It was all a bit of a blur. Melody had been quieter than usual. He didn't blame her. The scenes at Fort Kluff had been unsettling but necessary.

"We need some ground rules," He said as the coffee kicked in.

"I like rules. Thank you for signing the pre-nuptial agreement."

That must have been one of the documents he'd put his name to during the evening, signing his family name for the promise of a future.

"Daddy says most of the money will flow when there are grandchildren. He thinks becoming a mother will be good for me."

That brought a chunk of bacon flying up Vincent's throat. He swallowed it down, hard. It was one thing to marry for mercenary reasons, but quite another to bring children into it.

"Good. You are listening," she said. "I am not having children. Not to you or anyone."

"We don't have to talk about that. I'm sure we'll find some way to work around it later."

"You are not listening!" She banged the table with her fist. "This," she pointed to her stomach, "is not for getting babies. Full stop!"

Vincent retreated into sarcasm. "Oh my sweet. Our first tiff. However will we go on?"

A knock came at the door. Ruslana crossed her arms over her chest and refused to get it. Vincent went to the door.

"Good morning My Lord." It was Melody, making nice with a forced smile. "I trust you slept well. Here are your newspapers and schedule for the day. If you need anything, I shall be in the car."

"Thank you Melody," he said. "I will be right down in a minute."[30]

"I like her," Ruslana said after Vincent closed the door. "When Daddy's money starts to flow, you'll be able to pay her."

When her father's money began to flow, he'd be able to do a whole lot of things.

"He really likes you," Ruslana said. "If you hadn't come along, he probably would have bought another football team. And I so detest all that . . . *testosterone*."

"Good morning beautiful children!" A voice boomed at the door.

---

[30] "I'll be right down in a minute," means, "When I get around to it".

Babak came strolling in, sucking all the oxygen from the room simply by being in it.

Melody came trotting along in his wake. "He borrowed my key card."

Interesting. Melody must have had that key card earlier, yet she'd knocked.

"You are going to love this," Babak said as he handed a sheaf of papers to Vincent. No sign of any embarrassment on his part of walking right in to his future-son-in-law's hotel room. "This, my son, is how you win your crown back. Now, very important. Make sure your hand stays blue. Paint it. Colour it. Get a tattoo if you have to, but keep it blue."

He'd submerge his whole body in printer's ink for the amount of money Babak was offering.

Bakak said, "I have found a way to get your Aunt Anathea out of the picture, in a way that everyone benefits."

"She won't get hurt?" Vincent's mind darted back to Mrs Howser's deadly cadets, equal parts impressed with their brilliance and terrified of their power.

Babak looked at Vincent as if he were something stuck on his shoe. "It will only hurt if she does the wrong thing." He rubbed his hands together. "Now, I hope you have terrible taste in music, it's time to put on a show."

***

Ondine, Hamish and Old Col were in a constant state of worry about what Vincent and Mrs Howser were plotting, and doing their best not to let Ma and Da know they were worried about national affairs and royal intrigue. Because Ma had stated they were to have nothing more to do with Brugel's royal family, and Ondine didn't want her to know they'd ignored that edict.

Fortunately for Ondine, something else was happening in the pub to divert everyone's attentions. The music executive who had liked what she'd heard and seen in Cybelle and Margi several nights ago, was now encouraging them to enter BrugelMelody, which, if they won, would see them compete at PopEuroTube in May. [31]

All attention in the pub had since turned to music and performances and winning competitions, allowing Ondine, Old Col and Hamish to worry and fret about the nation's problems in private.

On this particular morning, they privately fretted while walking to the fresh produce market to buying food for their customers. For the next hour or so, Ondine and Hamish, along with Henrik and Cybelle, bought seasonal fruit and vegetables, hustling and haggling their way through the rows of traders. Spicy aromas assailed them at one market; stinking fish assaulted their senses in the next. At the end of one particularly stenchsome row, Ondine nudged Hamish out in to the fresh air, which just happened to be near a donut van.[32]

These were especially good donuts because they weren't always cooked right through, so the centre could be lush and gooey. For an extra schlip, you could have hot jam in the centre. Ondine always said yes because she was in love with the way they slammed the donuts onto the nose of a model dolphin to inject the jam in.

Hamish gave her a weird look. "Ye going tae eat that?"

---

[31] *BrugelMelody* is the local competition, held in early spring each year, to choose a song to represent Brugel at the PopEuroTube Song Contest in May. Some years the songs are even half good, but most years the competition is held in secret to spare viewers and participants from pain and humiliation.

[32] Every marketplace in the world has donut vans, it's the law. Dolphin-shaped jam injectors are optional.

"I bought plenty to share." She offered him one. "Watch out for the lava in the middle."

Screwing up his face, he took the tiniest bite then grimaced. "Pure carbs are nae good fer me."

"I know you can't eat sugar when you're . . ." she dropped her voice, "a ferret. But when you're you, you can, right?"

"Best not, just in case, eh?"

"Suit yourself," she shrugged then scoffed it. The heat burned her throat, pricking tears in her eyes. The heat moved to her tummy and radiated warmth as she licked her sugar-encrusted fingers, then wiped them on her coat. Bliss.

"Sign the petition?" A young woman about Ondine's age stepped in front of them with a clipboard and a pen. Behind her was a makeshift stall with more volunteers surrounded by signs and posters calling for the restoration of Lord Vincent's inheritance. Oh they were clever, standing near the donut van. A captive market or what?

Looking at the clipboard, Ondine saw pages and pages filled with signatures.

Hamish asked, "What's all this about?"

The volunteer brightened and said, "Lord Vincent should be Duke. We're collecting signatures to take to the Duchess and the Dentate, to show how much support Vincent has for his claim."

"But I thought everyone *loaved* Anathea?" Hamish said.

"Oh we do!" the woman said. "We think she's wonderful. But it should go to Vincent. We've collected three thousand signatures already. Sign here."

"Uh, I really don't get involved in politics," Ondine said.

"Yes you do." Somebody from the pro-Vincent team came over. "I saw you at the Snow Maze last year, you were there.”

Then he noticed Hamish and said, “and he was there, you were both up on the stage in the end.”[33]

“Mistaken identity,” Hamish said, grabbing Ondine’s hand and dragging her away.

When they were safely beyond reach of Team Vincent, Ondine said, “They’re so organised already. It’s only been a couple months since Anathea was officially sworn in.”

“Aye, but he’s wanted this for years. Now he’s stepping up the campaign. Can’t let Anathea get too settled, people might start liking her too much.”

---

[33] They were on stage, separating Mrs Howser’s control from Lord Vincent, then separating Mrs Howser’s soul from her body, with the help of Duchess Anathea’s intervention with a vacuum cleaner.

~ Chapter Six ~

Weeks of worry passed for Ondine. The spring equinox
had come and gone, but winter refused to let go. Grey skies
above only added to her gloomy mood. Hamish had taken
to sleeping as a ferret in order to stay young, which meant
even less time to sneak in cuddles and kisses with his
human self.

Her older sister's songs were getting frequent airplay on
the radio, which drew the crowds to the *Duke and Ferret*
hotel, making Ondine work even harder and wash even
more dishes than before.

Which meant she had no time to sneak off and warn
Duchess Anathea about what Vincent was up to. Instead,
she wrote letters. Old fashioned letters that required
proper handwriting, an envelope and a stamp.[34]

---

[34] Sure everyone has email and Snapchat accounts now, but this is
Brugel before the turn of the century. (Which is to say, the turn into the
21st century.) The first novel was about events that happened "exactly
twelve years ago today."

Each letter sent earned Ondine no reply, which added to her already growing list of worries, which she had to squeeze in between her regular classes at school and her increasing workload at home.

Thankfully, they had a rare night off with nobody for dinner and no guests staying overnight. It was a Monday night, and for the first time in Ondine's memory, her entire family were out together. They were at VTV6 studios, located in the foothills of Mt Verka Serduchka, to the east of Venzelemma.[35]

The air hummed with nervous tension as the television crews moved cameras into positions and checked lighting and sound levels. All the production people wore headphones with microphones attached. Turning to the very back of the studio, Ondine could see a row of people sitting behind a glass wall, the lights of an enormous control panel reflected on their concentrating faces.

Sitting – but mostly fidgeting – along a row of flip-down seating sat Ma and Da, looking proud and incredibly nervous. Next to them sat Henrik and Thomas, along with Thomas' parents and his younger brother Alexei. Ondine and Hamish sat on the other end of the row. Old Col had warned Ondine not to flirt or canoodle outrageously with Hamish in public, lest their 'make other people's wishes come true' magic got out of hand.

------

[35] Mt Verka Serduchka is one of Brugel's highest points, being almost four hundred meters above sea level and one of the last remaining hills that hasn't been excavated into a castle or fort of some kind. Hiking to the summit is popular all year, as is having your photo taken 'holding up' the leaning broadcast towers of VTV6 and BrugStereoFM. The towers were constructed in the early 1950s and began leaning almost straight away. They were straightened in the 1970s, with much fanfare and even greater expense. However this resulted in weaker transmission signals and a reduction in tourism, so they leaned the towers back to the way they were.

She'd also put a dampening field around Hamish to make sure Ondine's emotions didn't run wild. Even though Ondine knew she loved Hamish with all her heart, she didn't have the slightest inclination to sneak off somewhere privately with him. Drat that witchy great auntie of hers for having such strong magic.

"To think we paid full price for these seats, when we're only using the edge of them," Da said.

Margi and Cybelle were somewhere backstage, waiting to perform, along with several other acts representing the length and breadth of Brugel's musical talent. Being a proud nation, the rules of BrugelMelody stipulated that the music, lyrics and performers all had to come from citizens of Brugel, or at least permanent residents, to compete.[36]

A woman with auburn hair so shiny you could see the audience reflected in it, took to the stage. "Good evening ladies and gentlemen, I am your warm-up host, Marta Pompeii. Tonight's search for Brugel's next PopEuroTube star will be recorded completely live, which in real terms means it will be broadcast later tonight after editing out the mistakes and slotting in the adverts. We would not be able to put on such a wonderful show without you, the audience. So can I have your very best round of applause when I say, "go", so that we can record it. Okay, go!"

Everyone clapped, cheered, whistled and stamped their feet, shaking the studio.

"Thank you thank you. One more time to make sure we get it, and go!"

It didn't seem possible but the audience was even louder.

____

[36] Other countries in PopEuroTube Song Contest have no such qualms about their performers or composers being from another country, but Brugel is fiercely Brugelish. If the performers don't meet this criteria, visa arrangements are quickly made.

Ondine's hands smarted from slapping them together.

"Better keep yer powder dry for yer sisters," Hamish said.

Marta raised her hands, "OK, everyone, great job. Now please get ready to welcome your host to this evening, Me! Yes, I'm so cheap I do my own warm-up act!"

Marta paused and the audience gave a smattering of laughter.

"Tonight is BrugelMelody, our judges and voters at home will be sending Brugel's next act to PopEuroTube in May!" Another pause for applause. Ondine wasn't sure how much longer her flayed palms could take this.

"In order to get there the fairest way possible tonight, we have three judges, all experts in the field of performance, composition and technique. They will score each act, and in the case of a tie we'll call on the services of a mystery judge!"

The studio lights shone on the three judges. One extra chair sat further along, with its back to the audience. From the side of the chair, a hand came out and waved.

Ondine gasped. The waving hand had a familiar blue stain to it. "Did you see that?" She nudged Hamish.

"Aye. D'ye think it's him?"

"I'd bet my last fried cheeseball on it." That Vincent, he was getting into everything. Burrowing his way into Brugel like a botfly.[37] Meanwhile, where was Anathea? She should be here, so the people could see her and love her.

The music contest, when it eventually started, was pretty awesome. Nerves writhed in Ondine's belly as the first act finished their song. Then the next.

------

[37] Botflies are hideous parasites that grow under an animal's skin. You really don't want to look it up on a search engine. No please don't. OK, fine, I'm not your mother.

Every performance sounded better than the last.

Can we have one dud, just so Margi and Belle have a better shot at winning this?

Ondine's wish was granted with the next group. Five lads in white boiler suits danced so hard they couldn't carry their notes properly. Plus their choreography looked five years out of date.[38]

"Give me the code to your heart and I will give you mine.
Girl you're so fine,
You're always on my mind."

"They're so bad they could win it," Hamish teased.

Ondine shuddered. Hamish lifted the armrest that formed a barrier between them and pulled her in for a snuggle. She used his shoulder to block sound in one ear, then snuck her hand under her long hair to block the other ear.

Much better. The crowd damned the boiler-suited boys with polite applause when the song finished.

The next group was a proper rock outfit with two massive drum kits, three violins, a cello, three guitars and a robust woman out the front on vocals.[39]

She didn't merely belt out a song, she gave them an *anthem.*

A flag-waving, chest-thumping, patriotic-as-Brugeldirt rallying cry.

The chorus was so memorable that when they came to it a second time, people stood up and joined in.

———

[38] Five years out of date in Brugel is the equivalent to fifteen for the rest of us.

[39] Anyone familiar with the PopEuroTube Song Contest rules knows that the maximum number of performers on stage is six, so if the rock outfit gets through, they'll have to cull performers. There is, however, no limit on the number of drum kits allowed on stage.

If we go then we go.
If we fight, then we fight,
If it's the end of the world my friend, let it be tonight.

Jupiter's Moons, Margi and Belle were sunk and they were up next. Ondine forgot to breathe as her sisters took their respective places behind the microphone and piano. They looked like superstars; their hair perfect, their makeup glamorous but not overdone, their outfits timeless.

"We've seen some incredible acts tonight," Marta Pompeii said as she walked out in front of Margi and Belle. "Remember, voting will open in ten minutes, and you can only vote once. Don't go away, we're going to take a quick word from our sponsors and be right back."[40]

Ondine wished she could dash home and make a phone call. Then she wished she could be sick. Did they have to drag things out so much?

"It's all right dear," Ma leaned over to reassure her. "Auntie Col is voting for us."

But as much as Ondine adored her great-aunt, who had been there for her through many adventures in the past year, how would one vote make a difference?

"She's made sure all her Coven buddies are watching and voting as well," Ma said, in answer to Ondine's thoughts. Relief rolled over Ondine. Then, a fresh burst of panic. "What about –"

"– The phone lines? If a witch can't get through, nobody can."

OK, her mother's reassurances would have to do for now. Hamish squeezed her hand for luck as Marta Pompeii started talking again.

---

[40] Any more than one phone call per household and the BrugelTel system will collapse under the onslaught.

"Welcome back to BrugelMelody. It's been an insanely great show tonight, but we have more to come. And now, ladies and gentlemen, the song you have all heard and fallen in love with already. It's Margibelle with *You Are My Star!*"

The applause was so intense it smacked Ondine inside her head. As one, the crowd was on its feet.

"Margibelle?" Ondine mouthed to her parents.

Ma shrugged and shouted back, "It's better than Cybguerite."

Ondine could hardly breathe as the audience fell silent. Cybelle caressed the keys to start the song.

How could her sisters look so relaxed when Ondine couldn't breathe for the knots in her belly?

But, oh what beautiful music her sisters made! Margi's voice wrapped the audience in a collective hug. The crowd swayed and moved as one, then started clapping and stamping their feet as the song reached the bridge. When Margi hit the first big note of the chorus, the crowd screamed with delight. They knew the words and sang along.

Tears verily *spritzed* from Ondine. Hamish wiped his cheek. An unspoken bond united the audience, Cybelle, Marguerite and the nation itself.

Magic. It had to be magic. How else to explain the overwhelming sense of love in the studio?

Please win, please win, please win!

Margi sang true. Her voice united everyone as they moved from the verse into the coda with its incredible endnote.

Get the note, get the note.

Not a flicker of worry on Margi's face, not a wobble in her voice as she belted it out.

A silent beat as the audience let the song finish, before they erupted in delight. The noise bounced inside Ondine's chest as she let out her long held-in breath. Had she breathed at all during the song?

"They did it!" Hamish grabbed Ondine in a massive hug and lifted her off the ground. Ma and Da hugged and kissed each other and grinned and cried. Both of them. Down the line, Thomas and Henrik chest-bumped and jumped up and down and waved to their beloveds on stage. Thomas stuck his fingers in his mouth for an ear-splitting whistle.

The next ten minutes were going to be the longest in Ondine's life as they waited for viewers at home to cast their votes. Marta came back on stage and held up her palms to calm the audience down. She was enjoying herself, as if the applause was for her.

"Remember. Viewers' votes will be worth fifty percent, and the jury votes will be worth the other fifty percent. You have nine minutes left to vote."

"'Scuse I." Henrik nudged past them, Thomas in close pursuit.

Ondine climbed on her seat to make room for them. They had their 'visitor' passes clearly visible. "Give them our love," Ma cried as they headed off towards the green rooms.

What now?

Ondine was on such a high she didn't know what she'd do if Margi and Cybelle – *Margibelle* – didn't win. Leaning into Hamish, she said, "I think I'm going to be sick."

"Ye need fresh air, lass."

"Tell you what," Da handed him a lanyard with a spare house key. "Why don't you both go home and relax. There's nothing more we can do now except wait. We won't know the outcome for hours."

Ondine shook her head. "Hours? But the voting ends soon."

Da gave her a wink. "Yes, but remember they said it would be delayed so they could put the ads in and all that. Proper voting might not start for another hour. This way, you have time to get home and get on the phone."

A thrill charged through Ondine at the thought she could actually do something productive to help her sisters.

"Aye, I'll keep the pub safe till ye get back." Hamish looped the key around his neck and ushered Ondine towards the exit.

The cool evening air slapped Ondine's cheeks. "I'm not cut out for this. It's too intense!" Keeping her breathing even, her pulse finally stabilised. The nausea that had earlier threatened to swamp her eased away. Chills moved in and she shivered involuntarily. "If I'm this nervous now, what will I be like if they actually make it to PopEuroTube?"

With a chuckle, Hamish squished her sideways and kissed her on the cheek. "Ye'll be a mess."

"Aww. Have I told you lately how wonderful you are?"

"Aye." He tilted her face and properly kissed her on the lips. "And I'll never get tired of hearing it."

Just as they were about to walk away from the studios to catch the next train home, Lord Vincent came around the corner.

All three stopped and stared at each other.

Hurk, went Ondine's stomach. Luckily nothing but air flew out, although in hindsight she wouldn't have minded throwing up on him. A moment's hesitation, then Vincent confidently smiled. "Ondine, Hamish, how lovely to see you both. How have you been?"

Nothing came to Ondine, as she looked around to make sure there were no cameras or other people nearby. It wouldn't do to have witnesses if this ended badly.

"Aye, Vincent, yer the secret judge then?"

He winked. Actually *winked*, as if they were old chums

in some kind of prank together. "If I told you, it wouldn't be a secret, would it?"

"Shouldn't you be back in there, judging or something?" Ondine said, massively impressed with how sensible she sounded considering the emotions tumbling inside her. Vincent was a slimy toad of a person who had caused her nearly a year's worth of strife. This was as polite as she could possibly be.[41]

Vincent kept his gaze locked with Ondine's. "The public voting will be close. Very close. It might come down to the wire. It *may* come down to my vote deciding who goes to PopEuroTube and who misses out."

"Why are ye talking tae us then, lad?"

He sighed. "Time was, I could order you to call me 'My Lord' and you'd have to. Now I must endure your Scottish insults. You might not believe it, but I have matured. I harbour no ill feeling towards either of you, or your family. Everything I do now is for the good of Brugel, not myself. It's ironic, don't you think, that I have lost my title and yet become a more responsible man?"

He really expected them to believe that? Ondine stilled her eyes so they wouldn't roll in contempt. She cast a look to Hamish to see if he believed any of this either.

"I deserve your derision," Vincent said. "And your pity, if you have any. There is no easy way to build up to this so I may as well straight-out ask. I need your help."

Jolt! Ondine had to take a step backwards to steady against the shock. "You –?" she started

"– Need our help?" Hamish finished.

"Yes," Vincent confirmed.

Stunned, Ondine shook her head. "Saturn's rings! Why would I help you?"

---

[41] See previous *Ondine* titles: *The Summer of Shambles, The Autumn Palace* and *The Winter of Magic.*

Palms forward in surrender, Vincent said, "For the good of Brugel."

"Fer the good of yerself ye mean," Hamish said.

"Let's not be churlish. Ondine, you and Hamish helped my Aunt Anathea become loved and popular. I saw what you did and despite having scant resources, you managed to make my batty auntie respectable to the majority of people. Now I find I'm in need of something similar."

The images of the cadets at Fort Kluff, which Melody had terrified her with via astral projection, chilled Ondine more than the cold evening air. Not that she could say anything right now, because Vincent would then know Melody had blabbed.

Hamish scoffed. "Ye want to bump yer auntie off and ye want everyone to love ye while ye do it?"

Careful, she wanted to say to her beloved.

"Nothing of the sort. I truly believe Anathea is good for Brugel. She's had a steadying influence on the nation, and the public has a fondness for her, which would have seemed unfathomable only a year ago. I have absolutely no intention of curtailing her reign either."

He had to be lying so she'd lie right back. "I've got news for you Vincent. We can't make people's dreams come true any more. Look, I'll prove it." She kissed Hamish squarely on the mouth and it felt . . . weird! Not exactly wrong, but the zings and rushes of blood she normally felt were curiously absent. Pulling away, she checked the traffic. No double sets of green lights. The weather didn't become warmer. The people walking on the other side of the street were not suddenly drinking hot chocolate. Vincent was still standing in front of them, and he didn't have the smug expression of someone who had everything he wanted.

No magic.

Wow, Auntie Col's dampening spell must be doing

double-time.

"Told you," she said, needing to appear triumphant while her belly swooped with fear. Old Col's extra spell was working, but what if it kept on working and she and Hamish lost their love for each other? That would be terrible! "I don't want to get involved in political intrigues any more, I just want to be normal and boring."

"Your sisters don't," Vincent said.

His words were like an arrow to her heart. If Ondine didn't help him, would he vote Margibelle down? Just because he could?

"But how could I help you?" Ondine asked.

"Oh goodness," Vincent's face brightened, "you came around much faster than I thought."

"No!" Ondine spat the word out like bad food. "I didn't mean how *can* I help, I mean, *how*, exactly? Logistically and all that, because we don't have magic any more."

"The irony is, I don't actually need magic."

"No?"

"No. What I need is a miracle."

Morbid curiosity took hold. As much as Ondine didn't want to help Lord Vincent, she couldn't stop wondering exactly what he needed their help for. Plus, he held Margi and Belle's future in his palm. Competing in PopEuroTube was Margi and Cybelle's dream. Could Ondine really stand in their way because of her antagonism towards Vincent?

Against her better judgement, she found herself saying, "Show me what you need."

~ Chapter Seven ~

Ondine's muscles felt as weak as failed soufflé as Lord
Vincent guided her and Hamish back into the studios.
Knowing all she knew about Vincent, she must be insane
or have some kind of death wish to be helping him. The
second she thought about turning around and running out
of there, an image of her sisters shone brightly in her mind.
If she walked out on Vincent, she'd be walking out on
Margibelle too.

Vincent led them through a rabbit warren of narrow
corridors until they arrived at his private dressing room.
"Brace yourselves. This is messy."

He opened the door. Ondine's jaw dropped as there, in
front of a mirror sat the *orangest* looking woman she had
ever seen. Who was this citrus creature? On the sofa,
sitting behind her, sat Melody with her face in her hands,
quietly weeping.

With a firm 'snick', Vincent closed the door on the five
of them. "You see my problem now?"

Turmoil churned Ondine's stomach. She moved to the

couch and gave Melody a hug. It was good to see her, and if there was any chance she could get Melody alone, she might be able to get her away from Vincent.

"I failed," Melody said.

Ondine hugged her friend and whispered low, "You're doing great. We'll get you out of here."

Vincent cleared his throat. "This is my fiancé Ruslana Balakhan."

Ondine looked at the woman whose skin bore a striking resemblance to a glass of breakfast juice.

Vincent nodded and made something of a grimace. "She needs to look the part of a proper Brugel bride-to-be."

"I see what ye mean," Hamish said, casting a worried grimace towards Vincent and then Ondine.

Ondine had heard the name Balakhan from somewhere. Melody murmured, "Her father owns a football club." A twig figuratively snapped in her head as Ondine made the connections; Lord Vincent with all those cadets, plus the Balakhan money, would be unstoppable.

With Melody here in the room, they already had a powerful witch. Yet she obviously hadn't been able to help transform Ruslana into something presentable. Vincent was right, they'd need more than mere magic to convince the people of Brugel to accept Ruslana as their next Duchess.

"I don't mean to be rude, but what have you done to your face?" Ondine asked.[42]

Ruslana looked up. "My face is my fortune."

The twig snapped again. Ondine – and Melody – knew magic could only work if the magic-ee willingly went along with it. Or deep down believed it to be true. Free will always won out against magic. How could they change Ruslana if she wasn't willing?

---

[42] Anything couched with an "I don't need to be rude, but," is apt to be rude.

Hamish piped up. "At Margi's weddin' ye all looked like royalty, so ye did."

"My sisters!" Ondine suddenly remembered they would be in their dressing room. And they'd looked stunning on stage. Even better than on the day of Margi's wedding. They must have had help. "I'll be right back."

With that, she darted out of Vincent's dressing room and charged towards the performers' green rooms. Excellent! There was Margi and Belle, and Thomas and Henrik. She rushed forward and hugged them all. "You were perfect tonight. Beyond amazing!"

"I'm so nervous I could puke for Brugel," Cybelle said.

Seeing their faces, knowing how much they wanted this, galvanised Ondine's decision. She'd already agreed to help the hideous Vincent, if it meant her sisters' dreams came true. Yes, it was cheating, but if she didn't do it, Vincent could just as easily vote her sisters down out of spite. It didn't make it right, but she'd have to live with it. The sooner she put this incident behind her, the better. The make-up lady they'd hired for the wedding was in her sisters' change room, in her familiar pleather pants and jacket. Excellent.[43]

"You were great, but I need to borrow her for a bit. S'cuse me," Ondine grabbed the woman's pleather-clad arm and said, "Your country needs you."

Her sisters, brother-in-law and brother-in-law-to-be all shouted at once,

"What's going on?"

"Steady on."

"What?"

---

[43] Pleather is a wonderful substitute for leather and earns a bovine stamp of approval from the BBB, the Brugel Board of Bovines. Not actually chaired by bovines but humans, obviously. Cows cannot sign documents, as they lack opposable thumbs.

"Ondi, what's the –"

"Sorry everyone," Ondine said as she guided the confused make-up lady out of the dressing room. "State secret." With that, she bundled the woman down the corridor towards Lord Vincent's dressing room.

"Thank you for coming along. You can't tell anyone about this, OK?"

"Where are you taking me?"

"You'll see soon enough. It's all above board, nothing dangerous, but you'll need every skill you possess . . . and maybe even some you don't."

The woman pulled up. "Is this dangerous?"

"Oh, not in the least," Ondine grabbed her arm again and marched her down the corridor, then stopped and said to her, "Although you might end up traumatised."

Bursting in to Lord Vincent's room, Ondine found everyone where she'd left them. Melody, on the couch, hiding behind a curtain of hair. Vincent pacing the room. Hamish leaning against the wall. Ruslana sitting in front of the mirror, pressing on a set of false eyelashes.

"Everything is going to be OK," Ondine said, then turned to the make-up lady and lowered her voice. "I'm sorry, I've forgotten your name."

"Charlene," she said.

"OK." Ondine quickly made introductions, then guided Charlene towards Ruslana. The faster she did this, the less time she'd have to acknowledge how much she was helping her sworn enemy. "This er . . . lovely . . . young woman is engaged to Lord Vincent. Please do your very best to make her look like a future Duchess of Brugel."

With a sideways tilt of her head, Charlene took in Ruslana and said, "I'm not used to working with such a ... colourful canvas."

Ruslana ignored her, turned to the light-studded mirror

and brushed a layer of glitter across her décolletage.

Charlene took a few steps towards Ruslana and narrowed her eyes, then lifted her hair in places and studied her features. "I'm going to need help. I don't suppose anyone in here is a witch?"

With a sigh, Melody raised her hand. "I've tried, but she's too wilful for the magic to work."

"Let's start with the face, shall we?" Charlene picked up a swab. "We'll get the layers off first and see what we have to work with."

"You're not touching my face!"

"Wait a minute," Ondine beamed at her own cleverness. "Ruslana might be fighting the magic, but Charlene's the one who needs it. Melody, if you cast a spell on Charlene, it won't matter how much Ruslana complains or tries to fight it, right?"

Hamish grabbed her in a hug and kissed her cheek. "Have I mentioned lately how clever ye are, lass?"

Ondine glowed from the compliment.

Sizing up the situation, Vincent rubbed his chin in thought. "Melody, can you do it?"

"Of course I can do it. Take a look?"

While they'd been asking Melody to perform, she was already on it. Buzzing vibrations and sprinkles of green light infused the room. Charlene worked at mega-magical speed, spinning Ruslana around in her chair, dabbing cotton pads into industrial strength make-up remover and scraping off layers of *slap* from Ruslana's face. As each stripe of bronzed orange came away, they caught a glimpse of Ruslana's pinked skin underneath.

"There's a real woman under there after all," Vincent said.

Then Charlene's hands flew through Ruslana's hair, denuding the mass of synthetic extensions from the real tresses.

"Stop it!" Ruslana slapped at Charlene's hands. "I look like I crawled out a crypt!"

"Don't stop now, whatever you do," Vincent said.

In mere seconds, the hair extensions were a skanky pile on the floor.

"Is it real hair?" Ondine leaned forward and massaged the fibres between her fingers. "It's so dry." Then she sniffed it and wished she hadn't. "Smells worse than you, Hamish, when you're a ferret."

He inhaled the piece Ondine offered. "Urgh! That's mockit!"

Meanwhile, Charlene kept up her pace. Ruslana's face turned clean and shiny pink, her hair stripped of extensions and back to its natural length.

Ondine held her breath as she watched Melody, still sitting on the couch, still hiding behind her curtain of hair, muttering incantations to bind Charlene to the swirls of magic so she could get the job done.

"Moisturiser," Charlene said, finding a tub of the stuff on the bench beneath the mirror. She slathered it all over Ruslana, turning her white. Then she wiped most of it off again and the last smears of mascara released their hold. "Let's go for a more natural look, eh?" Charlene dabbed foundation on Ruslana's jaw, then her hands vanished into a blur of activity as she applied fresh make-up.

Ruslana tried to climb out of the chair. Lord Vincent put his hands on her shoulders and pressed her down. "Sit."

More magic swirls and activity continued until a triumphant "Done!" from Charlene, as she stood back to admire her work.

"I'm invisible," Ruslana said.

Vincent looked at his fiancé in the mirror and shook his head, his words croaking with heartfelt emotion. "You look beautiful."

Melody slumped on the sofa.

Ondine gave her a hug. "You're doing great. I know you're exhausted, but please keep going. We're nearly there."

"Stage two, the hair." Charlene's hands worked her magic – or more precisely, Melody's Magic – styling Ruslana's 'do' into a regal helmet of coiffidly curled perfection.

"You turned me into my mother," she grumbled.

"Exactly," Vincent said. "Keep going my good woman. Melody, you have my deepest gratitude."

"I know," Melody said with a sigh.

Although fascinated with the Charlene's skills, Ondine noticed the lingering sadness in her friend. "Oh Melody!" Keeping her voice incredibly low so that nobody else would hear, Ondine said, "You love him, don't you?"

With a dramatic sniff, Melody nodded and then wiped at her face, tugging her hair away in the process. Her eyes were red and puffy. "I'm such an idiot."

"You poor, poor thing." Ondine gave her another hug. "And you're not an idiot. You're amazing."

Somebody rapped on the door. A stage assistant walked in before anyone could say, "Don't come in!"[44] "Five minutes until you and Ruslana are needed on stage, Sir," he said to Vincent.

"We'll be right there in a minute," Vincent said, ushering the man out and closing the door behind them. Looking to Charlene and then to Melody, he said, "Hurry up."

"I'm using all the magic I have," Melody said.

"Then use more."

---

[44] It's not barging in unannounced, as long as you make two firm knocks first before you barge in.

Hadn't he heard her? What did he want, the last breath in her lungs? Looking at her rapidly exhausting friend, Ondine wondered if Melody might end up giving him exactly that.

"Nearly there," Charlene's hands were utter blurs as she finished Ruslana's makeup. "Do you have any better clothes?"

"What's wrong with my clothes?" Ruslana could have broken the mirror with her daggered look.

Another quick double-knock and the stage assistant came straight back in. "Four minutes."

Vincent tisked and said, "Yes, yes, I said I'd be there."

"It's just that it takes two minutes to walk from here to the stage. Let's get the microphones hooked up." The assistant walked over to Vincent and put his hand up the back of his shirt to connect a tiny microphone at the front of his lapel.

"Done!" The make-up lady turned the chair around so everyone could see Ruslana.

The stage assistant clipped a transmitter block on the back of Vincent's belt. "Can you say 'testing one two three,' please?"

"You're beautiful!" Vincent said, ignoring the stage assistant.

Not that Ondine was in the habit of agreeing with Lord Vincent, but Ruslana did look stunning.

"I'll be in the car," Melody said as she hauled herself off the couch and walked out.

"We really have to go, Sir, it's –" the stage assistant caught sight of Ruslana and became stutteringly lost for words.

Vincent beamed. "Come, Ruslana, it's time for Brugelers to meet their future Duchess."

Ondine glanced at him, silently reminding them of their deal. He made a slow blink, as if to say "I know" as he left the room.

Would he stick to his word? Ondine didn't trust him as far as she could throw a cheese ball.

***

Eerie quiet greeted Ondine and Hamish as they returned to the empty pub. In the past, there was always some kind of "goings-on" going on. Guests in the hotel, Chef preparing food, and the general noise of noisy people, even in their sleep. They checked the premises to make sure everything was where it should be and that thieves hadn't taken advantage of their absence. But then, according to the television promotions, everyone would be watching BrugelMelody. That had to include thieves too?[45]

"Put the telly on and let's find out who wins, eh lass?"

"Good idea." It would provide noise so they wouldn't have to talk. Because talking would invariably lead to a discussion about Lord Vincent, and whether or not they should have helped him. It hadn't felt right at the time, and now Ondine felt nothing but remorse. She kept herself busy making hot chocolates, took a deep breath, fixed a smile in place and joined Hamish on the couch.[46]

They'd tuned in to find Marta Pompeii announcing the top five finalists. Battlefront's *Anthem* made it to the top five, as did the boy band in boiler suits that Ondine was sure would disappear without a trace.

"Vincent had better come good on his promise," she said. Oh dear, she'd said it out loud.

"Aye," was all Hamish said.

---

[45] Even thieves need a night off from time to time.

[46] With marshmallows = hot chocolate. No marshmallows = hot cocoa. It's the rules.

91

"I did the right thing, didn't I? I mean, I didn't really have a choice."

"Aye," he said, giving her a rub on the shoulder. But no bone-melting kisses. Did that mean Old Col's anti-magic magic was still working, or was Hamish upset with her?

A rock outfit made it to the top five. As did the krumpers on skateboards. One place left, Ondine forgot how to breathe. Nerves stretched tighter than a slingshot, Ondine held her breath until she nearly passed out. Watching this at home was killing her.

"Margibelle!" Marta finally announced. Ondine and Hamish cheered at the screen and hugged each other, spilling their drinks and not caring. They hugged and kissed and bounced in their seats. A top five finish! Amazing! Maybe they really could win this?

Marta, all white of teeth and bouffant of hair, stood in front of the five acts. There, on the telly, were her sisters known as Margibelle, standing amongst the winners, smiling and waving at the crowd.

"Ladies and gentlemen and special guests," the Marta said, "These are our top five finalists!" She paused to allow the audience to go crazy for a while. "This is truly an historical night. In the first time ever at BrugelMelody, we have a three-way tie for first place!"

Ondine choked. Hamish patted her on the back to help her recover.

"As much as we'd like, we cannot send our top three acts to PopEuroTube. Although the quality was so high this year, it would be a crime if Slaegal and Craviç didn't immediately grab the runners up to represent them. This of course means we'll need to call in our mystery judge to make the final decision of who will represent Brugel at the PopEuroTube Song Contest."

The crowd went wild. Ondine and Hamish held each other, afraid to let go. On the telly, the curtains to the side parted, to reveal Lord Vincent, waving his blue hand to the crowd, a stunning Ruslana by his side, every millimetre the future Duchess of Brugel.

The presenter beamed and asked Vincent if he'd made his decision.

"I have," he said, then smiled again.

"Then may we have the result please?"

Would Vincent stick to his side of the bargain?

Ondine couldn't breathe for nerves. Margibelle had to win. They simply had to.

~ Chapter Eight ~

Pain lanced Ondine's chest as she waited for the result of Lord Vincent's casting vote. He had to come good on his promise.

"We have a three-way tie." Marta said, hamming it up for the audience. "Would you like to know who our three winners are?"

The crowd went insane. Ondine's head was going to explode from the tension.

"Our three winning performers, in no particular order are, Margibelle! Battlefront and –"

Ondine didn't hear the third band. It didn't matter. She squealed and squished Hamish, who cried out with joy as well. They'd won. Well, they'd equally won. They were tied for first.

Making a great show of the results, Marta Pompeii on the television turned to Vincent, who handed over the envelope with his casting vote. Marta then opened it slowly, dragging the tension out so long it breached the

Geneva Convention. "This year's winner, with Lord Vincent's casting vote, to represent Brugel at PopEuroTube is . . ." she paused and looked at the three final finalists. Margi and Belle were holding hands and turning blue from holding their breaths. Marta turned back to the camera and said, "Battlefront!"

Blood rushed through Ondine's ears. "What? What!" Her jaw dropped, further opening her ears as the noise of the televised crowd poured into her brain.

"It's a mistake," Hamish said.

"But Vincent said –"

"– The toe rag –"

"– that they'd get in."

"– lying piece of scum."

She couldn't hear properly over her thundering pulse, but her eyes weren't lying. There on TV, the members of Battlefront, who'd sung *Anthem*, were leaping with joy. They would represent Brugel at PopEuroTube. Not Margibelle. Who were hugging and consoling each other and then being absolute troopers and congratulating the members of Battlefront.

Deflated and defeated, Ondine fell back on to the couch and kept shaking her head at Vincent's deception. "He said he'd help. Why did I trust him? He used us!"

"Can I turn it off now lass, it's nae gointae get any better."

"I want to flip tables and start a riot!" Tears of frustration blurred everything as the words, 'he lied to us!' rang in her ears.

"We have plenty of tables in the dining room if ye want tae make a start."

Molten lava-anger fried Ondine's brain as she kicked over the side table. Then she quickly righted it again because flipping tables didn't solve anything. Except make her feel marginally better for having done it.

But still.

What else could she kick?

Noise wafted in from outside. A group of people were singing *Anthem* out in the street, as if they'd deliberately burst into song just to drive her mad. The singing became louder as it reached the back door. They were carousing now, right outside her family home. Talk about rubbing menthol into her eyeballs![47]

Hamish did what Hamish did best and wrapped Ondine in a hug. She howled out the unfairness of the world into his chest. Encased in Hamish's arms, his biceps should have smothered the sound of other people singing. But it became even louder. How was that possible? Then the noise came inside their room and she pulled away from Hamish to see her family walking in, twirling sparklers in the air and popping streamers!

They were singing *Anthem!* Had they fallen into a vat of plütz? Margi and Cybelle were hugging their men and singing. Ma was making strange ululations like a gypsy queen and Da was singing the low notes in some bizarre attempt to harmonise.

The Bergers joined in as well, as their son Alexei lit a fresh sparkler.

They looked . . . happy?

Eventually Ondine's family paused for breath, giving Hamish the chance to ask, "Have ye all lawst yer minds?"

"Watch the sparks on the carpet!" Ma said.

Margi broke away from Thomas and grabbed Ondine in an embrace. "Oh Ondi, it's wonderful!"

That would be yes.

"They haven't seen it yet," Thomas said. "Turn the box back on, you'll see what happened."

---

[47] If you've ever rubbed any brand of mentholated gel on an aching muscle, then accidentally rubbed your eyes, you'll know the pain.

Mute with confusion, Ondine did Thomas's bidding and switched the set back on. But by now they'd finished the broadcast and were showing an old movie.

Margi's smile grew larger. "Ondi, we're going to PopEuroTube anyway. We'll be representing Slaegal! Isn't that wonderful?" At which point Margi squealed, grabbed Cybelle and the two of them bounced around and made giddy noises. They moved into the beer garden to continue the party. Alexei had a fresh box of small fireworks that he was keen to set on fire.

The world had officially stopped making sense.

"You'll never believe it, darling," Ma said, coming over to smother Ondine in a hug. "Lord Vincent cast the vote for Battlefront to sing for Brugel, and we were crushed let me tell you. But then he told us the good news."

Ondine came up for air. "But how does he have any say in what Slaegal does?"

"It wasn't him, it was his fiancé Ruslana. Her dad's the head of the Slaegal delegation and they want Margibelle to sing for them."

"But . . . *Slaegal*?" [48]

Eyes fever-bright, Cybelle said, "Don't you see? This means we've got an even better chance of winning. Brugelers can't vote for Brugel, but they *can* vote for us because we'll be Slaegal. Just for one night."

Whooshing weirdness filled Ondine's head. "I guess that's good then." All the while she couldn't shake the feeling Vincent had tricked her. Margibelle were supposed to represent Brugel, not their enemies across the border.

"Good?" Cybelle said. "It's *amazing*."

------

[48] Brugel and Slaegal have had a frosty relationship at the best of times, which often manifests into 'nemesis status' during times of national competitions.

Henrik kissed Cybelle on the cheek and spun her around.

Hamish whispered in Ondine's ear. "Ye done good, lass. Vincent came through after all."

"Yoo hoo!" Came a familiar voice. Old Col sauntered out to the garden, "I came as soon as I could to join in the party!"

Old Col's eyes lit on Alexei and his box of exploding tricks. "Oh yes, let's set them off!" The matriarch and the newcomer to Ondine's extended family then set about setting fire to things.

At least they weren't doing it inside!

The excitement in the garden broke through Ondine's glumness. As a firework launched into the sky, Col waved her hands casting a spell. Vibrant red and gold sparks exploded outward creating a picture of Margi and Cybelle's faces against the starry night.

Ondine's sisters screamed with delight at the impromptu pyrotechnics display. She'd never seen the family so happy. Their emotions proved contagious and Ondine found herself grinning and hugging her sisters for the sheer joy of it.

Nobody needed to know about her deal with Vincent.

Bang! Another magic firework illuminated the sky, this time with Ondine and Hamish's virtual visages beaming down at everyone below in brilliant blue and purple.

"Oh how lovely Col!" Ma exclaimed, clapping with delight.

As the real Ondine gazed up in wonder, her sparkly-likeness broke into a smile. Then Hamish's apparition winked, morphed into a ferret and then faded away into smoke.

A heat wave swept through the garden, as if the trees had caught fire.

"Be careful, Alex," Mrs Berger said.

"Now that was a hot flash!" Ma said.

No harm done, everyone laughed and kept partying.

"Whoops, must have given it a little too much!" Old Col said.

More family phantasms flew across the sky above the pub, bringing gasps of joy to all. Alexei stuck a pinwheel to the decorative lamppost and set it blazing. Flames and sparks flew out in all directions as it whizzed around.

Creak! The pinwheel's heat buckled the lamppost.

Mr Berger said, "You've done your dash boy, get inside."

"We'll pay for the damages," Mrs Berger said.

"Not Alexei's fault!" Old Col jumped in. "I gave it a little extra. Sometimes I don't know my own strength."

"Is everything all right auntie?" Ma asked.

"Perfectly fine!" Old Col sounded way too defensive. "Josef, why not break out the plütz? The good stuff this time."

***

Rehearsals for the abnormal formal continued apace, but the Duchess Anathea did not appear at them, making Ondine even more worried as they trudged back to the family pub after an afternoon of dancing. Hamish winced as he held the door open for Ondine.

"Are you all right, darling?"

"Jus' me shoulders hen, on account of gettin' me posture right."

Old Col swished past. "Posture is the most important part."

"Aye," he said with a dramatic sigh. "After a good sleep I'll get the blood flow back into my arms sharpish."

"You could be a little more appreciative, Col," Ondine said, then suddenly felt terrible about speaking so harshly.

"Considering he ruined my first debutante ball, yes, Ondine, I *appreciate* that Hamish is at last making amends for his appalling behaviour all those years ago."[49]

Twigs figuratively snapped inside Ondine's head. Her great aunt had never sounded so tetchy before. She'd always been playful and full of mischief. Even when things were crazy, Ondine had always been able to rely on Old Col to steer them right. Now she looked and sounded downright mean. It wasn't like her at all. "Auntie Col, are you, y'know, all right?"

"Course I'm all right," she snapped.

"No need to snap."

"I didn't snap," she snapped. Again.

Ping, went Ondine's brain. "It's the ball, isn't it? You're getting worked up about it."

"Nonsense."

"It's going to be all right, you know." Ondine hoped Old Col would calm down. She needed her great auntie to be her great self. Not this snappish . . . *snapper*. "Hamish is working his shoulders off so that he'll be ready on the night. He wants it to be a success just as much as you do." And Ondine wanted the Duchess Anathea to be there so she could warn her again of what Vincent was up to. Honestly, sometimes she felt like everyone else had become so caught up in their personal issues they'd forgotten about what was really important. Protecting Brugel from Vincent!

People began filling the streets, heading towards the city centre. Dread filled Ondine's belly as the crowds kept coming during the late afternoon, with dozens of people waving flags as they walked. On the flags were blue hands.

---

[49] That ball. Where Hamish (as a young lad) had offended Old Col (as a young Colette Romano) and she'd turned him into a ferret (the evergreen Shambles).

This was a rally *for* Vincent.

Jolted into action, Ondine raced upstairs and grabbed her camera, although what she'd be able to do with the footage was anyone's guess.[50] She had to at least document what was going on. Maybe, when she showed the footage to Anathea, the Duchess might start to do something.

Music played, the spring sun beamed from the sky and the air filled with delicious fragrances of fried cheese balls. Although they were tired from rehearsals, Ondine and Hamish slipped out the side gate and followed the tide of people. They soon found themselves in Savo Plaza, where music and fun filled the air. Cadets created a percussion of precision drumbeats, streamers caught on tree branches filling them with colour. It was the biggest street party Ondine had ever seen.

"Gotta hand it to the lord, he does throw a fine céilidh,' Hamish said.[51]

If Vincent kept up this charm offensive, there would soon be a tipping point, which would tip Duchess Anathea out of Brugel entirely.

***

In order to avoid his palm fading back to whitish pink, Vincent plunged his hand into the toilet cistern, which had an old-style dark blue hygiene block in it. His skin came out a rich shade of blue.

---

[50] Most people these days would simply grab their phone, which comes with a camera on it, but this is Brugel, and technology takes a while to arrive. If Ondine had grabbed her phone, the cord wouldn't have reached the doorway.

[51] An enormous party to celebrate something big, like a wedding or your team winning a football game. When your team loses, you have a wake.

This was his symbol, as Babak Balakhan had decreed. Having a blue hand linked him to his ancestor Elmaree. And it looked great on the banners.[52]

For the briefest moment he wondered if the chemicals might not be entirely good for him, but staining his hand wouldn't be forever, just until he had the Dukedom back.

"Ready? Let's go," his bride-to-be said as he walked back into the hotel suite.

Happy crowds gathered in the plaza below their window. So many were dressed in blue, or holding banners of blue hands. There had to be a few thousand people already. Impressive. Babak had paid for everything. The security guards, the traffic management, the stage, the public address system, the entertainment and the food vans giving away free cheeseballs.

A second-tier celebrity presenter introduced the acts. "And now, ladies and gentlemen, boys and girls of all ages . . ." A troop of Fort Kluff cadets beat out a drum roll to build excitement.

In the hotel suite, two security guards, a male and a female knocked and entered. They wore identical, dark blue suits, aviator sunglasses and little clear coils of audio equipment clipped into their ears.

"We're ready to escort you to the stage, My Lord," the woman said.

"Excellent," Vincent said, "I'll be right with –"

A rock crashed through the window, shattering glass over the carpet.

---

[52] Elmaree the First had broken the quill she used to sign a marriage agreement with Prince Faddei of Slaegal. The phrase 'Elmaree's Stain' refers to the blue ink spilled over her writing hand, and the 'stain' on her reputation for reneging on a deal. It was never going to be a good deal for Elmaree anyway, but historians can be so cruel. For more details, read *All For Love: The Life and Times of Elmaree, the First Grand Duchess of Brugel.*

The woman pushed Vincent to the floor and shielded him with her body. "Stay down!" she yelled.

The noise and drama sent Vincent's pulse soaring.

"Breach in Lord Vincent's hotel room!" the man said, moving sideways to the window.

"Don't suppose anyone's going to jump on me?" Ruslana said with a petulant hand on her hip.

Squashed under the protective guard, Vincent tried to steady his breathing. He had to beat this panic, he couldn't let this spoil his day. He hissed out, "You're wrinkling my suit."

The woman let him up. "We need to get you somewhere safer."

"I don't think so," Vincent heard the wobble in his voice, so he played with his cuffs until his nerves calmed down. "The show must go on and all that."

Ruslana walked over and picked up the rock, which had a note secured with an elastic band. "Anathea forever," she read out. "Oh look, they've made all the letters from cut up newspapers. Bless."

Ruslana's sarcasm in the face of adversity gave Vincent the boost of confidence he needed. He held his arm out to her. "Shall we face the music?"

"We'll get this cleaned up right away," the woman said. "And replace the window."

With no glass in the window, the noise from the plaza came through clearly. The MC was whipping the crowd into a frenzy. Perhaps the crowd was so distracted, nobody had heard or seen the pro-Anathea rock?

The MC put on a strange voice and elongated every vowel " . . . Pleeeeease give a thumping great welcoooooooome to the band representing Brugel at this year's PopEuroTube, Baaaaaaattlefrooooooooont!"

The crowd cheered. The band members walked on, waving and blowing kisses to the crowd.

"Hello Venzelemma," the lead singer boomed out. "Are we ready for a good time?"

"Right," Vincent adjusted his tie in the mirror. Hmmm. Was this a tie type of occasion or not? Nah, too formal. He wrenched it off and popped open the top button on his shirt.

Melody piped up from behind the sofa, where she must have leapt when the rock came through. "If it's all right with you, I'll stay. I can see the stage from here if you need any magic."

Ruslana went to the phone and dialled.

"What are y –"

"– I'd like a basket of cheeseballs delivered to room two twenty please. Oh, and a bowl of potato wedges with three dipping sauces." Placing the receiver down, she turned to Melody. "Carbohydrates are on their way."

Of course. Ruslana was looking particularly attractive today. Her skin looked human, her hair shiny and healthy, her make up classic and understated. Melody must have been using a lot of magic to achieve that, and Ruslana must have been letting her.

"You are the luckiest son-of-a-duke in the world," Ruslana said as she took his hand and walked him into the hallway towards the lift. "You have me and you have Melody. The best of both worlds."

There was that.

"Looking at you now makes me appreciate Melody all the more," he said.

"When we break up, I'm keeping her," Ruslana said.

The lift made the universal 'ping' to let them know the car was at their floor.

"Shouldn't that be Melody's decision?" Vincent said as they stepped in. He hit the ground floor button with the knuckle of his non-blue index finger. It wasn't that he was particularly germ-phobic, but he'd seen stories about pathogens on everyday items such as lift buttons, mobile telephones and supermarket trolley handles. It turned his stomach. Sure, and he'd had his other hand in the toilet cistern only a few moments ago. All part of the sacrifice to get his inheritance back. [53]

Ruslana broke into his thoughts. "Don't tell me you actually care about Melody?"

It made him uncomfortable. "I care enough not to treat her like a commodity."

She gave him a single raised eyebrow.

He was saved from saying anything more by the 'ping' as the doors opened to the hotel's reception.

A barrage of media jumped into their way, lights on, cameras running, microphones at mouth height.
"Smile and wave dear," Ruslana said, giving his hand a squeeze, "I've got this."

As if born to the role of Duchess, Ruslana put them all at ease, her tone at just the right pitch to be heard, but not raucous.

The reporters, however, shouted over one another as they fired fresh questions at Vincent and Ruslana as they headed towards the stage outside in the plaza.

Outside, Battlefront's lead singer finishing another song to huge cheers. Then, as she looked back and acknowledged Vincent, she turned to the crowd and got them really excited.

"I know the song you want to hear. We can't wait to perform it for the rest of Europe!"

------

[53] Hygienically cautious people endeavour not to touch anything with their palms or finger pads, as this is the fastest way to transmit bacteria and viruses, which adore warm, moist conditions. Comparatively, the knuckles are usually drier and less conducive to harboring germs. This dovetails neatly with Brugel's public health announcement series: "Stop Touching Your Face!"

The crowd made piercing whistles, blasting Vincent's eardrums. The singer rocked out *Anthem*, the audience went berzerk in support. If Battlefront performed like this at PopEuroTube, they'd collect dozens of 'treize-points'. [54]

"Thank you Venzelemma! Thank you Brugel!" the singer cried out to the crowds. "See you at PopEuroTube!"

The MC revved the crowd into pure mania, gearing them up for Vincent's appearance. "And now, it's my absolute pleasure to introduce our next guest on the bill." The MC said. "He's the reason we're here today, to show our support. Ladies and Gentlemen, I bring you the next Duke of Brugel, Lord Vincent!"

The crowd went completely insane. Fried cheese balls flew through the air.

He turned to Ruslana and held out his hand. "You coming with me or staying here?"

"Oh sweetheart," she gave him a cold wink, "we're in this together."

He helped her take the stairs first, then followed. She waited for him on the side of the stage, before taking his hand again and holding it aloft, like a winner.

The crowd was delirious, taking five minutes to quieten down enough to listen to anything he had to say. The clouds parted. A brilliant shaft of sunlight played upon Savo Plaza. Wild and passionate applause broke out. He hadn't even said anything yet.

"Thank you," he said, waving with both hands to the crowd, who cheered again. Beside him, Ruslana took a respectful step backwards, demonstrating that he was the important one here.

---

[54] Trieze-points (pronounced 'trez-pwa') is thirteen points, the highest score any country can give a contestant on PopEuroTube.

"How fantastic is Battlefront, right?" It wasn't in the speech at all, but it matched the mood. Adoring whistles and cheers filled the plaza.

"I want to thank everyone for coming out today, your support is humbling and I'm incredibly grateful. As you know, I have dedicated my life to Brugel and will continue to do so for as long as the people of Brugel will have me." The goodwill from the crowd told him he was saying all the right things. Movement to the side caught his attention. He looked over and felt stones pour into his gut at the sight of Ondine and Hamish in the crowd. For the briefest second their eyes locked. They weren't here to support him; he knew that much. But he wasn't going to let them ruin his big moment. They were but two people in a sea of supporters. It was important to stay positive.

"I appreciate everyone being here today. Thank you Venzelemma. Thank you Brugel." He stepped back from the microphone and waved as the crowd made crazy noises. Groups of people were stamping their feet on the cobblestones to make a drum roll sound. The cadets from Fort Kluff, looking resplendent in their military uniforms, set up another precise drum roll that lead into the start of a classic marching beat. The MC rushed to the empty microphone "Let's hear it for Lord Vincent!" People cheered and whistled so loudly, Vincent could barely hear what the journalists were asking him as he stepped off the stage.

Oh, they weren't asking him anything. It was for his bride-to-be.

"Ruslana, what's it like being engaged to Brugel's next Duke?"

"It's wonderful," she said without missing a beat. "Because he is a wonderful, caring, considerate man."

Laughing out loud would expose them both. Vincent blushed and looked to the ground in an effort to compose himself. Who knew she'd be such a good blagger?[55]

"When we met I didn't know who he was," she added.

That was true.

"Where did you meet?" A woman asked.

"We meet at a charity function in Norange," she said.

That wasn't a lie either, really. If he had to describe how he was feeling about Ruslana right now, Vincent came perilously close to admiration.

"When is the wedding?"

"Late summer," they both said on top of each other.

Their audience laughed and Vincent found himself smiling at Ruslana. She was handling herself beautifully in front of the media. Without a trace of orange skin, she was lovely to look at. All Vincent had to do was stand beside her looking supportive. Just as it had been on stage, where he'd said very little. The voice in his head said, "I have a feeling this is all going to work out beautifully."

____

[55] Blagger is Brugelish for telling very big fibs, which are very similar to the things that come out of the back-end of a bull.

Blagger is not to be confused with Blogger, although the results can often be the same.

~ Chapter Nine ~

On the first Sunday in April, the clocks moved forward by two hours to herald the beginning of Brugel Summer Time, even though it was still spring, and only just if the weather outside was any guide. Ondine loved having hours of light in the evenings, but it came with a price of woefully dark mornings. And two hours' less sleep that first night.

"Up you get darling, it's already nine o'clock." Ma shook her shoulder to rouse her from her bed. "Even though it's really only seven."

Defensively Ondine slapped the pillow over her head. "Lemme sleep in."

"You say that every year. Come on lazybones, get up."

"Not lazy, sleep deprived."

"You say *that* every year as well. Come on. We have guests for breakfast."

Why did her parents take bookings for the first weekend in April? It was always chaos in the morning as everyone felt the effects of the time change. Bumping into the doorframe on her way out, Ondine staggered from her bedroom and turned down the hall, finding herself outside Hamish's bedroom. Huh? Her brain hadn't consciously decided that, she'd just found herself here. Oh well, now she was here, she may as well see if Hamish was up.

She rapped on the door, "Has Ma come and shouted at you yet?"

No reply.

Another rap and repeat question. Another bout of silence. Curiosity eating at her, Ondine half-covered her eyes with her hand and turned the handle. "I'm coming in, hope you're decent. No reply at all. She pulled her hand away and looked at the bed. At first it appeared empty, but then she saw the hint of movement. Pulling back the covers, she found Shambles the ferret curled into a knot of fur where Hamish the man should have been.

"How dare you!" The words flew out in a burst of disappointment.

The ferret didn't move. She picked him up by the middle, and he sagged at both ends like gloppy pizza dough. "I can't believe you're doing this to me!"

The ferret twisted and spun in her hand. "I'mawakeIpromise," he jumbled and then dived under the covers. As he transformed into his gorgeous Hamishness, Ondine grew more and more furious. "You don't need to sleep as a ferret. You're not sick, you're not injured. Why are you doing this?"

"Awww lass, it's too early."

He mustn't have adjusted his clock. She'd caught him before he'd had the chance to wake up and change himself back. "You slept all night as a ferret, didn't you?"

Being so tired, his accent sounded thicker and even less understandable than normal. "Mustae had a wee tummy ache in the night and turned in mah sleep, so I did."

"In your sleep? Then where are your pyjamas?" They

should have been mushed up under the covers somewhere, but instead they sat there like the incriminating evidence they were, folded on the side chair.

Normally when Ondine was right, she felt victorious. Now she felt hollow. "Don't lie to me."

"I'm sorry lass, I didnae mean to. Honest. I just panicked a wee bit."

"So you *were* sleeping as a ferret?"

"Aye, I was. But I did it fer you! You've seen me grey hairs and all. I'm turning into an old man in front of yer eyes. Between you and me, I think Old Col's magic is warping out of control. I'm scared that if I don't sleep as a ferret every night, I may not wake up at all!"

***

With so many stressful scenarios about her like spinning plates on bamboo canes, Ondine had to get at least one of the worst worries off her list. That afternoon she made a personal visit to Duchess Anathea.[56] After that, her conscience would be clear about state matters and she could get back to more important fretting about her great aunt losing her magic and her beloved Hamish turning into a wrinkly old prune.

"Ondine dear, how lovely to see you," Anathea said, as if they were old friends.

They were in a private room on the southern side of the building, to make the most of the light. At least, that's what Ondine assumed as there were no curtains at the windows. The room had a two-bar heater sitting in the hearth of an open fireplace, but only one bar was active.

____

[56] There was a half-hour wait to gain an audience. Because even though Ondine considered herself a friend of the duchess, she was still a member of the public and she didn't have a prior appointment.

The last time Ondine had been in the ducal estate in Venzelemma had been summer. She'd come with her father and Shambles – the ferret wrapped around her neck like a scarf – to warn Duke Pavla about a threat to his life. This time it was to warn the Duchess of something much worse. Vincent was about to overthrow her, of that Ondine was certain.

"Thank you ever so much for seeing me."

"I assume you're here because you have news?"

"Yes, and it's all about Vincent I'm sorry to say. I have been sending you regular reports but I'm not sure you're getting them?"

"Marvellous," Anathea said as she walked to her desk and began flicking through a diary. Not the reaction Ondine expected. Anathea carried on as if she'd simply been told the lunch menu for the day. "Has all your school work been finished for the term?"

"Err . . . My finals will be in a few weeks. I'm going to Business College, which starts in September. I want to run the family pub when my parents retire. But that's not important. You must know what Vincent's up to. You saw the rally, didn't you? And all the cadets?"

Flicking a page in her diary, Anathea looked up and said, "Summer will be a busy time for you."

It was like they were talking about completely different things. "You don't seem worried?"

Anathea nodded. "Walk with me, I am to be fitted for a dress in ten minutes."

They left that marginally-warmer-than-an-igloo office and stepped into a chilled hallway. As they walked, Anathea fired questions at her. "What sort of following does he *really* have?"

So she *had* been listening. Perhaps she was worried about somebody else listening to them?

"His popularity is getting bigger every day, and you

know how Mrs Howser is free. She's training cadets at Fort Kluff and I've got to tell you they terrify me. They're totally mutated by magic."

Anathea grabbed a door handle to lead them into a new room. Strange that nobody opened the door for the Duchess of Brugel. Perhaps she'd had to cut back on staff? They walked in to find a dressmaker with a tape measure for a scarf, and a wardrobe on castors, with racks of clothes inside zippered bags. She wore a heavy fur-lined cloak and matching hat with the earflaps turned down, which she quickly turned up as Anathea neared. There was no heating in here at all.

"Ondine, you may keep talking as I have pins stuck in me by Luminita here. Be careful, Luminita, there is padding to be had, but it is not to be pricked at."

"So I guess you need a plan to counter Vincent's popularity?" Ondine offered.

"Do I? I can't do much about other people being popular with the mob, can I?"

A twig snapped in Ondine's brain. This was not the Anathea of old. "Yes you can. Making you popular is all we've been doing for the past few months. Why are you slacking off now?"

Anathea glared. "You forget your place. I will not be spoken to in that way."

Ondine shrank at the rebuke. The dressmaker ducked out of the way, pretending she wasn't there. Ondine wanted to say, "You're not nearly as worried as you should be and I'm starting to think there's some kind of magic spell on you. Vincent suddenly has loads of money and is incredibly popular and people are taking to the streets to show their support." Instead, all she could manage was, "I'm sorry, Your Lordship, but I'm worried about you, and I'm worried about Brugel."

A slow smile spread over Anathea's face. "So you *do*

care."

Ondine blurted, "Of course I do."

"Good." Anathea's expression softened. "Then you will understand why I need to look my best at all times. I can tell by the way you're locking your hands together that you're cold. The circulation in my feet may never be felt again. But to the outside world, I look the part. Plus, the law is on my side."

"But he's loaded and you're broke!"

The dressmaker's mouth dropped open. Pins fell to the threadbare carpet.

"You will be paid," Anathea assured her.

"Cash," Luminita said.

"Of course." Anathea shook her head.

"Today," Luminita said.

"The bursar will be given your invoice on the way out."

Luminita asked, "Which one is the bursar?"

Anathea quietly cleared her throat. "The one behind the desk."

Luminita began packing her things. "You mean the one who drives your car and opens doors and answers phones and makes your tea as well?"

Anathea sighed. "Yes, that's the one."

"I will go now," Luminita said.

Anathea held her hand out. "The dress will be ready in time for the opera tonight?"

"When I get paid, I'll come back." With that, Luminita zipped the duchess's jacket into a protective clothing bag. "I'll see myself out."

"You're going to the opera?" Ondine gulped with worry.

"The premiere of *The Cholera Tourer*. An historical piece loosely based on the story of Black Sonja."[57]

"You will be safe, won't you?"

"I have my earplugs at the ready." A dreamy look clouded her features, "and I shall have Valentin at my side."

"Is he the handsome man you brought to dance rehearsals?"

Anathea's face glowed. "He's such a silver fox, don't you think?"

If she were into older men, Ondine would agree. She nodded anyway, just to be diplomatic. Strange thoughts drifted through Ondine's mind as she looked at the Duchess's expression and realised how very lonely Anathea must have been all these years. Then her gaze drifted to the peeling wallpaper, the dust-encrusted furniture and worn carpets. For a moment she wondered if being the Duchess of Brugel was more a burden than a blessing.

"You think this room is bad?" Anathea broke into her thoughts. "State dinners cannot be hosted because the floorboards in the dining room are beyond repair."

From a side door, Biscuit the dog barrelled in and ran for his mother. She cuddled him and buried her face in his fur.

Saving Anathea felt like such an impossible task, until a stray thought took root in Ondine's brain. "Vincent's got money now, if he's so determined to take all of this. Get him to start paying for repairs."

That made Anathea stop for a moment and look at Ondine. "Did Vincent send you?"

"I'm not working for Vincent." Ondine tensed. "As if that would ever happen."

------

[57] 'Loosely based' in that Black Sonja was responsible for the spread of Bubonic Plague, not cholera, throughout the Black Sea region. People caught cholera from drinking contaminated water, whereas the plague was spread from person to person from sneezing, shaking hands and touching one's face.

Guilt swamped her and she looked at the floor.

"I won't be lied to," Anathea said.

Gulp. "I'm not lying. And I'm not working for him."

"But?"

Since when was Anathea so astute? With a sigh of defeat Ondine said, "I helped him. But only a bit. And I wasn't really helping him, I was helping Ruslana. All I did was grab our makeup and hair lady to make Ruslana look presentable. Because Vincent said if I helped him, he'd help my sisters get in to Pop Euro Tube." It felt so good to get that off her chest.

"People can be persuaded with the right motivation," Anathea said.

They walked back to Anathea's office. Somebody had turned off the little bar heater while they'd been out. It was the kind of cold Ondine felt right between her shoulders after she'd been sitting at her desk for an hour, doing homework.

"Rurururu," Biscuit barked. Anathea let him down and he trotted over to a little bed underneath her desk.

"Where are you daughters, by the way," Ondine asked.

"Why do you ask?"

"Because they should be here, working for you. That way they will save you money on hiring staff, and they'll learn what's involved in being Duchess. And you can do a media charm offensive yourself, so people will see your daughters here, putting in the hours, and they'll get used to them being around."

"Why should my daughters work?"

Ondine scrunched her brows in confusion. "Everyone needs to work. I've worked for my parents my whole life. It's normal."

"Ah but Ondine, your normal is very different to *my* normal. And my daughters will not be subjected to merchant-class expectations of normal."

"But . . ."

"Mm?" Anathea's eyebrow rose in smugness.

Ondine couldn't help staring at Anathea for longer than was strictly polite. Now they were back in her office, the duchess was back to being obscure and a little rude again. "Are you sure you're not under some kind of spell?"

"Positive."

Ondine's hope deflated like a day-old balloon. "That's a real shame."

"Why is that?"

"Because I don't think you're taking the threat from Vincent seriously enough. And . . . I don't know! You're not *you* any more." If this was Anathea's real nature, how had it taken Ondine so long to see the Venn diagram, where Anathea appeared in one circle and 'The real world' took up another, but they only crossed over in the middle for a millimetre?

"My dear Ondine," The Duchess said, her face tightening, "There is so little we agree about, I can't see why you're still here."

Chills buzzed her system. "I guess I should go then."

"See yourself out, there's a good girl."

Numb with shock and disillusionment, Ondine staggered towards the door. "Oh, before I go. Thank you for your time, My Lord Duchess."

"Keep the door closed, you're letting the heat out."

"What heat?" Ondine said as she shut the door with a snick.

The whole way home on the train, Ondine couldn't help wondering where it had all gone so horribly wrong. She may have backed the wrong horse in Anathea, but there was no possible way she'd transfer her allegiances to Vincent. If Anathea was batty, Vincent was positively poisonous.

Which left her exactly where?

Through the keyhole in the wardrobe door, Lord Vincent watched as his aunt took her position behind her desk. The dog slept beneath, barely snuffling when Anathea placed her stockinged feet on him. "Nicely done." He stepped into the room and gave a slow clap. "I thought you'd never get rid of her."

"That poor girl's had her heart broken. I hope you're happy."

"Very. Now, where were we?"

"My daughters' educations, my clothing allowance and the restoration of this crumbling old pile."

Looking around, all he could see were the faded signs of a once proud room. "If we get started on the renovations, it should be ready by my twenty-first birthday."

She gave him one of those looks, it silently said, "I have so much to say I don't know where to begin."

He waited. Eventually she said, "Those renovations should have been done by your father."

"We both know he was broke. That's why he married my mother."

"Ah yes. We come from a long line of marrying into money. I see the tradition is being carried on."

"I'm nothing if not practical."

The dog under the desk stirred.

When he was sure she had nothing else to say, Vincent asked, "Speaking of daughters, where are my beautiful cousins?"

Another sigh from Anathea, making the dog wake up and grizzle. "My daughters are in school, as you know. Have the tuition fees been paid for the term?"

Vincent stroked his chin where a beard might one day be. Should he grow the split moustache like his father?

"They have been enrolled for the past year, have they not?"

"They've been home for holidays and such. They have not completely lost touch with Brugel. What's your point?"

"My point is, you enrolled them before you had any known way of paying for it. What would you have done if I had not become engaged to a means of income?"

A shrug. "Their father would have been petitioned. In fact, I think *your* father was petitioned as well, and he didn't get back to me before . . . well, before he was poisoned by your mother. My, what a lovely family we have."

"My father's passing was to your benefit as much as mine." He couldn't help a little snort of contempt escape. He could have sworn he saw a plume of steam from his nose it was so cold in here. "Let's take a walk, dear aunt." He offered his arm. It wasn't so much that he thought a stroll in the gardens would change things, but standing around in this cold room did nothing for his circulation.

"Everyone can see what you're doing, you know." Anathea said as she walked through the doorway.

"I'm doing what's best for Brugel," Vincent said.

"You keep telling yourself that."

"Because it's true." Why couldn't she see that? "It's far better to have stability at the helm."

"Saying stability implies I am unstable. Anyone can see I am being actively undermined."

"All I propose is a smooth transition period and a respectful handover, which will be beneficial to everyone."

They reached the double doors that lead out to the parterre garden. It crimped his heart to see the overgrown edging of the flower beds where once had been laser-straight lines. He held his arm to the side in the hope she'd take it. She did, and he drew her closer as they stepped out into the weak spring sunshine. If there were any photographers around, they would capture them looking friendly and comfortable. The pictures would also capture the dilapidated garden, which would not hurt his cause one bit.

"How are my darling nephews?" Anathea asked.

"The nannies at Bellreeve tell me my brothers are doing well."

"Are they taken to see their mother?"

"Yes. I'm told they have supervised visits to the asylum on a regular basis."

"How often has Kerala been visited by you? I'm sure you're missed."

Something dried his throat, but he had to look calm and in control, just in case somebody in the public saw him. Because he had his public face on, the one that told the world that everything was all right. "As much as I miss her, it will do none of us any good to be seen with her."

"You're sounding very grown up about it."

"I don't have a choice."

"There are choices. You could retire from public life to grieve in private. To deal with the mess your mother left behind. To help your brothers. Instead you pursue attention as if the death of your father were a springboard to be taken into public life."

"It sounds so calculated, coming from you" he tucked his head down and caught sight of another overgrown garden bed. Green shoots of . . . something . . . fought through a tangled blanket of weeds. He tried to remember what was there last year. They were red and white flowers of some kind.

"The first thing you're going to do is hire a gardener. Or ten. Send me the bill."

"Dearest of nephews. The building is falling to bits, and you're worried about geraniums?"

"It's the first thing people see when they visit. That's

another thing. You're going to open the gardens to the public."

"I don't think that should be done," she pulled up short and glared at him.

"Dearest of aunts," he shot back, "This garden is public, therefore it should always look its best."

"There are so many more pressing things that need to –"

"– There always are, but they are on the inside, and the public will not see it." He felt so proud of the way he didn't let any of the disappointment or upset show on his face. At least, he was fairly sure it wasn't showing on his face. Those muscle relaxants he'd borrowed from Ruslana were really messing with his head.

***

If Ondine had a thesaurus with her for the train journey home from visiting the Duchess of Brugel, she would have found herself feeling flat, cheerless, dejected, despondent and all-over generally *blah*.

But she didn't have one with her, so she had a hard time knowing exactly what she should call the melancholy settling over her. It was the kind of thing that made her want to listen to sad songs.

Once she reached the warm embrace of the family pub, she followed her nose to the kitchen. It wasn't her eyes that told her something was wrong but her nose. There was nothing on the cooker. (Nor were there any people).

The only thing she could detect were remnants of cold scrambled eggs and toast scrapings. They carried the distinct scent of having been cooked some time ago and were now congealing.

Peeking into the dining room, she found her family helping Margi with some vague ideas of choreography that would allow her to move around while also singing and hitting her notes.[58] Cybelle, of course, was excused from any dancing because she would be on piano the whole time. No sign of Hamish anywhere, which added to her growing list of disappointments. Nor Old Col. Maybe they were at the dance hall.

"You look like you're at a loose end," Ma said as she came into the kitchen and turned the coffee maker on. "There are always dishes to do."

"I have a stack of homework." Which was absolutely true.

"Everything all right?" Ma gave her a funny look, as if she knew something was up but was waiting for Ondine to confess.

"Just tired I guess," she said with a shrug. The tremble in her jaw gave her away.

"Darling, what's wrong?" Ma put one arm around her and directed her to their private room behind the kitchen. Then she did the most bizarre thing. Ma closed the door to the kitchen, blocking out the sound of her sisters' music to give them real privacy.

"Everything." Ondine slumped into the nearest chair.

"Did the meeting with the Duchess go badly?"

"How did you know?" Of course her mother knew everything.

"You've had so much excitement this past year, it's not surprising you're feeling flat now. Best get your homework done while there's time. Thank goodness Every Pop Top will be over soon."

"PopEuroTube."

"That's the one. I never thought I'd say this but, hooray for Slaegal."

------

[58] Sure, Margibelle's performance is about the song, but it's also about putting on a show. Margi doesn't want to stand on stage like a lump if she can help it.

"Who are you and what have you done with my mother," Ondine said. Then she pulled herself together. "Seriously. The pub's closed; you're being wonderful and understanding and . . . really calm. Are we all under some kind of spell?"

Ma sighed and slumped her shoulders. "Not a spell, exactly."

Ondine forgot to breathe as she waited for Ma to tell the truth.

"Ruslana is being very supportive." Ma's palms went up in a defensive-yet-shushing motion to keep Ondine from jumping to conclusions. "Don't jump to conclusions. But she wants Margibelle to do well and for that to happen they need time to rehearse, which means turning customers away from time to time."

"You don't have to call them Margibelle when it's just us at home, you know."

Ma shrugged, "It's kind of catchy."

Ondine got up and said, "I have homework to do." As she reached the foot of the stairs she turned back. "Exactly how much support is Ruslana giving us?"

"Enough. She wants Slaegal to win. And you have exams soon so you'll benefit with more time to study."

Shaking her head, Ondine knew she should be grateful. All the while she felt a horrible sense of unease, as if the very ground had shifted under her feet.

~ Chapter Ten ~

The next few weeks of April passed in a blur of essays, assignments and exams for Ondine, rehearsals and costume fittings for Cybelle and Margi and a whirl of chiffon and feathers for Col and Hamish. Great-Auntie Col was the one in chiffon, obviously, and she paraded herself around the closed dining room showing the gown to its best advantage. The dress had fluffy white ostrich feathers at the neckline, collars and hem; many of which became ensnared in Hamish's hair as he held her hand and practised their 'walk' they had to do for the presentation. The peach-coloured dress draped and flowed over Old Col's body like water over boulders (being as old as Old Col was, there were a several boulders). When she twirled, the skirts fluttered outwards, delicate and shimmery like a hibiscus flower. It hurt for Ondine to look at Hamish in his impossibly gorgeous suit. It was the same suit he'd worn to Margi's wedding, except now he had a matching peachy cummerbund and a rose bud in his lapel. It wasn't a real rose, because it wouldn't last the distance between the rehearsals and the big night.

Having finished her second last assignment in Brugelish Literature, Ondine had time to watch Hamish and Old Col rehearse. It was still light outside, thanks to Brugel's two-hour jump in to daylight saving time. This time of year they'd normally have customers in the dining room and the garden, if it were warm enough.

In the closed dining room, Margi and Cybelle had created something of an impromptu party. The girls were singing while Chef and Thomas clapped out a beat. Hamish and Old Col were performing a Brugelish three-step.

"Hey, Ondi!" Hamish said. At which point his footing slipped and took Col for a tumble.

Everyone gasped, all eyes turned to Old Col to see if she was hurt.

"Sorry Col," Hamish said, "I got distracted."

"Yes." Her voice was sharp enough to cut fabric. "Don't do that again."

"Aye-aye captain." He gave mocking salute, deflating some of the tension. Then he turned to Ondine and her heart melted a little more. He was under so much pressure to be the perfect partner for Old Col; the lady should be thanking him, not speaking daggers.

"Ondi, help me out of my dress," Old Col said as she approached her. "I can't let it get wrinkled before the big night."

"Of course. Auntie Col, when is the do-over deb?"

"Didn't I tell you? It's May twelve. Hamish you should have told her."

"The twelfth?" Hamish said, "I thought you said it was the Saturday afterwards?"

"No, they brought it forward."

Margi, Cybelle, Ondine and Hamish all looked back

and forth to each other. Eventually Margi expositioned, "But that's the same night as PopEuroTube!"

"Is it?" Old Col gave a nonchalant shrug. "I guess you won't be able to come then. No matter, I know my debutante ball is hardly something you younger folk'd be interested in."

"I don't think that's what she means, Aunty Col," Ondine said. "I think we'd all like to be at both events."

Another shrug. "Be a dear and get my zippered apparel bag would you, we'll need to put the dress in it the moment I take it off, so that it doesn't get any dirt from the floor. Come along."

Ondine followed Old Col to the private room behind the kitchen.

"I have a bone to pick with you, child. What is going on with Hamish? The more we rehearse, the worse he gets."

"Nothing," Ondine said feeling terribly disappointed. Because they'd been doing a whole lot of *nothing* lately, and she'd been rather hoping that they could have at least been doing a little bit of *something*. "I'm sure he's trying his absolute best. And I think you should have told us earlier that your dance would clash with PopEuroTube. Is there any way you could hold over the deb until next year?"

The woman scowled and her cheeks turned red. "There won't be a next year!"

"Are they not having one?" Or was there something about her great aunt's health she wasn't telling them?

"Stop pestering me," Old Col said.

Old Col had always been a fixture in the family. If she was sick, if something was wrong, she should tell them. Ondine's hands shook with worry as she helped her great-aunt out of the dress. Ostrich feathers came loose as she breathed in, causing her to splutter.

"Mind the dress!"

"Yes Col."

"Stop spitting on it!"

"I have feathers stuck in my mouth." It was a wonder Ondine didn't yell back. In fact, she could have sworn she was using up her very, *very* last reserves of *nice*. Right, the dress was safe. She handed it to Col and tried to keep her voice calm. "Something is wrong. You're being mean, and that's not like you. And I didn't want to worry you but your magic isn't as strong as it used to be so Hamish has been sleeping as a ferret."

"I am fine."

"No, you're not." They stared at each other, the tension in Ondine's chest growing by the second.

With a deep sigh, Old Col said, "I'm cross because there's so much to do. Hamish hasn't been getting any better and the dance is in two weeks!"

"Come and talk to me when you're out of denial." All the aggravation did Ondine no good, so she left Old Col to stew in her bad mood and followed the music back to the dining room. They'd pushed the tables and chairs into the corners to create a dance floor in the middle of the room, and the radio was on. Ma danced with Da, Cybelle danced with Chef and Margi danced with Thomas. Hamish was sitting it out, but he had a huge smile as he clapped along to the beat.

"Lassie, would ye do me the honour of this dance?" The power of seeing him in that formal suit turned her emotions to mush.

Nestled close in his arms, she saw sprigs of silver through his hair. More of those silvery strands grew along his temples. When he smiled at her, his eyes crinkled and twinkled, but then when he stopped smiling, the crinkles stayed exactly where they were.

Her heart flailed at the sight of his weary face. He'd be

sleeping as s ferret again tonight.

***

The day Ma re-opened the pub doors, everyone in Venzelemma wanted a table. They'd ask, "Is this the Margibelle Restaurant?" and her mother would beam and say, "It sure is!"

Lord Vincent, curse him, publicly said their pub was one of his favourite places to visit. The demographics in the dining room changed to a much younger, more demanding crowd. Customers didn't order as much, preferring an entree as their main. Then they'd stay in their seats when they were done, listening to Margibelle perform.

Ma carried a set of empty plates into the kitchen and turned to Ondine. "Can you head out to table three and get their dessert orders for me?"

Taking a peek at the table – a group of teens perhaps a year older than her – Ondine doubted she'd have any luck. "How much do you want to bet they get an ice cream on the way home instead."

"Recommend the *crème brûlée*. Nobody can resist that."

"We're out of *crème brûlée*," Henrik the chef said from down the end of the kitchen.

"We have lemon tarts, we can burn the top of them," Cybelle called back.

Ma took a breath and pushed the menus into Ondine's hands. "Improvise."

As luck would have it, right at that moment Lord Vincent, Ruslana, Melody and an older man came walking in to the restaurant. Ma dashed past Ondine in a blur and quickly cleared a table for them.

Ondine approached the table she'd been assigned,

128

doing her best to ignore her nemesis in the room.

One of the diners on her table said, "He'll make a great duke."

"Hello," Ondine interrupted brightly. "Would you like something for dessert or do you want the bill?" The unspoken part being, "so you can clear off."

They all said variations of "Oh yes, dessert," as they looked towards Vincent and decided to stay.

"What takes the longest to make?" One of them asked.

"The lemon-lime sorbet. We make it from scratch." Ondine said. Not a lie. They had made it from scratch. Four days ago. The diner should have asked, 'which dessert takes the longest to bring out to the customers?'

"Sorbets all round then."

Taking the menus back, Ondine headed to the kitchen to find everyone in their regular blur of activity. Hamish, bless his peach-coloured cummerbund, stepped in to the kitchen, having just returned from another rehearsal.

"Excellent," Ma said as she clapped eyes on him, "you can look after Vincent's table. He's just arrived for second dinner."

"Aye," he gave her a tap-to-the-head salute and peeked around the doorway into the dining room. "Who's that lummox with them?"

Being unable to look away from her beloved, Ondine only had eyes for Hamish. And the thick bands of silver hair at his temples that were not there this morning.

"Hush now," Ma said, "He's Ruslana's father, and with any luck, one of our new patrons. Whatever they order is on the house, by the way."

"Sorbets for table three," Cybelle dinged the service bell from the other end of the kitchen.

Ondine grinned as she settled each fluted bowl on her serving tray and made her way out to the table. The customers barely noticed her as she set their desserts down.

Too busy gawping at Vincent. "I took the liberty of bringing out the bill at the same time," she said.

No response.

Fine then.

Back in the kitchen, she sought out Hamish. "How are you feeling?"

"Not well. I found even more grey this afternoon."

She examined his temples, streaked with salt and pepper. "I can see that."

"I wasnae talking about me head."

Heat roared up her neck and she snarfled behind one hand. If she made too much noise, Ma would want to know why.[59]

"It was on me chest, lass. Where d'ye think I meant?"

She playfully swatted him on the arm. "Come on, let's see if table three has paid the bill." She lead him towards the wall partition, where they could look out onto the dining room without the diners feeling as if they were being monitored.

"For someone about to get married, she doesnae look so happy," Hamish said.

Ruslana sat there, all slumped of shoulders and pouted of lips. "And you say she only wants a salad?"

"Aye, and nothing to drink."

If Ondine could see the woman's dour expression from this far away, so must everyone else in the restaurant. "If she keeps cracking the sads, it will be bad for business," Ondine said. The moment her mother walked past, she pounced. "Ma, they're as miserable as a wet cardigan out there. I think Hamish should take them a complimentary bottle of plütz."

"A whole bottle? Best check with Da."

---

[59] Snarfled is the act of stifling a laugh while coughing a little. Spluttering may also be involved.

"Don't pick on Ruslana," Margi said as she joined the spying. "If it wasn't for her, Belle and I wouldn't be going to PopEuroTube."

"I helped," Ondine blurted, then wished she'd kept her mouth shut.

"Yes, your cheering in the audience made all the difference," Margi said with a roll of her eyes.

Hamish said, "You'd think they were planning a funeral, not a wedding."

"You're jumping at shadows." Margi took another peek at the table. "Is that your friend with her back to us?"

"That's Melody," Ondine said. "She's allowed to be miserable, because she's carrying a torch for Vincent."

"She likes the sauce," Margi said, indicating with a tilt of her head.

Oh dear, should Melody be having alcohol? Ondine thought they were the same age, which meant her friend shouldn't be touching the stuff for a couple of years yet.

"Any danger of the two of you getting any work done?" Ma asked as she stuck her head around the corner.

Ondine had never felt more hopeless. Melody was their insider in Vincent's camp, but she hadn't fed them anything useful for ages. "I'm not sitting by while Vincent swoops in and undoes all my hard work. I mean, *our* hard work."

"There's a fraudulent slip if ever I heard one," Hamish said.[60]

"We need Melody on our side. I'm going to get her." Ondine strolled out to the dining room, her pulse krump-dancing behind her ribs.

---

[60] A fraudulent slip is where you accidentally blurt out the truth. This is completely different from a Freudian slip, named after the enthusiastic 'father' of psychology, Sigmund Freud, who spent his lifetime reading naughty subtexts into everything.

Melody sat semi-slumped in her chair, enveloped by glum-fog. Ondine opted for her brightest tone. "How are your meals tonight? Is everything to your liking?"

"Beautiful. Delicious," Babak said. The man ate like a farm harvester, ploughing through the food in a solid line across his plate.

Vincent's knife and fork were resting on the side of his plate as he chatted to Ruslana. "It's as good as I remembered," he said, giving Ondine a smile that in an earlier season could have melted her heart.

Her insides shrivelled but she kept her smile steady. "I'll pass that on to the chef. Can I get you anything else? Desserts? More plütz?"

"Yes, more plütz." That was Babak. "Tell me, where do you get your supply? It's so hard to find in Norange."

"I'll send Da over, he's our resident expert on the best places to buy just about anything. Uh, Melody?" turning to her friend and placing a kind hand on her shoulder. Melody jumped, as if she'd been in a trance. Or perhaps she'd been busy making spells all this time? That would explain her distraction. But not the lack of eating. Using magic was supposed to make a witch ravenous, yet her friend had barely touched her meal. "Is everything all right?"

"Oh yes, it's fine. You gave me a really large serve, that's all."

"Are you sure?" Leaning in closer, "He is looking after you, isn't he?"

She nodded. "Yes."

"Perhaps you should lie down," Vincent interjected. "This is a hotel, there's bound to be a spare room where you can rest."

"She can stay." Ruslana placed her hand on Melody's wrist, clearly meaning to keep her at the table.

"I don't want to cause any trouble," Melody said. She

wasn't as twig-like and waifish as she had been with Mrs Howser, but there was no light in her eyes.

"No trouble at all, come and have a rest in our private lounge," Ondine said. Then they could be alone and have a good talk.

Vincent said, "It's absolutely fine with me. Take a break."

Chin puckering with emotion, Melody nodded and rose from her seat. All eyes fell upon them as Ondine lead her friend through the kitchen and out to the private lounge . "Have a slouch on the couch here and I'll build up the fire."

"I'm not cold," Melody said.

OK then. "I was going to ask if everything is all right, but I can see it's not." Ondine moved in for a hug and her friend's arms wrapped around her with the gusto of an orang-utan.

Eventually Melody pulled away. "Who's the psychic one now?"

Ondine shook her head. "I thought it would be like old times. A bit of spying here and there, feeding Anathea information and then somehow everything would fall into place and we'd save Brugel again."

Melody gave Ondine a strange look, crinkling her forehead into horizontal lines. "Save Brugel? From what?"

"From Vincent, obviously."

"But he's the best thing to ever happen to Brugel."

Something screeched in Ondine's brain. "No he's not. How can you say that?"

Silence stretched between them.

"Because it's true! Everyone loves him." Melody's eyes brightened. "He'll give Brugel stability."

Wait, what? "But he's *awful*. And he's done so many horrible things to my family –"

"Like make sure your sisters got a shot at fame and

riches in PopEuroTube? Yeah, I can see how badly that's working out for you."

Ouch! "I don't mean that." This was going off the rails superfast. "I mean all the things before. He's a power hungry . . . *I don't know what*. But he'll do whatever it takes and use whoever he needs to use to get there. We have to stop him. For the good of Brugel!"

Shaking her head, Melody said, "He would have been duke if Anathea hadn't interfered."

Ondine rocked back in shock. "She did not interfere! It always should have been hers except Pavla came along."

"And we're lucky he did!" Melody dragged her sleeve across her tear-stained face. "I can't believe you're trying to drive a wedge between Vincent and me!"

"Melody, please, why can't you see reason?"

"I was going to ask you the same thing! Now get out of my way. The Duke of Brugel needs me." Melody lifted her head and walked serenely to the dining room.

"That went about as bad as can be expected," Hamish said from the doorway.

Anger and frustration burned Ondine's heart. Nothing would change her mind about Vincent being bad for Brugel. But how in heaven's name could she make Melody see that?

"Ondi?" Margi showed her divine head around the corner and then she stepped closer. "What did Melody mean?"

Panic turned her brain numb. "What bit?" How much had she heard?

"The bit about making sure we had a shot at PopEuroTube?"

All of it then. Ma appeared. So did Old Col.

"What is going on?" Cybelle asked.

How many more people were going to crowd in here? Ondine blew her fringe in frustration. Tiredness seeped through her bones and she let go of the horrible secret that had tied her stomach in knots. "I helped Vincent that night at BrugelMelody. And in return, he made sure you went to PopEuroTube."

Silence chilled the air by several degrees.

Cybelle tilted her head. "Wow, you really do think it's all about you."

That was not the response she was expecting. She'd just bared Her Terrible Secret and they'd thrown it back in her face. "I'm not trying to take credit. He really did promise me he'd help you if I helped him."

"Aye, he put her right in it." Of course Hamish came to Ondine's defence. He was a champion like that. "Anyone else would have told him to sod off. Yer lucky to have a sister who cares so much about you."

Cybelle's hands curled into fists on her hips. "A sister who's so jealous she'll tell lies to make herself important."

"That's not what happened ye numpty eejit!" Hamish had never used bad words against any member of her family. Except perhaps for Old Col. "I was right there. And Vincent tightened the screws. Ye should be thanking Ondi fer helpin'."

Margi put her hand on Cybelle's arm to guide her away, but Cybelle shrugged her off. "You can't stand it that you're not in the spotlight! Don't you dare come to PopEuroTube, Ondine. I don't want you there. I don't want you pretending it has anything to do with you. This is *our* moment and you're not going to ruin it!"

They stormed off in high dudgeon. Hamish came over and gave Ondine a gentle hug.

"I'm an idiot," she said, her body crumpling into his. "I thought I was helping. I really did. It's only made things worse. My sisters hate me."

"And the country's charging headlong into Vincent's grip."

"Yeah, that too," she admitted. Up close, this late in the evening, Hamish's hair was more grey than black. His eyes that used to sparkle with mischief had a cloudy lining inside the lens. Cataracts? But only old people got them. As much as she wanted - needed - more hugs from her dearest love, she stepped out of the embrace. "You'd better get your sleep." The unspoken part being 'as a ferret'.

With everything falling apart around Ondine, she couldn't bear it if she lost Hamish.

~ Chapter Eleven ~

The day of PopEuroTube and the Abnormal Formal
dawned. Ondine stretched as she woke, all languid and
soft, and sleepy and at peace with the world. Then she
woke up and reality flooded her with all its recent
disappointments.

Her sisters had left for Craviç the week before so they
could attend rehearsals and media events. Today, Ma, Da,
Thomas and Henrik were heading off to Craviç in a rented
campervan. This was the first time Ondine could remember
her parents ever taking a holiday. It left Old Col, Hamish
and Ondine in by themselves in Venzelemma.

In their private room behind the kitchen, the television
was on, with the crew from *Good Morning Brugel* chatting
about events. It was one of those shows people left turned
on in case something interesting came up, a noisemaker in
the background to fill the silence. Ondine's ears pricked at
the sound of a familiar voice.

There on the screen was Lord Vincent, adding to the

saturation coverage of PopEuroTube promotion.

"The grand final will be so exciting. I encourage everyone in Venzelemma to come to Savo Plaza, it will be a huge party. We'll have a giant television screen to watch the whole event."

"Can I ask a question without notice My Lord? Will there be something extra special announced?" The co-host asked with a cheeky smile.

For a question 'without notice' it sounded awfully well rehearsed to Ondine.

Vincent positively beamed down the camera. *"There's no sneaking anything past you Cristina. Yes, we will be doing a live cross from Savo Plaza to announce Brugel's voting results!"*

A heavy sigh deflated Ondine. With most of her family away, she could have had all sorts of shenanigans with Hamish today, if only she didn't have the bone-deep certainty that Vincent would be staging a *coup d'état* tonight.

Old Col's hand fell sharply on Ondine's shoulder. "Don't worry about him. Let's move tables and chairs out the way so Hamish and I can dance."

Mouth dropping open in shock, Hamish said, "Won't that make us too tired for the real thing?"

"Nonsense. It will keep us in peak condition."

Shaking his head, Hamish said, "It's a deb ball, Col, not The World Cup."[61]

Throwing her hands in the air, Col yelled, "I knew it! I knew you'd ruin it! Why did I let you talk me into being my partner when I knew you didn't have your heart in it?"

---

[61] As with Eurovision, The World Cup (in either football, rugby or curling) is something Brugel has also failed to win.

"Steady." Ondine placed her palm on her great-auntie's upper arm. It wasn't Hamish that had done the convincing anyway, it was Old Col's idea.

"Don't touch me!" Col shrieked.

Ondine gulped. She'd never seen her great-auntie like this before. They'd been through some pretty stressful situations in the past but she'd never been so tightly wound up. "Calm down Old Col."

"Old Col. *Old!* That's all I am to you, an old woman, an inconvenience, someone to be humoured while the rest of you have a wonderful life and forget about me!"

"*Cummoan.*" Hamish crossed his arms over his chest. "Ondi's always been good to you and you're sponduletising."[62]

Ondine's forehead crinkled in confusion. So did Col's. But at least Col had stopped complaining for a moment, even if it was to wonder – as Ondine was – what in heaven's name Hamish was talking about.

"I'll get ye a wee nip of plütz. That will steady yer nerves."

"Nerves? I don't have nerves."

"Make it a bottle," Ondine said.

"I do not have nerves!"

"Oh, you've got nerves," Ondine said, "that's why you've been in a bad mood for weeks."

"I have not been in a –" Auntie Col stood to her full height and breathed hard. "It's true I have anticipated this night, but I do not have *nerves.*"

Not buying it. "You've been mean to Hamish ever since he said he'd be your partner, and the whole time he's been doing his best. And you've been tetchy with the rest of us.

---

[62] Sponduletise means to talk utter rubbish and be a right proper pain. Closely related to, spondylitis, which is a horrible affliction of the spine and muscles.

There's no need for you to be like this when you could just magic up a spell so you look awesome on the dance floor."

The old woman glared at Ondine.

"Here, drink this, it'll make ye feel better," Hamish handed Old Col a nip of plütz in a brandy glass.

"I don't need it," she said, drinking it anyway.

Ondine tried again. "Chef's left us plenty to eat. You must be starving, why don't we sit down and relax?"

"Not hungry," Col said.

"Any sausages?" Hamish asked.

"It must be nerves then if you're not hungry," Ondine said as she raided the refrigerator.

"How many times do I have to say, 'I don't have nerves'?" Old Col said.

"But you must be starving. Magic uses up so much energy and –" Ondine stopped, then looked hard into her great-auntie's eyes. "If you're not hungry, maybe you haven't been using magic. Why haven't you been using magic, Auntie Col?" Invisible hooks pulled Ondine's stomach as she waited for the woman to answer.

Col creased her brow, then jutted her chin. "There's nothing wrong with doing something the old-fashioned way from time to time. I want to do this right, that's all."

"Why aren't you using magic?" Ondine put the dish of leftover sausages on the bench.

"I told you, I don't want to –"

"Liar!" Ondine flung a cold sausage at her great-auntie.

The woman turned but the meat splodged onto her sleeve before dropping onto the floor.

"Five second rule." Hamish picked it up and ate it.

Ondine had seen enough. "You could have magicked that away, but you didn't. What's going on Col?"

"I simply fail to see why you're resorting to violence –"

"– Ease up, hen –" Hamish reached for the dish of

sausages to stop her flinging any more away.

"Why aren't you using Magic, Col?"

At first, Col's face held defiance. Were they in for more lies? Then a tightened top lip and chin tremble. "It's gone." Her eyes, surrounded by flaky-pastry skin, turned pink with the effort of holding back tears.

"Gone?" The truth bounced off Ondine's brain, refusing to go in.

Hamish stopped eating.

"Yes, gone," Col said with a whooshing sound as she let all her breath out and sagged before them. "I thought I was having a few senior moments, like at the wedding and, you know, afterwards a bit. But now it's . . . it comes and goes in flashes, I must be in wiccapause. It's only a matter of time before it's completely gone. I promised Anathea she'd be safe at the abnormal formal. That I'd look out for her. I can't stop thinking something terrible will happen tonight and I won't be able to do a thing to stop it."

"Col, I'm so sorry," Ondine stepped closer and wrapped her arms around her great auntie's shoulders. It helped to hide the stark terror freezing her inside. This was why Hamish was ageing so quickly each day, why he'd had to sleep as a ferret every night instead of sneaking in lovely cuddles and kisses with her. It was something Ondine had tried so very hard to ignore for so long. Sadly, denial could only last so long. More than half a century ago at her debutant ball, when Old Col placed the spell on Hamish that turned him into a ferret, he was just 17 year old. When Old Col died (hopefully not for a very long time) that staying spell would end and Hamish would revert to his original age.

If they didn't fix this magic issue, she could lose Hamish forever.

And the thing about Anathea's safety, that was important too.

"It's always been there in the back of my mind. That I could lose it one day," Col said.

Wetness slid along Ondine's arm. Was Auntie Col wiping her nose on her?

"When did this start?" Ondine asked.

"I think it started . . . or started to stop I suppose . . . at the autumn palace, back in September or October it must have been. It was coming and going, in fits and spurts. I guess I knew then it was only a matter of time." She looked around and found a chair, dragged it over and slumped into it. "Hand over the plütz."

Hamish asked, "Is that wise? It's still pretty early and we need to be on our feet all night?"

"Give her the plütz," Ondine said.

When Hamish gave Old Col an unsure look, the woman shrugged and said, "It's happy hour in Moldova." She took a few sips, coughed then cricked her neck from side to side. "OK kids, unless something radical happens tonight, we'll wake up to Vincent being Duke any day now. What in heaven's name are we going to do?"

***

Ondine slipped a lanyard with the hotel and house keys around her neck, then slung another lanyard over the first – this one had her video camera strapped to it. The spring day felt warm and inviting as they began their walk to the station. The perfect weather for street parties and kick-starting a coup. A short train ride later; the three of them were standing in the reception foyer at the Venzelemma *castlette*, asking for an audience with the Duchess.

Which is exactly when the wheels fell off their grand carriage of a plan.

"What do you mean she won't see us? Do you know who I am?" Old Col creaked and cracked as she stood to full height.

The assistant turned florid. "The err Duchess is . . . indisposed and can't be disturbed."

"She's not sick is she?" Ondine asked.

Giggles echoed from another room. The three of them turned as Duchess Anathea walked in, her hand set in the crook of Valentin's arm. So besotted with her middle-aged beau, the Duchess of Brugel kept right on giggling as she walked past Ondine and out to the balcony beyond.

"She completely ignored us," Ondine said.

"Aye. Terribly indisposed, so she is," Hamish said.

"That's not good," Old Col muttered. "Seriously not good."

The assistant bustled the trio out a servant's exit so they were once again out on the streets.

"He sure did pick a fine time to show up, don't you think?" Ondine asked. "It's like she doesn't care about Brugel any more."

"She's thoroughly distracted lass."

It made no sense to Ondine. "Being the Duchess is all she ever wanted. And she was so desperate to hang on to the position and . . . and be popular. How can she walk away from that? Oh!" She slapped herself on the forehead. "Maybe Vincent's asked Melody to put a spell on Anathea so that she doesn't care?"

Old Col tilted of her head. "I'd say it's Valentin who's put the spell on Anathea."

"He's a witch?" Ondine asked.

"No. But he's a charmingly attractive man, and they have a history."

Every one of Ondine's plans and ideas to help Anathea and thwart Vincent had fallen to bits. This was not how things were supposed to have happened! Depression weighed upon her. "This is doing my head in. Every time I've tried to help, it's either gone badly or gone nowhere."

"You can't save the world every time, lass," Hamish said. "Ye've done so much for Anathea, told her everything you learned about what Vincent's up to. Ye cannae do any more for her."

"But I have to try!" She said.

"And that's why I love you." Hamish tucked a tendril of hair behind her ear. "And I know ye won't stop trying to help, even if she won't listen. Tell ye what, we'll see Anathea again, at the debutante ball. We'll make her listen to reason."

"It will be too late by then," Ondine said. "There'll be thousands of people in Savo Plaza watching PopEuroTube on the big screen. I bet my next hot meal Vincent will be there, absorbing all that goodwill. We're sunk!"

"Nothing more to be done here. Let's get to the dance hall," Old Col said.

Deflated, they walked towards the nearest station. Which was exactly when their luck changed for the better as a well-dressed man stepped across the road a little way ahead of them.

Ondine whispered, "That's Valentin."

"Aye, where's he off tae?"

It looked like he was catching a train, just as they were. Ondine reached into her pocket, getting her camera ready to capture anything, should anything present itself as being capture-worthy.

"Wonder where he's off to?" Old Col asked. "The way he was making eyes at Anathea just before, you'd think he couldn't bear to part from her."

Keeping a respectable and not-at-all-stalkerish distance from Valentin, they followed him down a flight of steps and ended up on the same platform. Once again luck stepped in and saved them from having him notice they were there, as a crowd of teenagers in the middle of the platform talked in high-pitched squeals about how exciting everything was going to be tonight.

"Is he catching the same train?" Ondine whispered to Hamish.

Being a head taller, he could see more clearly. "Aye, I think so."

"The three of us together are too obvious," Ondine said. "Let's split up."

The train pulled in. It had seven carriages. Ondine slipped in with the noisy teens. Away from the protective reach of Old Col and Hamish she felt disconnected. Like her skin didn't fit properly and she couldn't get comfortable. Also, she couldn't see Valentin, and suddenly she wished she hadn't come up with the idea to separate. What if Valentin got off at another station?

The rowdy mob didn't take seats, preferring to stand and chat and giggle all the way. Ondine squished her way through the crowd to the connecting section to the front carriage, where she found Hamish and Old Col walking towards her. A smile burst free, so she stayed where she was and waited for the two of them to get to her.

"He's not in this carriage, is he lass?"

"No, so he must be further back," Ondine said.

He wasn't in the next one, or the one after that. How many more carriages were there again? Sneaking glances through the connector to the next carriage, Ondine searched for Valentin.

Another station came and went.

"Did he get off?" Ondine asked.

"I couldn't tell," Hamish said.

"He didn't." That was Col. "There are more people in the last carriage now, we could go in and nobody would notice three more."

They took the risk and walked through the remaining connectors until they were in the final carriage, trying desperately not to look like they were looking for someone. "That's him down by the doors," Ondine said as she turned her back to face Hamish. "I saw him just before I sat down."

"I think I can see him," Hamish said as he craned his neck. "Now he's checking his watch."

"And you know why he's doing that?" Ondine said.

"Tae tell the time?"

Rolling her eyes, "Because he's obviously meeting with someone."

"You're making it sound nefarious," Old Col said. "I like it. Who needs magic when you've got a brain like yours, eh?"

Hamish nudged her. "Course she's got a good brain, she chose me, dinshe?"

"Where is Valentin?" Old Col asked.

Ondine looked further down the carriage. "He's getting up. Bother, he's heading out."

"Owf we get then," Hamish said.

Heart thwacking against her ribs in the effort to execute her espionage, Ondine walked as casually as she could manage to the train door.

They stepped on to the platform and Col looked around. "He's not there?"

"Are you sure?" Hamish asked.

Old Col tisked. "I've lost my magic, not my eyesight."

"Oh no," sickness flipped Ondine's belly. The doors behind them closed with a swish-thud. "He didn't get off." They turned to see Valentin standing on the other side of the train door, waving to them.

Ondine said, "Saturn's rings!"

Old Col said, "Hogs and hazels."

Hamish said something that defied translation.

~ Chapter Twelve ~

Disappointment curdled Ondine's emotions as she struck 'espionage agent' off her imaginary list of future career opportunities. Dejected, they walked the rest of the way to Savo Plaza. The crowd soaked up the pre-PopEuroTube entertainment before the main even beamed in live from Craviç on the big screen. Hamish spotted two empty cafe chairs around a table. Old Col ordered the second cheapest thing on the menu, a tea and biscuit combination.[63]

If Ondine were being honest with herself, she had to admit things were looking more than hopeless for them. The thought of giving up made her all kinds of cross, but the way forward was more confusing than ever.

And yet they'd come so far, they couldn't give up now.

---

[63] This is a lovely trick, which cafes and restaurants often deploy. Customers feel less inclined to order the cheapest item on the menu, for fear of being judged a tight-wad. Clever establishments set their prices to make the second-cheapest item the most profitable for them.

Which meant the only course of action was to keep on going, hoping for a miracle.

As they sat there, taking sips from the one teacup and sharing the two biscuits between three, Ondine sitting on Hamish's lap because of the chair shortage, a man in a suit darted out of a laneway towards the Plaza Hotel entrance.

"Psst," Ondine said to Hamish and Col. "Look over there at your nine o'clock."

They both looked in different directions.

"Over there," she said, pointing. "It's Valentin. He went into that hotel."

Patting the camera around Ondine's neck, Old Col smiled. "Get to it then."

Ondine made sure her camera was ready. Steadying her breathing, she walked to the hotel, even though her body screamed for her to sprint.

In the hotel lobby, there wasn't anyone around who looked like Valentin. *Jupiter's Moons, I've lost him!* Needing to un-panic, she strode to the ladies' bathroom and locked herself into a cubicle. A moment later, two women came in and chose the cubicles either side of Ondine, both chatting all the way through relieving themselves. There was no option but to overhear all of it.

"I think you're being mean by not helping." One of them said. Her accent didn't sound entirely Brugelish, but it was hard to tell with their voices bouncing off the tiles.

"I hardly need to help, he's getting everything he wants." The other woman said. A woman who sounded exactly like Melody.

The video camera weighed heavily in her hands. Ondine really needed to get out of here. She also wanted to record the conversation but the machine made a little 'beep' sound when it came on, which would alert the ladies. She flushed to make enough white noise to drown out everything, then pressed the 'record' button. Which made her feel all kinds of sick in the head at the fact she was recording a conversation in a women's toilets.

Time to get out of here and leave the others to talk in private, so she could get it all on tape.

"Oh, hello!" Melody said far too loudly.

Quick, act surprised it's her. "Oh wow, what are you doing here?" *Real smooth, brain, thanks a lot.* "Hello, it's Ruslana, isn't it?" They went to shake hands, then Ondine remembered she's been in a bathroom. "I'd best wash them first." Mercury's wings, if she used the taps, the rushing water could drown all sound completely. Instead she wiped them on the tops of her skirt in slap-dash fashion. "Are you staying here at the hotel?"

Ruslana tilted her head. "Yes. Why don't you come up and take tea with us?"

"Sure? I just . . ." *I can't tell them I have a camera sitting on top of the toilet. Oh great, now they're washing their hands and leaving. So much for spying. Time to get back in the stall.* "Ah, I think I've eaten too many fried cheeseballs, I'll be another couple of minutes. Oh this is so embarrassing. S'cuse me."

"We'll wait for you out in the lounge then," Melody called out as they left.

"Thanks." Quickly Ondine locked herself behind the cubicle door and retrieved the camera. OK, the first attempt was a bust, but if she slipped the camera into her coat pocket – as bulky as it was – she could record whatever future conversation came along without alerting anyone to the giveaway 'bleep – you're being recorded' noise.

Not that she could see Ruslana or Melody when she walked out to the foyer. Where had they gone? There were plenty of people milling about, but none of them were who she wanted them to be. First she'd lost Valentin, now she'd lost Melody and Ruslana. Frustration twisted her lips as she headed to an area that looked more like a greenhouse than a lounge. Potted plants taller than the average person screened the guests, while golden spring sunlight poured in from the floor-to-ceiling windows.

There, relaxing on a lounge chairs with a glass of tea-coloured liquid (which obviously wasn't tea) was Anathea's second-ex and current beau, Valentin. Sitting across the low table from him was Lord Vincent. Sitting beside him was Ruslana's father, Babak Balakhan.

The body language was far too relaxed for people who had only just met. Heart threatening to leap out of her throat, Ondine breathed into her coat lapels to muffle her noisy breaths. With trembling hands, she checked the camera to make sure the little red light was still on. It was! Hooray, she'd done something right at last. As quietly as she could manage, she placed the camera into the coconut fibres at the base of the plant and checked the view. It captured all three men, Valentin front-on and Vincent and Babak from the back.

Time to retreat to the foyer.

"There you are!" Melody said, out of nowhere. Ruslana was standing beside her.

Ondine jumped, her pulse beating a tattoo in her brain. "I didn't hear you," and she patted her chest and laughed to show how silly she was. That should be enough to disguise how guilty she *really* was.

Melody embraced Ondine. "Are you all right?"

"Err, just feeling off colour, because of the, um, you know, the cheeseballs." Best lie ever.

"Why don't you stay with us for the night?" Melody asked. "We'll have a lovely time catching up. It's been so long since we've done that."

This was a completely different Melody from the love-struck misery she'd argued with back at the family pub. "Oh, you don't want me cluttering up the place. I'm too tense about tonight, I'll be a mess when Margibelle come on." Not a lie.

Ruslana quirked the corner of her mouth upwards. "Is that the only reason why you're tense?"

"Well . . ." Ondine looked at her feet. *Come on brain.* Nothing.

"Stay with us," Ruslana said, "we're going to watch the show from the hotel balcony. We have the best view of the big screen."

"Maybe um," she started again, fighting a sickening sense of panic that they would tie her up for the rest of the evening. Then a really, really good idea came to her. "Actually, perhaps we can catch up another time. Hamish is in the plaza and um," she felt herself blushing deeply, which reflected how she really felt, but also gave her enormous relief that her lie held a massive dollop of truth, "this is kind of the only privacy we've had for the longest time."

Ruslana and Melody made an 'O' with their mouths and blushed right along with her, before smirking behind their hands.

"Be good. Be safe," Melody said with a wink.

"Of course," Ondine replied, blushing even more furiously.

"Wait a minute," Melody looked her up and down. "You're not feeling funny in the tummy because you're –"

"– No way!" Ondine cut her off, then dropped her voice. "No, it's not that. Definitely not that."

"OK, well, be good, you hear?" Melody said.

"Yes ma'am," Ondine gave Melody and Ruslana a quick salute and headed back to the bathroom to:

a) breathe

b) laugh

c) buy time and work out how to get the camera out of the hotel's planter pots without anyone seeing her.

Sickly heat threatened to leap out of her mouth as Ondine waited for as long as she could in the bathroom. Hands slippery with fear-sweat, she stepped as quietly as she could towards the greenery. The seats were empty. At last! Something had gone her way! She wiped the coconut fibres off the camera. It was switched off. Had someone seen it and messed with it? Had it reached the end of the tape and switched itself off?

Desperate to review the footage, but doubly-desperate not to be sprung sneaking about with a camera, she slotted it into her coat pocket. *Please let there be something on this.* Just as she turned around the plants, Hamish appeared.

"Ah! You scared me!" Like she wasn't tightly wound enough!

"Sorry hen, but I was worried about ye. Ye've been gone so long and I lost sight of ye."

"You've been looking out for me?" Harp music played in her head and her heart soared.

"Of course I have," he kissed her for good measure. It was a really good measure. Then he tilted his forehead against hers and lowered his voice. "I saw Valentin leave, so I think we're safe. Col's gone to the dance hall already, she said she needed time to get dressed."

"Goody." They were unchaperoned. This earned a properly lovely kiss on the lips, which sent sweet shivers all the way through to her toes. She needed kisses like this, they were all-too-rare these days with Hamish spending a third of his life as a ferret.

Life was crazy, Brugel was crazy, her family was crazy. Ondine didn't even know what extra crazy tomorrow might bring. But one thing she did know for sure; in the midst of all the craziness, she and Hamish would still be together. They belonged together, and she'd do whatever it took to make sure they'd stay together. If their attempts to disrupt Vincent from his claim to the throne failed, and she was starting to suspect that they would, no matter what happened, she'd have Hamish.

And he'd have her.

Which lead to another, not altogether welcoming thought. They'd come too far on this crazy journey to go back to the way things used to be. Then a truth-bomb hit. They couldn't 'go back' to the way things were, even if they tried. Only now did. Ondine realise she and Hamish had to keep going. They'd do their best to stop Vincent, even if it meant going down in a big screaming heap. Because even if they failed, and that was looking like the most probable outcome, at least Ondine would know that she and Hamish had tried their hardest to stop him.

Together they walked further down the street to find another cafe – they'd lost their spots from before, as the crowds grew even more crowded in Savo Plaza – to grab a seat and check through the camera's little rectangular screen for anything usable.

"If you want to sit here, you have to buy something," the samovari said.[64] He had that tired look of someone who had to repeat himself all the time.

"Two teas, no sugar." Hamish said.

"Sugar's on the table anyway," the samovari said.

Ondine begged the heavens she'd captured something useful.

"You can clearly see it's Valentin," Hamish said. "You're amazing."

---

[64] In Brugel, a samovari is one who works behind the samovar; in the same way a barista (bar tender) works behind a bar. A samovari may be male or female, and their skills of brewing tea and cultivating a disdainful attitude towards customers takes years to cultivate.

"Your teas," the samovari turned up with a tray loaded with hot cups of deep brown liquid with floating slices of lemon.

Thanks," she said absently as she kept looking at the small picture, wondering how it could help them at all. "Saturn's rings!" She nearly knocked her tea over in excitement. "Look, they've giving him something in an envelope."

"It's *goat* to be loaded with cash, hen. Ye've got him."

"It's not enough." She worried her bottom lip against her teeth as she kept playing the footage. "We can't see who's giving him the envelope of money."

"Mebbe they get up in a wee bit and we'll see their faces?" As he said it, the three men in the image did indeed rise from their seats, their business transaction over. As they rose, they stood out of frame, so their heads weren't visible any more.

"I'm going to have to swear," Ondine said. "Really, properly scream and swear." But to make a liar out of herself, she buried her head in her hands, clamped her eyes shut and clenched her lips together.

"We havnae failed, yet," Hamish said as he rubbed her back in gentle circles. "Let's have another look and see if there's anything we've missed."

"And then I can swear?" Ondine said behind her hands.

"Aye, I'll teach ye a whole new set."

Sniffing, Ondine dragged her sleeve over her face, then set to making her tea sweet enough. She fished out the slice of lemon and added in two teaspoons of sugar. In her frazzled state, it wasn't enough. Two more teaspoons swiftly followed. Perfect.

If only a cup of tea could fix the sick feeling of failure coating her like a damp blanket. Deep in her bones she knew Lord Vincent was going to take over the country tonight. This tiny bit of footage was her only weapon against him.

"Let's have another look. Here's Valentin," Hamish said, replaying the footage. "And then we see Vincent give him the money."

"That's not Vincent, that's Babak," Ondine said. "He was sitting closer to the wall."

"Aye, so his hand is the one covered in bling."

A true observation, the man had chunky gold rings on every finger.

"That's Vincent now, shaking Valentin's hand," Ondine said with a heavy sigh.

"Wait a minute, is there a zoom on this? Aye, here it is. Let's get a closer look."

Each press of the zoom button made the centre of the picture larger, showing a familiar hand. "It's blue!" Ondine squealed.

"Way hey!"

Pure joy spun like a tornado through Ondine as she bounced up and down on her seat. Hamish threw his arms around her and kissed her all over.

"Ye did it lass, ye *goat* him!"

"Are you going to order more tea or what?" The samovari asked.

"Later," Hamish said as he pushed his chair back and drew Ondine to her feet. He kissed her solidly on the lips and said, "You're amazing."

When they eventually stopped kissing, reality snapped back into focus. It was dark and Savo Plaza was packed with people, many of them had blue hands and carried the Brugelish hexagonal flag. Some wore the flag like a cape, tied at the neck, which pushed patriotism over the line towards ranty-nationalism.

A column of drummers and Fort Kluff cadets marched past. In the distance, a clock 'bonged' five times.

"Let's get to Old Col," Ondine said, grabbing Hamish's

hand and leading them down a side street towards the direction of the ballroom. "We can't be late for the abnormal formal."

Running nearly the whole way, they reached the ballroom with lungs fit to burst. Fire and cramps greeted every breath Ondine dragged into her throat. "Haveto (gasp) find Anath (gulp) ea and show her (wheeze) the tape of Valentin."

"Aw naw hen," Hamish pulled up sharply. "She's already dancing with him in the ballroom."

How did he get back here so quickly? Ondine wondered. He must have had a car.

"I'd best get changed, sharpish," Hamish said, then disappeared into the gentlemen's rooms.

Like magic, he reappeared moments later in his formal clothes.

Old Col spotted them and came over. "I thought you'd never get here," she said to Hamish, while giving only the briefest nod to acknowledge Ondine. "I've waited a long time for this, I'm going to have my dance with Hamish."

It would be beyond rude to take this moment from Collette Romano, who had waited decades to right this old wrong.

Hamish, looking resplendent, guided her to the dance floor and they twirled and danced with charm and grace.

Last time they'd been here, the dance hall defined 'shabby chic'.

Now, filled with people dressed in their finery, it came to life.

Flower vases on pedestals added glamour and life.

A chandelier twinkled and sparkled, casting bubbles of light around the room.

The walls were festooned with streamers and rosettes, adding colour and vibrancy.

Couples danced, their skirts and suit tails swishing and

swaying with fairytale elegance.

I'll give you two minutes, Ondine thought. *Then we'd better get on with our mission.*

As if psychic – and there was every chance the elder witch had that ability – Old Col and Hamish approached Ondine about one minute and fifty seconds later.

Old Col said, "Thank you, Ondine and Hamish, for allowing me this lovely dream."

Tears welled up in Old Col's eyes, as she turned to her dance partner. "Hamish, you've made an old woman very happy. I forgave you a long time ago, but now you've truly redeemed yourself at last."

"Aye. This is how it should have been all those years ago. But if you hadn't cursed me and turned me into a ferret, I wouldn't have found my true love Ondi."

Old Col smiled with serenity, as if everything was right with the world. Then her faced snapped back and it was all business. "Right, moment's over, what's next?"

Hamish said, "Ondi's captured brilliant evidence of Vincent on tape. We need to show it to Anathea."

"Well then, we'd better show her." Col said. "I suggest we dance close to her, then swap partners so I'll dance with Valentin and you dance with Anathea. Guide her down here to the kitchen so Ondine can show her the tape."

Her great auntie had snapped into commander-in-chief-mode. Ondine liked it. "Sounds like a plan!"

Hamish and Old Col twirled closer and closer to Anathea and Valentin. They took light steps, making it look effortless as they homed in. Then the switch! Old Col stepped to the side, then she and Hamish bowed to Anathea and Valentin.

Shame Hamish had his back to Ondine, she couldn't see what he was saying, nor his expression. After a painful heartbeat of time, Anathea accepted the offer and swayed into Hamish's arms. Auntie Col smiled, tilted her head then turned to Valentin to await his offer.[65]

Gliding across the floor, Hamish steered Anathea neatly through the guests, moving her surreptitiously towards Ondine. Meanwhile, Valentin hadn't offered for Auntie Col's hand. She stood in the middle of the dance floor, waiting. The expression on her face somewhere between expectant and mortified.

Ask her you clod, Ondine silently begged. A heavy ball of doubt rose in Ondine's throat. If Old Col waited any longer, she'd turn into a statue. People were looking, craning their necks this way and that.

Then, horribly, Auntie Col made a bow to Valentin, even though he had no rank over her. Jupiter's moons, Valentin turned his back and returned to his table. In a cloud of peach chiffon and ostrich feathers, Old Col glided towards the powder rooms. At that moment, Hamish guided Anathea into the kitchen. *Oh, the camera!*

"What is so important that it must be seen right away?" Anathea asked.

"It's this, My Lord Duchess." Ondine held the viewing screen out so she could see what they had. "I recorded it today. I'm so sorry to be the bearer of bad news, but your Valentin is taking payoffs from Babak and Vincent."

As Anathea watched the footage her breathing became more rapid, then her face froze. For a second Ondine thought their beloved leader would flip a table and storm out.

"Valentin has been properly identified?" She asked. "It looks like him, but without my glasses I cannot be sure."

____

[65] Brugel's debutante balls are so old fashioned, guests must follow exacting rules of propriety. Only men may ask women for a dance, not the other way around. If a woman is asked for a dance, she may politely decline, although this seldom happens.

"You wear glasses?" Ondine and Hamish asked together.

"There's nothing wrong with wearing glasses," Anathea said. "Although I am on the young side."

"Yeas," Hamish agreed with her. "Far too young to need glasses."

"And how will people know that this is Vincent giving him the money?"

"It's not Vincent, it's Babak, you can tell because of all the rings on his fingers. Vincent's the one who is shaking his hand just . . . now. See that."

Anathea shook her head. "It's just a hand. It cannot be proved that it's Vincent."

"When it zooms in, you can tell it's him, because the hand is blue."

The Duchess of Brugel frowned enough to make a tiny crease in her forehead. Then she took a step backwards and held the edge of the table. *Grrrrk!* The table skidded on the floor under Anathea's weight. Ondine stepped in to steady her.

"It's a horrible shock, I'm so sorry My Lordship," Ondine said. "But we had to show it to you. You needed to know the truth."

Steadying herself, Anathea removed some invisible lint from her sleeve and took a deep breath. Then she made a pathetic sigh and her voice came out so softly Ondine had to strain to hear her. "That lying bucket of wee. He was supposed to be helping."

"Eh, which one, Valentin or Vincent, Me Lordship?" Hamish asked.

Anathea made a dismissive sniff. "Both of them. I should have twigged Valentin's timing was too perfect. Same with Vincent, offering to pay for renovations, all the while he was paying for Valentin to romance the throne away from me."

"Aye. But aside from the obvious heartbreak, it's amazing news, wouldn't ye say?" Hamish asked, his face full of hope. "This exposes Vincent. Once we show this to the world, nobody will trust him ever again."

Anathea's chin wobbled.

"We have tae find a way to play it on the big screen in the plaza tonight, then everyone will see what Vincent's been up to, so they will," Hamish said.

"No!" Anathea stood straight up, knocking the table backwards again. "It cannot be played."

"What?" Hamish and Ondine said as one.

"It is humiliating." Anathea said. "Dear heavens, I will be laughed at. I will be derided. I will be seen to have no judgement. No, it cannot be played. You are expressly forbidden."

The figurative plates Ondine had been spinning on bendy poles came crashing around her. "But if people don't see it, Vincent will win."

"I won't be held to ridicule," Anathea protested.

Old Col joined in, having clearly heard a fair bit of the conversation. "Then say the footage is yours, My Lordship. Tell Brugel *you* managed to catch Vincent doing these horrible things."

Anathea's chin wobbled again. "Because horrible things *are* being done to me! I am being taken for a fool!"

"Naw hen, not like that. You'll be the messenger, and if ye sell it right, folks'll think you were on to Valentin the whole time." Hamish said.

Had he just called The Duchess of Brugel 'hen'?

Silence passed between them, before Anathea finally said, "You want me to get on stage, in front of everyone, and say my suspicions were confirmed and Vincent cannot be trusted?"

"Yes," Ondine nodded.

"That will not do," Anathea said. "Vincent needs to be

spoken to. I will go to him at once."

"He wilnae listen," Hamish said with a headshake.

"What about the rest of the debutante ball?" Old Col asked.

Ondine said, "We can tell the orchestra to play faster."

Colour draining from her face, Anathea said, "Would it be terribly unducal of me to have a quick puke?"

***

If the only worries Ondine had that night were making sure Hamish danced beautifully for the entire evening, she would have been nervous. But the situation with Valentin taking bribes to fall back in love with Anathea chewed her confidence to shreds. Then there was the extra matter of stopping Vincent from taking over the country. That thought poured a fresh cup of acid into the churning washing machine of her stomach.

But most of all she had no idea how her sisters were doing at PopEuroTube because the ballroom's kitchen, where she spent most of her time, did not have a television. She made her way to the women's changing rooms and discovered several ladies crowded around a portable television set. Oooooh! They could catch glimpses of the acts between dance sets.

"There you are," Old Col said to Ondine, "Call me when Margibelle comes on."

"Shush!" Somebody shushed.

Anathea walked in and everyone sprang away from each other and pretended they weren't doing anything wrong, even though they looked incredibly guilty.

"When are Margibelle on?" Anathea asked the room. "The suspense is killing me."

"Another quarter hour, My Lordship," one of the debutantes said.

"I'm so tense!" Anathea said, then put a broad grin to her strained face. The Duchess looked tense all right, but it surely had more to do with her ex-husband accepting bribes to woo, and her nephew planning a coup, than anything happening in the world of music.

The debutantes exited but left the television on. Their partners, no doubt, were huddled over a radio or television in the men's room.

"I had no idea the room could be cleared so quickly," Anathea said as she moved towards the basin and played cold running water over her wrists.

"Have you burned yourself?"

"No dear, stemming the nausea. I'd make a cold compress, but that could trickle water onto the dress and a stained dress can't be returned."

Ondine's nerves hitched and she checked the door to make sure nobody else was coming in, then she took up position at the basin next to Anathea. "Valentin doesn't suspect anything, does he?"

"No. He's being charming tonight. Just as he was when we first met." Anathea righted herself and tucked a stray hair behind a pin. "On with the show, eh?"

In the ballroom, the duchess was a picture of a serene, regal woman, smiling and enjoying the company of the elegant man seated next to her. She looked so comfortable and at ease, the polar opposite to the nauseated wreck Ondine had witnessed in the restrooms.

From the side of the room, a couple of men in tuxedos guided in a television set on a trolley and plugged it in. People looked confused and glanced from it to their partners and then to the duchess.

The dance set finished with a swirl of strings from the orchestra. Anathea rose and walked to the podium. "Ladies and Gentlemen, it has been my delight and honour to receive you this evening. It's a special night for everyone here, but it is also a very special night for Brugel. I too am guilty of stealing away to keep track of events concerning PopEuroTube."

Nervous laughter washed through the crowd.

"Rather than keep you exiled from our marvellous performers, let formalities be suspended for a short while so we may enjoy Brugel's moment."

A huge cheer rang through the ballroom as people crowd-rushed the television set. It was on, it was in colour and someone had turned the sound up so high it distorted.

Wait a minute. They were supposed to be speeding things up so they could get out of here early, not delaying proceedings. Did this mean Anathea had lost her nerve about confronting Vincent?

Nevertheless, she squished in to watch the performers from Craviç sing their boppy melody. The Craviçians were dressed in long frilly peasant-skirts and overblown blousy tops. Absolutely ripe for a sudden costume change mid-song. A cheer erupted as the Craviç singers hit the chorus, spun around and revealed their sparkly under-costumes of mini skirts and tube tops. It didn't take long for Craviç's song to be over.[66] The next group, from the Kingdom of Radzvilla, were interminable with their wheezing piano accordions and spiky hats that looked like giant red pine cones.

"Radzvilla's a real place?" Hamish asked.

"I'll check an atlas," Ondine said.

Oh joy, at last it was time for Slaegal's entry to come on. Normally Ondine zoned out when the neighbouring country appeared, but this was different.

"I'm sorry we cannae be there for real," Hamish said, rubbing circles on her back.

---

[66] The maximum song length on PopEuroTube is four minutes. When the song is particularly terrible, it feels longer.

"Ah well." Ondine tried to forget the blow-out argument she'd had with her sisters. "At least I'm with you."

He kissed the top of her ear and gave her a squishy hug as the lights dimmed. Margibelle took their places. The auditorium at PopEuroTube was silent. Watching on television, the ballroom for the abnormal formal was silent too. Ondine felt her ribs cramp as she forgot how to breathe.

Be amazing. Just. Be. Amazing.

"Shhhh!" Someone said. As if they needed reminding. It might be their neighbour on screen, but everyone knew Margibelle were home-grown Brugelers.

The note. Oh the glorious note Margi hit to launch into the song. It was sublime. It was soaring. It was heartbreaking. It hit true and strong and set everything in motion.

Someone turned the volume down to stop the distortion, so they could enjoy it for the magical music it was. Nobody in the ballroom spoke. Nobody even moved. Ladies held their taffeta gowns in their fists to stop them rustling. The musical bridge built the song and took it soaring into the chorus. The chorus had the PopEuroTube auditorium on their feet, waving flags and singing along.

Tears sprang from Ondine. She didn't dare sniff as the noise would disrupt the transcendent music. Music her sisters had made. There was no fear on Margi's face. She was one with the music, and the music united everyone in this little patch of Eastern Europe. The last note came on sure and strong. The crowd went crazy. Margi came out of her musical-dream-state to acknowledge the crowd. Now her voice broke, now her eyes shone with unshed tears. *"Thank you, I love you!"* She cried out.

The ballroom, filled with everyone in their finest and

on their very best behaviour erupted with howls of joy and sheer relief for Margibelle's amazing performance. Ondine grabbed Hamish in a bear hug and knocked him sideways with a mash-pash. They kissed and laughed with relief and kissed some more.

The commentator on the television said, *"And they've done it, the firecrackers representing Slaegal have brought the house down with that wonderful ballad."*

"Just when I was losing the will to live, we get a reminder of what PopEuroTube is all about," his partner in the commentary box said.

"Yes. Poaching acts from other countries." They both chuckled at how clever they were.

"Now here comes something we've all been waiting for. If you ever need a theme for stealing a tank and liberating a city, this is it."

"It's the band from Brugel, with a song that will get people marching in the streets. It's Battlefront with Anthem."

On screen, people of all nations waved flags, whistled and cheered. As the first chord blared out, noise dropped to a hush. In the dance hall, they were silent as well, swaying in time with the stirring music. Grudgingly, Ondine had to respect Battlefront. It was an amazing song. It made you want to cheer, carouse, smile and weep. The chorus boomed through the speakers. Everyone around Ondine and Hamish joined in. Any other year, Ondine would have sung along, but she couldn't stop the knives of jealousy stabbing her heart. Her sisters should have been singing for Brugel instead of Slaegal.

Somebody turned the volume up even louder. The drumbeats came in so strong and heavy Ondine could felt it all the way from her feet.

Boom-boom, boom-boom-boom. Thump-thump, thump-thump, thump-thump.

Wait a minute. The thumping wasn't from the television. It was the floor rattling. The walls too. Looking up, the chandelier shuddered and shook, the lights flickered. The doors burst open. A group of cadets marched in. Armed cadets. With serious looking weapons.

Everyone screamed.

Hamish grabbed Ondine and made a run for the rear door, just as more cadets burst through this entrance too. Standing before all was Birgit Howser, dressed in a traditional Brugelish travelling witch cloak, the shoulders trimmed with epaulettes. Her eyes lit upon Ondine and she gave a slow shake of her head. "Run along now, silly girl."

"I'm not going anywhere," Ondine shot back, her heart rate doubling, her breathing coming hard and scared. Because despite the brave words, she was terrified of what Mrs Howser might do. What the cadets might do. "Why can't you leave us alone?"

"Oh bless, she's still talking," Mrs Howser said. The witch turned to a cadet and said, "Shut her up for me."

The cadet, a lad who looked younger than Ondine, nodded, then thrust his hand out.

Ondine tried to scream, but nothing came out. Hamish said a horrible swear word.

Mrs Howser smiled. "Well done." Then her gaze roved the crowd until it rested on Duchess Anathea with a bone-freezing smile of victory.

"Protect the Duchess," Old Col said to anyone who would listen.

All heads turned to Anathea, standing completely still beside Valentin. "Something must be done," she squeaked out.

"Of course," Valentin said. He took Anathea's hand and kissed it. Then he spun her around so fast he pinned her arm behind her back.

Ondine screamed, "Let her go!" Except nothing came out.

"Nobody move!" Valentin said, pinning Anathea's arm even tighter and making her yelp.

Mrs Howser scoffed, "That's *my* line!"

Valentin nudged Anathea towards the cadets and Mrs Howser.

"Good," Mrs Howser said. "If everyone behaves, nobody will get hurt."

"Really Birgit," Old Col marched towards her witchy foe. "You could have at least waited until we'd finished the ball and been presented. And to think we used to be friends!"

Mrs Howser rolled her eyes. "Of course. It's *always* about you."

"You have to take your spell off Hamish as well" Old Col acted as if she and Mrs Howser were alone, having a friendly old spat, instead of being surrounded by armed cadets.

"As if I'd ever do that!" Mrs Howser said. "Now get out of my way, I have so much to do, and so little time!"

"You know the spell!" Old Col was shouting now.

Everyone was looking at Col as if she were a few nuts short of a trail mix. The twig snapped for Ondine. "Oh! *That* spell!" She would have said it out loud, if she'd had a voice. Instead, she said it in her head. But, at least she knew what to do now. She grabbed Hamish, placed her palms on either side of his face and drew him down for a kiss. The spell, which Old Col had been referring, was the one that made other people's wishes come true whenever she and Hamish became amorous. The magically contagious spell that had caused so much mayhem in Brugel in the first place.

Many times in the past, Ondine had kissed Hamish good and proper. Tonight, she kissed him with the hope of a happy future for the two of them, and for Brugel. Which had her quietly thinking how clever and selfless she was. For his part, Hamish kissed her back with all the passion she'd come to love. What a kiss. Behind her closed eyes, searing bright lights flashed around the room.

Something slumped to the floor. It sounded like a sack of potatoes. Ondine broke away from the kiss to see Great-Auntie Col on the ground in a crumpled heap.

"No!" Ondine silently cried.

"This is too good," Mrs Howser said, leaning over Old Col, lifting her arm and letting it flop back onto the ground with a soft *thud*.

Fear jarred Ondine's joints. Old Col didn't move. Didn't make a sound. Her once proud expression fell sideways under the weight of gravity. Her closed lips didn't move, her nostrils didn't flare.

In her mind Ondine cried out, "What have you done?!" Wailing grief poured through her. "No, no no no! Col! Aunty Col! Wake up . . . the dance isn't over yet."

"Trying to use my magic against me. *Honestly*!" Mrs Howser shrugged. "Once a witch is past wiccapause, you're better off dead anyway."

Furious, Ondine sprang at the witch. The cadets leapt to defend their leader. Things got messy quickly. Behind her, Hamish shouted. Something solid and heavy bashed Ondine's shoulder, the pain sharp and hot. Something else equally heavy smacked the back of her knees, sending her to the ground in a screaming heap. Pain immobilised her. Looking up, she saw Hamish leaping at Mrs Howser's throat. Mid-air, he transformed into a ferret, his claws and teeth bared for maximum damage.

A cadet swiped him with a rifle butt, sending him flailing.

Ondine scrambled to her feet despite the searing pain in her shoulder. With a desperate lunge, she slid along the parquet floor, catching him millimetres from impact. Momentum kept her sliding. Ferret in hand, she could not stop the wall coming closer. She hit it. Hard. If the world had turned black it would have been a relief. Instead she felt every twisted tendon, every bruised bone and every bleeding muscle. Concussion wouldn't take her out, all she could do was curl into the pain, close her eyes and groan pathetically.

Mrs Howser shouted, "Everybody out!"

At which point, Ondine prised one eye open to see the cadets marching Duchess Anathea, Valentin and the rest of the guests into the street.

"Her too," Mrs Howser pointed to the prone form of Old Col on the ground. "Bring her, she could still be useful."

A cadet who looked like nothing more than string and gristle in a uniform, crouched down to Old Col and lifted her into his arms.

Was it the flickering lighting? The stress? The pain? Ondine wasn't sure, but she could have sworn she saw Old Col wink at her.

~ Chapter Thirteen ~

The view from the hotel suite filled Vincent with a
palpable sense of something ominously good waiting for
him. Everything was coming together. On the television
behind him in the hotel suite, and on the enormous screen
down in Savo Plaza, the PopEuroTube presenters talked in
rhyming couplets.

The man said, *"That is the end of the music and art."*
The woman said, *"Now it is time to play your part."*
"The voting will open in just a minute."
"Phone us now to see who will win it!"
Shudder.

"We go now?" Babak said, slapping a meaty hand onto
Vincent's shoulder.

Ruslana remained on the couch, nibbling pistachios.
Crick, tink they went, as she cracked each green nut, then
tossed the hard shells into a stainless steel bin by her feet.
Melody sat by the window, sending glimmering waves of
green and silver sparkles wafting into the crowd gathered

in the plaza.

The PopEuroTube co-hosts recapped the performances from the night.

> *"It's been such a night, we don't want to stop."*
> *"Here are the songs again, right from the top!"*

"Rhyming ham and cheese. We'll be lucky not to get a riot," Babak said.

Melody turned to Vincent. "They're ready now." She looked sweaty and grey, like she'd been locked in a sauna and force-fed green bananas.

"All right, everyone," Vincent clapped his hands, revving himself up. "Let's meet the people."

Babak took his daughter's manicured hand, wiped the pistachio salt from it, then guide-yanked her out of the chair until she was on her feet. "The people are ready for their new Duchess."

"She needs her wig," Melody said no louder than a breath.

"Good catch," Vincent said.

Unsteady as she may be, Melody picked up the exquisite helmet of hair from where it rested on a polystyrene head on the sideboard.

"Coming." Ruslana stood before the mirror to make the hair sit the right way.

If they timed this correctly, when Battlefront's song recap came on with *Anthem*, Vincent would step out in front of the big screen and take the microphone. Not that he liked to brag in clichés, but he'd have the mob eating out of the palm of his hand.

***

Waking up in the abandoned ballroom, Ondine fought

through multiple layers of soreness to get on her feet. Everyone was gone, which angered Ondine all the more as it denied her a long-awaited showdown with Howser. Damn that witch! Her voice came out as a croak, but at least it was back. "Hamish, where are you?"

"In here, lass," he said from a darkened cloakroom.

Her eyes adjusted quickly to the darkness and she made out his human shape as he rifled through a pile of clothing.

"We'll need warmth if we're tae venture out." He returned to her with an overcoat and slipped it over her shoulders.

"Whose is this?" She asked as she creaked her bruised arms into the sleeves.

He shrugged. "Somebody else's. They left in a hurry."

Heavy rumbling shook the floor again. Grabbing her hand, Hamish dragged her to the doorway. "I never knew ye got earthquakes in Brugel."

"We don't," Ondine's whole body shook. The windows rattled and paint flaked off the walls. It hurt to talk, but the more she did the easier her voice came back. "Let's see what it is."

It didn't take long. Shrinking themselves into the darkened doorway, they watched a tank roll through the cobblestone street. Its caterpillar tracks rattled and shuddered past, the main gun pointed ominously forward.

The question, 'where is it going?' formed, but the moment she'd thought it, Ondine knew. "The plaza," she said, running out onto the street as soon as the tank was gone.

Realisation smacked Ondine upside the head. "Jupiter's moons! Half of Brugel is in the plaza tonight! This was Vincent's plan all along. Everyone is penned in! It's a trap!"

"Aye, ye worked it out faster than me."

"This way, I know a shortcut."

The pair jogged at a heavy-breathing pace towards Savo Plaza, taking alleyways too narrow for a tank to pass through. The cool air of the spring evening, and the mission to save her country invigorated Ondine. But they could only keep going so far before they had to stop. They turned to find a wall of people blocking the road. People waving banners with blue hands printed on them.

"Wait a minute," Hamish pulled her into the shadows of a doorway. "There's a bloke with a megaphone instructing them."

These were no PopEuroTube revellers, they were an organised gang. A gang supporting Lord Vincent and heading straight for the plaza. Skirting around the blue hand mob, Ondine and Hamish took a side alleyway heaving with people. "Excuse me, sorry, please let me through? Can I just . . ." Ondine said on a repeating pattern as she budged and nudged her way closer to the big screen to see what was going on. The further they pushed, the thicker the crowd, until it became impossible to breathe for the crush of people.

On the big screen, countries took it in turns to deliver their scores. Someone just gave the ultimate thirteen votes for Slaegal. Zings of happiness zipped through Ondine on behalf of her sisters.

Hamish squished her around the middle. "Margibelle are in front lass!"

The crowd roared enough to shatter the roof. Luckily they were outdoors and there was no roof to shatter.

The next set of votes came in, and the voice giving those votes sounded hideously familiar.

"Good evening Europe, this is Venzelemma calling!"

The crowd's enthusiasm flew off the scale.

There on the screen was Lord Vincent's face, five times larger than life. He had his back to the rapturous audience in Savo Plaza, delivering his long-winded time-wasting piece about how wonderful the night had been and what a brilliant show everyone had put on.

Ondine's eyes moved from the big screen, to see Vincent in the flesh on the stage below. He was speaking into a camera, a chunky cable trailed from the back of it. That cable had to lead somewhere, and it had to be plugged into *something* in order for Vincent to get his live messages across to the millions of people watching PopEuroTube all over Europe.

"I've got a plan," she said, grabbing Hamish by the hand. "Let's unplug him!"

Pulling the plug wouldn't stop the show, but it would stop Vincent's grandstanding by killing his live feed.

The crowd hushed as Lord Vincent delivered the lowest five scores. Ondine hoped he'd drag it out so they'd have time to get to whichever power socket that cable was connected to.

Keep talking, wind bag.

Then Vincent announced, with a long drawn out pause, that Brugel was giving nine points to Craviç.

A small part of Ondine wanted to know the rest of the results, but they had to pull the plug on Vincent and get people out of the plaza before the Fort Kluff cadets and Mrs Howser arrived.

There it was! The cable fed straight into an outside broadcast van.

Bang bang bang Ondine smacked the van's door with her palm. A frazzled woman wearing a headset opened the door and glared at them. "What do you want?"

"Who are *you*?" Ondine said, fuelled with bluster and adrenaline. "Where are Yovanna and Berol?" There was no Yovanna and Berol, she'd made those names up, but she hoped the tone of her voice would confuse the staff inside.

Vincent dragged the points out, delivering "Ten points

to the outstandingly wonderful performance from Haute Montagne."

"Never mind who I am, who are *you*?" The woman said. "And what do you think you're doing banging on the door during a live broadcast?"

Not falling for it, then.

"Ondi lass, will ye hold me?" Hamish said, one eyebrow raised as he held the door wide so the woman inside couldn't slam it closed.

"Yes darling. Of course." Ondine wrapped her arms around his waist, threading her thumbs through his belt loops as she did so. The man she loved made a howl of pain and crumpled into her chest. His clothes fluttered in the cold air and she quickly rolled them into a ball in her hands.

"On guaaaard!" Hamish cried out, leaping his Shambles-ferrety self up the steps and into the van.

The woman's screams pierced the sky. Madness filled the van. Shambles leapt from shelf to shelf, down to the floor, spun in the air, leapt onto his feet, twisted and tumbled, scarpered up a wall and somersaulted down again. A mesmerising display of agility and insanity.

Outside, Vincent delivered Brugel's eleven points to Moldova. A small part of her wanted to know who Brugel would give thirteen points to, but there was an army on the way and she had to act now.

The frazzled woman screamed again and charged after the furry intruder.

Ondine slipped inside the van and looked for the 'live' video feed amongst the technology and the wizz-bangery. There! She saw a label stating "LIVE CROSS UPLINK." That had to be it.

Flick!

People outside in the plaza hollered and booed.

She must have done something right.

The van rocked. With a crunching thud Ondine landed on her tailbone. The van door slammed shut as the mob outside rocked them back and forth.

"What have you done?" The woman held on to the walls for balance as she rounded on Ondine. "You've cut the live cross. Get everything back the way it was or we'll have a riot on our hands!" The woman, who should now be called The Furious Woman, turned to Ondine and yelled, "Get out!"

Shambles leapt onto the (furious) woman's lap. She yelped and jumped into the air, all arms and legs and pointy angles. "Get it off!"

"I've called security," a man said. He must have been in the van all along. His cardigan was so dirty and worn only the stains held it together. "I don't know what your game is love, but we've got no money. No point robbing us at ferret-point."

Ondine took a desperate look at the array of buttons and knobs and things that slid up and down, and little windows with needles that wobbled from side to side. Why could there not be a simple master switch? It was one thing to silence Lord Vincent, but if the big screen kept on playing the rest of PopEuroTube, people would stay in the plaza and be trapped by the tanks.

Great Pluto's Ghost. There it was! A fuse box with a master lever.

Flick!

Everything switched off. The world turned black. Ondine groped for the door and shoved it open. Light spilled from outside as she scrambled to collect Hamish's abandoned clothes. A blur whisked beside her; Shambles leapt clear out of the van and scarpered up a nearby pole. In the plaza, the great screen stood like a monolithic art installation. Impressive but useless. The crowd grew restless, throwing empty cheeseball cups and drink cans at the screen.

Hope bloomed. She'd stopped it. The party in the plaza and the big screen showing PopEuroTube. All of it came to a shuddering stop. Surely everyone would go home now, right?

***

Standing on the blacked-out stage confirmed Vincent's deep-seated fears that he wasn't allowed to have nice things. "Melody! Fix this now!"

"On it!" she called out from somewhere. It was so dark he couldn't tell where that somewhere was. With a flash and a *bzzt*, the lights came back on, along with the rest of PopEuroTube on the big screen. The crowd behind him cheered and whistled. He kept looking down the barrel of the camera, waiting for the red light to come on.

The operator behind the camera pulled his headphones off his ear and said, "After the live cross cut out, the show's hosts in Craviç read out Brugel's final votes going to Slaegal. So they're not crossing back unless the vote is close at the end of the night."

Damn.

The live feed restored, the big screen showed the delegate from Trajikstan announcing her votes. Thirteen points to Brugel.

The crowd in Savo Plaza, so distracted by the power cut, were now firmly back on board, cheering and hollering Brugel's top vote.

The leader board had Druvitzia first, Slaegal second and Brugel third, then a huge gap of thirty votes to fourth place, Craviç.

The broadcast went to a quick replay of all the acts during the night. On stage in front of the big screen Vincent grabbed a spare microphone from his jacket, flicked it on and spoke to the crowd.

"Ladies and Gentlemen, no matter the result, Battlefront has made Brugel proud tonight."

The crowd roared its approval.

Adrenaline charged through Vincent. "Straight after the results, we will have a special announcement, but for now, try not to bite your nails off while we wait to see who wins!"

It should be Brugel, but to Vincent's disdain, the last two countries' votes – and they took their sweet time delivering them – did not go their way.

Then the PopEuroTube masters of ceremonies were back on screen with their rhyming couplets.

> *"It's the end of the night,*
> *we've had so much fun.*
> *It's our pleasure to say*
> *Druvitzia won!"*

Savo Plaza erupted with howls of disapproval and deep rumbling booing noises. Looking out at the crowd, Vincent knew he had to keep things upbeat. It would have played out so much better had Brugel won, but things were already set in motion, so it didn't matter in the grand scheme of things.

That's when he looked out at the broadcast van and saw Ondine and Hamish standing nearby. Right then he knew they must have been responsible for the blackout a few minutes ago.

He didn't think he could hate them any more than he could right now.

***

Staring Lord Vincent right in the face, Ondine crossed her

arms and willed herself not to leap on stage and strangle him with the microphone cord. Then she remembered she was a nice person who didn't go in for public displays of aggression. Even though she was sorely provoked. Yet there he was, standing in front of the big screen, hogging the limelight and all the goodwill.

"Ladies and gentlemen, Battlefront was amazing tonight!" Vincent said.

Behind him, the big screen changed from showing images of the winners at PopEuroTube to something very different. The interior of a public building.

Huh?

Ondine tried to work out where she'd seen this building before. It was cavernous, with dozens of well-cushioned chairs arranged in a u-shape around a long central table. That's when it hit her. The inside of Brugel's dentate building. At the centre of the room, near a long table, stood Brugel's First Minister Natalia Cebotari. Beside her Duchess Anathea stood trembling, a sheet of paper in her hand.

Ondine's bile rose.

The crowd hushed as they listened to the quavering voice of their Duchess.

"To the people of Brugel. Congratulations on an outstanding performance at tonight's PopEuroTube. You have done your country and yourselves proud. Brugel's future on the world stage stands strong and assured.

"Tonight, it is with an eye on such a future that I announce my abdication as Duchess of Brugel, effective immediately, handing over rule to my nephew, Lord Vincent, who will from this moment on be known as Duke Vincent the third.

"I have also resolved to disband the dentate and open the government to free and fair elections at a time of Lord

Vincent's choosing.

"I must stress that I arrived at this decision myself. The decision was mine alone to make.

Thank you for being the best people in the world, from the best country in the world. I will as ever, be your humble servant, Anathea."

A pretty speech that hushed the crowd watching it in Savo Plaza.

Ondine knew the duchess had not written it herself. For a start, it wasn't written in that passive style of *things being done by someone else* that Anathea favoured. But mostly it didn't ring true because of the way Valentin and Mrs Howser had treated Anathea at the ballroom earlier tonight.

On stage Vincent spoke into the microphone again.

"Ladies and gentlemen, people of Brugel. I accept this honour. I must now travel to the Dentate and sign the necessary paperwork. Thank you for making history tonight!"

Ondine wanted to throw up, cry and tear her hair out all at the same time. The very worst thing had happened and she hadn't been able to stop it.

The mood in the plaza changed from friendly to confused in the snap of a twig.

A metallic rattling noise came closer. But from which direction? Craning their necks, Ondine and Hamish looked around.

"It's over that way lass," Hamish said, pointing to the right as a tank pushed its way down a street.

"No, it's this way," Ondine said, pointing to the left as another tank creaked into the edges of the plaza. Cadets flanked both the tanks, blocking the exits.

More tanks and cadets arrived and clotted access to the remaining streets. Riding on the top of one, came an all too familiar old witch. Mrs Howser, her cape flowing behind, looking like the queen of the world.

"Mercury's wings! We're trapped like rats in a cage!"

Wasting no time, Mrs Howser stood at the front of her tank and waved her arms. Sparks of dark magic flew through the air and landed like snow on people's heads, melting into their clothes and hair.

Any confusion evaporated as the crowd's mood switched firmly into full-on support for Vincent. Cadet's moved through the crowd, giving out blue banners and noisemakers. People chanted for Vincent in not-quite-unison (like they would properly chant at a football match). The original supporters held placards on sticks in favour of Vincent, yet covered their mouths with bandanas or surgical masks. Some of them wore those rictus-grinning face-masks from an inexplicably popular movie.

The giant screen showed the buoyant mood, as the cameras captured the pro-Vincent crowd and broadcast it to the rest of Brugel.

For a moment, Ondine lost her mind as euphoria for a new leader took hold. But wait, this couldn't be right. Mentally shaking herself, she dug deep, all the way to her boots, to remember why she and Hamish were here in the first place. They were here to stop Vincent, not support him.

No magic spell could counter-act such strongly held free will, and when it came to battling Lord Vincent, Ondine had an over-supply of free will.

Uh-oh, Hamish's face had already glazed over as he fell under Mrs Howser's spell.

"Snap out of it!" she yelled to her beloved.

He did not snap, nor did he come round when Ondine gave him a shake.

"Hamish, remember why we're here! We can do this, this spell can't stop us!"

But he looked so far gone, as if he'd become another person. "Come back to me, Hamish!"

With every fibre of her love, Ondine kissed Hamish, hoping it would knock some sense into him. If things weren't so desperate, it could have been a timeless kiss that developed into a lovely snog session. But Ondine didn't have that luxury.

When they eventually pulled away, Hamish smiled, then winked at her. "I needed that. Right, let's see what's to do?"

"Howser's put a spell on everyone, taking the goodwill in the crowd and turning it into a pro-Vincent rally. Our kiss hasn't affected anyone else. I can't very well go around kissing everyone in the entire crowd to break the spell!"

Looking about them, Hamish nodded. "We're in the thick of it now, lass."

The tanks cranked up again and began reversing down the streets. The cadets marching along side them. The mesmerised crowd stayed behind, watching events unfold on the giant screen.

A chant broke out in the plaza as someone started shouting on a loudspeaker, "Blue hand group. Blue hand group."

"I wish I had one of them," Ondine wailed.

"Like this?" Hamish produced a megaphone from behind his back.

"Oh my stars I love you so much!" Ondine threw her arms around his neck and kissed him all over the face, including, obviously, the lips. Her lips stayed on his for a while longer, because she loved him *that* much. It was Hamish who pulled back, and handed Ondine the megaphone.

Climbing onto the top of a stone plinth, Ondine cried out, "People! People, listen to me!"

They weren't listening.

"Helps if ye turn it on," Hamish said.

"Oh." Feedback whine. Take two. "People, listen to me!"

Great volume!

The people stopped. Actually stopped. Whoa, power! Ondine's nerves jangled as the crowd turned to her.

"It doesn't have to be like this! You're all under a spell, but it won't last! It was obvious that Vincent forced Anathea to make that speech. She's still our Duchess!"

Hundreds of revellers looked at Ondine. Waiting for her . . . to do what? To know the right thing to say? To give them answers?

"This is not the Brugel way. I love our country and I know everyone here loves our country too. Brugel . . . is what makes Brugel great."

Not the best start, because her brain hadn't caught up to the situation yet. "I'm sorry Vincent and Anathea are fighting. But we can sort this out. Life will go on tomorrow. Because we are a thoughtful people, and we look after each other. We have so much love to give. That's what our country needs now. We don't need to kick out the Duchess, we need love!"

Voice cracking with emotion, she flicked the button off so that she wouldn't amplify her aside to Hamish: "D'ye think it's working?"

"Keep giving it laldy," Which was Hamish's way of saying, 'give it all you've got.'

She flicked the loudspeaker back on again. "I love my country, I love our Duchess Anathea, she is a national treasure. She needs us and we need her."

People lowered their blue fists and banners. Having their attention made Ondine bolder. "Go home to your families and loved ones. Show the people closest to you how much they mean to you. That's the spirit of Brugel.

That's *love*."

One by one, people turned to each other, as if waking from Mrs Howser's spell. They were shaking their heads, confused about what was going on.

"It's worked," Ondine turned to Hamish.

The crowd dropped their banners and signs.

"Love is the answer!" Ondine cried out.

She'd done it!

As one, the crowd suddenly let out an almighty roar and charged towards Ondine and Hamish, turning on them. Panicked, Ondine dropped the loudspeaker. Hamish grabbed her free hand, hauling her away from the angry mob bearing down on them.

"Up," Hamish said as they reached a tree. He linked his palms together to make a step. Ondine slotted her foot in and he *hoiked* her up. She hauled herself into higher branches, the crowd forming a sea of people below.

"Hamish?" She glanced at the base of the tree. Panic shot through her. He was nowhere. "Hamish!"

"Right here lass," he said, as his ferret form shot out of his clothes and scarpered up the trunk. "They're raging now."

People began pushing each other up the tree. The branch Ondine clung to, now with a Shambles ferret on her shoulder, leaned over the awnings of a shop. She crawled along the branch, her weight bending the arm low. Splinters bit her hand. There wasn't time to check for injuries as she scrambled from the branch onto the makeshift balcony. With a satisfying twang, the branch sprang back, throwing the other climber into the crowd below.

"That went about as well as could be expected," Shambles said.

Now they were higher up, they had a better view of the rioters. More people climbed the tree to get closer to

Ondine. Someone else shimmied up a nearby flagpole.

Claws digging into Ondine's shoulder, Shambles yelled, "Run!"

Clang, clang, her feet crashed over the metal awnings as Ondine ran away. Then she came to a halt. The next awning was made of canvas, with huge mould and moss patches. No way would it take her weight. *Clang, clang*, someone else's feet closed in on them. Holding on to whatever parts of the wall she could, Ondine shuffled and hauled herself along, using window sills as footholds and –

Riiiip!

The person following had tried running across the awning, only to tear straight through it and land on the ground.

"The drainpipe!" Shambles yelled in her ear.

"Easy for you!" Ondine yelled straight back.

The claws left her shoulder and the ferret scarpered up the drain, all scritches and scratches as he found footholds in the rust. The rioters below were screaming and hollering now. She'd become the fox and they were a pack of slavering dogs.

"Hurry!" Shambles again.

"What do you think I'm doing? Taking a leisurely stroll?" Desperate for something to grab on to, Ondine reached up and clutched the lip of the guttering with one hand. Then she wedged her foot between the downpipe and the bracket holding it to the wall, pushing herself up. Her other hand grabbed more guttering.

"Gotcha!" Someone grabbed Ondine by the other foot and pulled on her.

Desperately she clung to the guttering, her arms burning in pain.

The crowd erupted in screams.

Claws raced down her arms. It had to be Shambles. Ondine felt but couldn't see Shambles scarpering down her body towards her attacker. The other person suddenly screamed in agony and let got. Shambles must have bitten him good and proper.

"Get up lass," Shambles yelled.

Muscles burned as she clung to the guttering and scrambled to the roof. "That's it, nearly –"

Whoosh!

The guttering buckled, sending freezing dirty water and last autumn's slimy leaves over them. Rivers of sludge poured into Ondine's armpits, then drizzled down her torso. Somehow – probably adrenaline coursing through her from the fear –instinct had her hanging on. With a few more shuffles and shimmies, she found a new section of guttering that held her weight. Her legs found the top of a window for purchase and she pushed with all her might.

A hand grabbed her by the wrist. "I've got ye."

She looked up into Hamish's smiling face. Hamish back in his human form, with both his hands around hers, hauling her up onto the roof.

She fell against him, breathing hard with relief. He spluttered as her wet hair fell across his face. Her wet, stinky, slimy hair.

The crowd below them hollered. People were climbing trees to get onto the shop awnings – avoiding the ripped canvas – and clawing their way up the side of the buildings. No way did Ondine want to hang around to see if they reached the roof.

The solid body of Hamish vanished out from under her and his ferret form scarpered to the roof ridge. "This way. Come on."

All things considered, it made a frustrating kind of sense to Ondine that he'd reverted straight back into a ferret. The sight of a naked man crawling over the roof wouldn't exactly be a calming influence on the mob, would it?

Spreading her weight out to minimise the chances of falling through, Ondine crawled on all fours, following Shambles. On the other side of the roof ridge, several shops opened out to a courtyard below. At the back of the buildings they found a narrow ladder, but the rungs were too far apart for Shambles to climb down safely, so he scrambled onto Ondine's shoulder and took the easy way down.

"Don't take this the wrong way, lass, but ye stink."

"You're hardly a rose garden yourself," she shot back.

He rewarded her with a ferrety kiss on the cheek. Shame it wasn't a human one. She could really do with one of them right about now.

~ Chapter Fourteen ~

The irritatingly slow drive to the Dentate had Vincent chewing at the nubby bits of skin on the side of his nails. If they went any slower they'd go backwards, but the crowds made it impossible to get momentum. Despite Babak's security detail, supporters leapt too close to the car, slapping the panels and windows in support.

"I'm getting out to walk," he said.

"No," Babak's hand slapped hard on his shoulder, welding him to the seat. "You are in no rush. You are patient and wise beyond your years. Yes?"

"Yes, you're right."

"You're going to be wonderful," Ruslana said.

"Where's Melody?" He hadn't seen her since the lights had gone out during the glitch.

"She said she was going back to the hotel for a rest."

Had she abandoned him at his moment of triumph? "What if I need her?"

"All good," Babak said. "It's all done now, you're the

Duke. Relax and enjoy it."

Finally (had it only been ten minutes?) they reached the Dentate. A row of cadets stood guard by the side of the road, with a tank behind them. Floodlights lit the neo-classical facade with its fluted columns and stone steps.

The driver pulled up. Babak, Ruslana and Vincent slid along the leather seat and climbed out the car, to a phalanx of flashing lights as the media throng jostled for the best shot. Vincent took his time, smiling and waving, as if greeting an invisible friend just on the other side of the photographers.

He took the steps at a regal pace as reporters fired a barrage of questions at him:

"Did you convince the Duchess to resign?"

"Have you been planning this?"

"What about democracy?"

Keep looking relaxed and unhurried. Keep looking in control. Because you are in control.

The reporters kept firing questions, he kept right on walking and waving.

"What will happen to Anathea now?"

"Is this against the constitution?"

"How do you feel, now that you're Duke?"

The media crush managed to move aside enough for Vincent to make his way to the Dentate floor. Anathea and the First Minister would be waiting there for him. He'd sign the papers and dismiss them. Then he really would be Duke.

One foot in front of the other. It was a miracle he could see at all thanks to the flash burns in his vision. Gradually the black rectangles faded to reddish blotches. Anathea came towards him, hand out to shake his. "Be good for Brugel," she said.

Before he could respond, she stepped away. The camera-flash blotches in his vision cleared enough to see

Mrs Howser in the gallery, along with a few cadets. They'd been brilliant tonight, turning up and lending support at just the right moment.

Melody may have bunked off earlier tonight, but maybe he didn't need her any more as long as he had Birgit Howser in his corner?

Natalia Cebotari, the first minister, guided him towards a table, where a series of papers waited for his signature. The fact the first minister had said nothing in protest only proved how powerful Mrs Howser's magic could be. He'd reward the witch accordingly.

Vincent took his seat and picked up a pen. Cameras clicked and flashed. Reporters kept firing questions but he ignored them. The only thing people needed was to see him signing papers. One by one he set his name to the space on each page, confirming his ascension.

Quietly, Ruslana appeared at his side, her manicured hand lightly touching his shoulder in a show of support.

***

Keeping to the shadows and away from the rioting mob, a dejected and defeated Ondine trudged home with the ferret on her shoulder. The mob had heard her message of love and utterly rejected it. Everything they'd done to help Anathea had failed.

"We'll be all right lass," Shambles said with forced cheeriness. He'd taken up position on her shoulder. "As soon as we get home, I'm running ye a nice hot bath with lots of bubbles."

Soaking in something clean and hot would be heavenly.

"Aye, and I'll wash yer hair for ye."

How lush. "Thanks."

"Although I cannae promise I'll be able to stay out of the bath meself."

Despite the chill, heat bloomed on her cheeks. When he was Shambles, he could be so delightfully inappropriate. On they trudged, the cloudless sky sucking any remaining city warmth into the stars. Trembles and chills filled her body.

"Only a few kilometres to go, hen. We'll be there soon."

Shame having no clothes meant he couldn't become his Hamish-self and give her a piggyback instead. She turned her collar up against the cold, only to find it wet and slimy from the gutter splash.

"Mebbe if ye jog it will warm ye from the inside."

Lights twinkled up ahead from a mobile food van. The enticing smell of fried cheese balls carried on the wind. "Lend me a fiver will you?"

"Err . . . I dinnae have any."

Now she really would cry. From the cold, from her wet clothes, from her sore feet and her all-over misery. "But you had money –"

"– In meh pocket, when I had meh pants on, so I did."

The pocket of his pants, which were now lying somewhere at the bottom of a tree in central Venzelemma.

"I could go back for them. If ye want me to?"

"No point," she said with a huge sigh. Honestly, she could sigh for Brugel at this rate. She couldn't face walking all the way back to the base of the tree they'd climbed, in the forlorn hope of finding the pants Hamish had abandoned, let alone finding any money left in the pockets. The mob could still be there. They might recognise her. And she did *not* have the energy to go though all that again.

"I'm just glad I have the keys." Reaching inside her soggy clothes, she pulled out the lanyard. Where the keys had been were now the tattered edges of torn polyester. They must have ripped off during the tree climb. Or the roof climb. Or scrambling over the guttering.

"I give up," she slumped to the kerb. Any second now sobs would rack through her body and she'd be a blubbering mess on the cobblestones.

"Whoa!" Shambles nearly fell off her shoulder. "Lass, dinnae give up. We've had a setback, that's all. When we get to yer pub, I ken still scarper in and unlock the door from the inside."

Trudge home they did. Being an old city, many of Venzelemma's streets were made from cobblestones. Beautiful for postcards but hell on the ankles. They came across cadets on street corners, moving people on.

"Where are you going?" One of them asked Ondine.

Dread filled her stomach. "Home," she snuffled.

"You go straight home then, and stay out of trouble," the cadet said.

She wasn't going to argue with them. Finally they made it to the family pub. "I'll be right back," Shambles said as he scurried over the gate at the back of the family pub.

Snick went the lock and the gate opened with a satisfyingly old creak. Good. At least they were in the beer garden. But still outside. Oh, hello, Hamish was his Hamishness. He'd pulled a tablecloth from the clothesline and draped it around himself, for modestly. What a shame. "Right, now, where do ye parents leave the spare key?" Hamish looked about the potted plants and checked under the back doormat.

She drew the tattered ends of lanyard from her pocket. "They used to keep it on this."

"Right." Hamish chewed on the inside of his cheek. Lost in thought. Then a look of determination came over his face and he stepped in and gave her a kiss. "I'm gointae get ye that bath I promised. Hold this for me."

He gave her the edge of the tablecloth. Just as she thought she might see something saucy, he flashed back into a ferret. A few minutes later, she heard footsteps from inside the hotel and a partially dressed Hamish opened the door. In his other hand – oh bliss – was an enormous bath towel.

"I've *goat* the bath running already, so up ye get. I'll get yer pyjamas for ye."

In the bathroom she shucked her slimy cold clothes off and climbed in. It was cold.

Of course it was cold. It would be generous to even call the temperature tepid. The lack of steam should have given that away, but she hadn't noticed. At least the water wasn't freezing, because then she would have screamed. She turned the cold water tap off completely and stuck her head directly under the hot – but really tepid – water to get the slime out of her hair.

It was her fault the water was cold. Because the rest of her family were away and it was just herself and Hamish, she'd turned the hot water service to mornings only, because they didn't have guests and for once, she wouldn't spend evenings up to her armpits in hot soapy water, washing dishes. She'd give anything for some hot water now. But the system was in the laundry, and that was in the room next door. That would mean getting out of the bath and getting *really* cold. Instead, she stayed under the hot tap until it got so cold she couldn't stand it, then she turned it off and grabbed a fresh towel and rubbed her skin raw to help warm it up.

There was a radio in here, against the wall. It crackled as she turned it on, which wasn't surprising considering the years of condensation turning its belly to rust.

"*. . . reeling from the sudden abdication of Anathea, Duchess of Brugel in favour of her nephew Lord Vincent.*" A man's dulcet tones said.

Ondine's feet were so cold they'd started burning, which only served to boggle her all the more. How could a body part be so cold it felt like it was on fire? Wrapped in towels, she opened the door to find Hamish with a pile of nightwear in his arms. "I wasnae sure what ye wanted, so I brought a selection."

"You're so sweet," she gave him a kiss. "Put them on the chair over here."

On the radio, the reporter gave a description of what was happening in the streets of Venzelemma. *"There's a carnival atmosphere down here, as if people know they're part of something momentous. It could be the excitement of the night, or it could be the need for youth to express their individuality."*

"Howser's spell sure did a number on everyone in the plaza, even the reporters," Ondine said.

"Aye. No mention of the tanks, or the confusion. The world has gone whirlypits."[67]

The report mentioned only the excitement of the night, and Vincent's triumph.

Ondine slipped an oversized nightshirt over her head, then modestly wriggled her towel out from beneath it. "Let's get a fire going."

An hour or so later, they sat together, staring into the flickering light of the small fire. So much upheaval in one day meant neither of them would get much sleep.

"Sometimes I feel so selfish," Ondine said in a scared voice. Admitting the truth did that. "I want us to run away from all this . . . this mess. Just so I can be with you and to hell with the world. The trouble is, the next minute I want to storm the streets and liberate Brugel in a tank."

He rubbed her back but didn't interrupt. That's how wonderful he was.

---

[67] Whirlypits means nothing is making any sense, which is par for the course in Brugel.

"What kind of person am I Hamish? Am I a coward or a fighter? I'm so scared this is it. That I'm not going to survive whatever crazy thing happens next."

He kissed her softly on the lips. "I'm so glad you said that, lass. I've been thinking the same, and thinking meself a scaredy cat for having thunk it."

He understood. Of course he did. He was her soul mate. With a shaky sigh, she admitted another truth. "Then there's the devil on my shoulder not wanting to die a virgin."

He made a soft (but never condescending) chuckle. "Aye. I have one of them too saying the same thing."

As difficult as it was admitting her fears, she loved Hamish even more for accepting them and sharing his. That's why they would always be together. They understood each other.

They kissed with a mixture of passion and sorrow, until reality crept back in, thanks to a sudden rapping at the pub door.

"Stay here, lass I'll sort it." Hamish's footsteps disappeared down the hall.

Ignoring his instructions, Ondine padded after him, just in time to see Hamish untying the rope from a lumpy hessian sack on the doorstep. Old Col climbed out!

She spluttered and complained. "Birgit Howser better sleep with one eye open from now on. Look at my beautiful dress, it's ruined!"

Overcome with relief and delight, Ondine flew at her great-auntie and wrapped her in a solid hug.

"Don't blubber on the bodice!" But there was no venom in Col's words as she folded her arms around Ondine, her frail body shuddering with sobs.

"It's good tae see ye Old Col, ye must be fair puckled."

Wiping her eyes, Old Col looked at Hamish. "If you mean exhausted, you're right. I could sleep for a week."

"We've lost, haven't we?" Ondine said as they drew Old Col towards the fire so she could warm up too. She spoke the words she never thought possible, her voice cracking with exhaustion and disbelief. "It's all over. Vincent's won."

"Weil get through this lass." Hamish gave her hand a squeeze. "It might be rubbish for a while, but we've still *goat* each other."

Such kind words did little to balm her ragged nerves.

"Anybody home?" A shaky voice said.

"Melody?" Ondine and Hamish said together.

There she was, slumping against the doorframe.

Hamish went to her, offering his arm for support. "Ye look done-in."

"I'm so sorry. For everything. I thought I could make him better. I thought maybe if I loved him enough he'd change. But he didn't, and I had to leave or I would have lost my mind."

Ondine wasn't entirely sure Melody hadn't lost her mind already. Why had she arrived now, of all times? Was she here under Vincent's orders or had she really left him?

Hamish grabbed an extra chair while Ondine piled more logs on the fire to keep the warmth coming.

"I'm so sorry for behaving so badly," Melody said without prompting. "I lost sight of what was important. And I know I let you down."

It sounded genuine to Ondine, what with the contrite look on Melody's face and the complete absence of 'ifs'. "What if Vincent asks you to come back and work for him again?"

She shook her head. "He won't. Well, he'd better not, because I'll send him off with a flea in his ear."

"A what?" Ondine asked.

"I'll tell him to shove it," Melody said. "Anyway, he doesn't know where I am. I left a note saying I'd gone to my grandparents in Craviç."

Old Col said nothing as she looked into the flames, but her worn face told Ondine all she needed to know. They were well and truly defeated. Vincent had won and nothing would ever be the same in Brugel again.

~ Part Two ~
Eight Months Later

~ Chapter Fifteen ~

If life could be measured in suckage, Ondine's life easily
out-sucked the most powerful vacuums in the world.
Every day of Vincent's reign brought fresh bad news.

The morning after Lord Vincent had become Duke of
Brugel, a palpable sense of dread descended as they waited
to see what would happen to their country. At first it was
the little things. The newspapers Da loved to read each
morning suddenly weren't available at the shop. In the
afternoon, when they'd tuned the radio to their favourite
music channel, they'd heard nothing but static.

Then things became much more blatant. Cadets turned
up at intersections all across the city. They weren't doing
anything, as far as Ondine could tell, but seeing them in
such public positions, in such great numbers, made her
uneasy. As if she couldn't simply go for a walk down the
street without someone watching over her.

Reporting on her.

The seasons passed in a blur of misery. Summer had

been brief and hot, giving everyone sunburn and sleepless nights. Not that people enjoyed walking in the late afternoons as the streets were full of mean-looking cadets. Autumn had been pretty with all its changing leaves, but Ondine's mood was too sour to enjoy it. Her mood didn't improve in winter either. Instead of glorious snow dusting the world with magic, it had rained something rotten, making everything soggy. The winter festivals and the snow maze didn't happen, on account of the lack of snow. Christmas had come and gone with few customers in the pub and scant tips.

And now it was heading into spring again, but Ondine didn't dare hope for anything good happening any time soon. Life was too crapulent for that. They weren't living. They were existing.

"It's called 'outrage fatigue' dear," Ma had said one morning over breakfast. "One unrelentingly ghastly thing after another tends to wear you down."

Eight months of 'unrelentingly ghastly' things had worn Ondine down, that was for sure.

The worst of 'the ghastlies' had to be the curfew at sundown. All citizens had to be off the streets by five at night and they couldn't emerge until seven the next morning. Which made evening travel and socializing near impossible! This had devastated the DeGroot's earnings immediately, as most of their business came from the dinner crowd and overnight guests. Although everyone had been equally affected by the massive changes to Brugel daily life, Ondine couldn't help thinking Vincent had targeted her family in particular.

Education had gone by the wayside, too. Ondine had planned to enrol in a business degree in the autumn, so she could learn even more about running a business and one day take over the family pub. Alas, the college she'd chosen had tripled its fees and closed half its courses. This necessitated taking a gap year to defer her studies. Officially she was working in her parents' hotel. Unofficially she was just as broke and unemployed as everyone else.

The private family room behind the kitchen was often overcrowded. They could eat in the dining room, where there were plenty of tables and chairs, but they had to keep the restaurant clean and tidy on the off chance a paying customer might come in. So they huddled together in their little private room, taking breakfast in shifts.

On this particularly miserable spring morning, Ondine and Hamish took first shift with Melody, Margi and her husband Thomas Berger. Adding to the squeeze was Thomas's younger brother, Alexei. Alexei was a brash young thing, full of grand ideas about where Brugel had gone wrong, and how to fix it. He loved regaling them with historical facts about revolutions, which he'd learned about in school the previous year. He'd make a wonderful lecturer in politics, when things returned to normal.

Whenever that was.

Fortunately for Alexei, he had terribly sensitive skin, so he was unable to submerge his hands into hot soapy water. Alexei and his parents had moved in with Ondine's family during the miserable winter just past. The Bergers had worked at the Brugel Science Institute all their careers. A month after taking office, Lord Vincent declared a budget emergency and cut all science funding. With months of no income, the Bergers put their house up for sale and moved in with Ondine's family. After all, the pub had plenty of vacant bedrooms.

Ordinarily, having a crowd of people in the pub was no big deal. But these were not paying guests, they were extended family, and that meant Ondine had to spend extra time finding useful things for people to do. This in turn gave her less time with Hamish. Much to her continued frustrations, Hamish had even less time for Ondine. His 'staying spell' that Old Col had put him under from the very beginning was losing its potency. Hamish aged far too quickly during the day and had to recuperate as a ferret all night.

Melody, who'd also come to stay, was earning her keep by creating health spells for Hamish.

Ma and Da had taken in family on Ma's side – GrannyMa and GrandDa had come home from their retirement travels, because their pensions had been cut off. They'd parked their caravan in the beer garden. Old Col had also come to live with them full-time, which was excellent as it meant they could keep an eye on her health, both magical and physical. And her mental health, truth be told.

Old Col and the grandparents were in the second breakfast shift with Ma, Da, Cybelle and Henrik. Col had always been batty, but since her horrible night with Mrs Howser, which she still refused to talk about in any detail, she'd been even battier.

At least she was still with them, which was more than they could say for Anathea. Ever since her abdication, there had been no sight of Brugel's former duchess. Rumours swirled about her fate, from living in exile with her ex-husband in the mountainous kingdom of Haute Montagne (the kindest outcome) to not being amongst the living at all (an awful outcome) to being kept prisoner in a rat infested cellar (the awfullest).

The only nice thing to happen was when Margi and Thomas announced they were having a baby. That had at least shone some light into their dim world. They'd announced the news soon after Christmas, and all the oldies had immediately burst into tears of joy and love and they kept hugging all afternoon. This conveniently overshadowed how miserly their Christmas had been.

Now, each time Da walked past Margi, he stopped her, kissed her on the head and then said, "see you soon my little Berger," directly to her belly.[68]

A creaking door and chiming bell told them someone had walked into the dining room.

A customer?

Wiping the breakfast egg from her mouth (the family had brought in chickens and were raising them in the laundry, where it was warm and the hens could produce all year round), Ondine headed out to see who had walked in. It was Ms Cebotari! "First Minister, how wonderful to see you!"

"Just Natalia these days," she said with forced smile. Her dark hair had grown longer, revealing a wide parting of grey roots. Without makeup, her skin looked spottier, with little red blotches along her jawline. She slipped on a pair of glasses and looked closer. "Ondine? It is you. I'm so glad you're still here."

With a mirthless laugh, Ondine said, "Where else would I be?"

"I've come to see how you are faring."

" 'Badly' pretty much sums it up." Then Ondine remembered her customer service training. "Would you like breakfast? Coffee? We still have real coffee if you'd like."

Natalia creased her mascara-free eyes in seriousness. "You're not cutting it with chicory are you?"

"No ma'am. We'd sooner close for good than do that."

"I always knew you were a good sort," Natalia embraced Ondine in a hug. Then she dropped her voice into conspiracy territory.

"Is Vincent still your patron?"

---

[68] Da's idea of Margi having a 'bun in the oven', proving that 'Dad Jokes' afflict fathers the world over.

"No way." Ondine kept her voice low as well. "We haven't seen him for months and I hope we never see him again."

Natalia sighed and smiled. "I'm so glad you said that." Then she released Ondine, dashed for the front door, opened it again and said to somebody waiting outside, "The coast is clear."

In the next minute a dozen people walking in singles and pairs entered the dining room. Natalia made the introductions. "Everybody, this is Ondine DeGroot, a true friend of Brugel. Ondine, it's my pleasure to introduce you to the Brugelish Resistance."

As the Brugelish resistance ambled in, Ma entered the dining room and clapped her hands with delight, instantly mistaking them for people with money. "New customers, how wonderful!"

***

Vincent could not remember ever being so happy. Which was saying a lot considering how well things had been ticking over this past year. He'd refinanced his life thanks to the generous Balakhans, removed his annoying aunt and become the Duke of Brugel. All before his twenty-first birthday.

He sat behind a Brugel Oak desk, admiring the grain and the glossy finish. This was the desk his father Pavla had inherited from his father and his father before him. It wasn't in such great shape when Vincent found it, covered in dust. Dented. Stained. That's why he'd had the surface replaced, and the drawers remade and all the neglect sanded out and varnished. Some of the original Brugel Oak was still in the desk, and really, that's all that mattered. The connection to history. Thankfully, he hadn't had to keep dying his hand blue every couple of days, so that connection didn't have to remain.

Like many over-achievers, Vincent didn't want to rest after his early victories. What would be the point? Resting meant stopping, and he wasn't for stopping. Stopping would mean he'd peaked too early. The door to his office creaked open. Babak Balakhan and Birgit Howser walked silently across the thick carpet, folios tucked under their arms ready for their weekly meeting. From another door came a quick rapping sound, then a waiter walked in with a tiered tray of fruit, cheese and crackers. Unlike Vincent's desk, the meeting table in the middle of the room was not made of Brugel Oak. That sacred timber was getting harder to obtain. Apparently the dust from Brugel Oak sawmills played havoc with people's allergies.

Vincent took a seat at the head of the meeting table. Once he sat down, Birgit and Babak took their seats. He nodded to both of them and said, "How goes our fair Brugel this week?"

"More petitions to end the curfew, or at least drive it back by a few hours," Babak said. "There are claims it's bad for business to have to close so early."

"Most businesses close at five o'clock, don't they?"

"Yes, Your Lordship, they do, but the petitioners are saying their staff need to be home well before curfew, so many are closing as early as three. I have to say I can see it from their point of view."

Vincent shrugged. "What's our next item?"

"I'm proceeding with the database of all witches, as per your request," Mrs Howser said. "And the *normals* who caught mutating magic. It's enabling us to keep track of citizens with useful magic, now and in many years to come, when I am not here."

It was the first time she'd hinted at an inability to carry out her tasks. "You're planning on leaving?"

"I serve at the Your Lordship's pleasure. But age catches

up with us all, and there are some things not even magic can cure."

For a moment he'd thought she was planning on leaving. Now he understood it was more about her mortality, he wasn't so concerned. "Let's not get melodramatic about it." He turned to Babak. "How are the negotiations proceeding with Slaegal?"

"We're on target for the merge in the next six months. We should work out a timetable for releasing information to the public. Advance warning runs the risk of stirring outrage."

"So? We closed all the media outlets critical to us."

"That is true," Babak said with a satisfied smile. "My concern is any lingering doubters."

"I'm fixing that," Mrs Howser jumped in. "The dampening field will be ready ahead of schedule, so we won't have to worry about assemblies via astral projection."

Vincent loved the way Babak and Howser competed with each other to be the favourite. "We shan't have to worry at all if we sell the merger right. Bringing Brugel and Slaegal together will make us stronger. What about Craviç, any feelers out there to see how that will be received?"

"Their ramshackle protest movement is voicing concerns about us," Babak said. "They're putting the blue-flowered flags on their homes and cars."[69]

Vincent shrugged, "Blue flowers go well with blue hands." Then he thought some more and came up with something better. "Let's make new flags. We'll put the blue hand holding the blue flower as a sign of our friendship."

———————

[69] The blue flowers of the chicory plant, which grow wild across the Craviçian landscape.

"I like where you're going with this," Babak said.

"What shall we do about the elections?" Mrs Howser asked.

Vincent frowned. "Who's banging on about timetabling them now?"[70]

"Nobody. Or at least, nobody publicly. My thoughts are that we set a date in late summer –"

"– That will give them far too much time to prepare." Babak interrupted.

"Not if we don't tell them until August." Mrs Howser said. "Say, four weeks' notice?"

"I've always liked the way you do business, Birgit," Babak said. "Four weeks sounds perfect."

Nobody had touched the platter, fruit or otherwise. It was a game Vincent liked to play, knowing Babak and Birgit wouldn't dare eat before he did. He made himself wait longer and longer without eating, to the point where his tummy cramped as the smell of the softly warming cheese teased his nose. "Do you have anything for me to sign?"

Mrs Howser produced several pieces of legislation. "These are from your edicts last week."

"Good." A government of three people was so efficient.

---

[70] Timetabling isn't even a proper word, let alone a verbing of a noun. But of course Birgit and Babak let Vincent get away with it, because he's the Duke.

~ Chapter Sixteen ~

It didn't look in any way suspicious to have members of the newly formed Brugelish Resistance taking afternoon tea at Ondine's family pub, *The Duke and Ferret*. This is because nobody, aside from the members themselves, knew of the existence of the Brugelish Resistance. To people on the street, walking past the pub, it simply looked as if *The Duke and Ferret* had customers in the dining room.

"It's so lovely to have guests here for afternoon tea," Ma gushed as she wheeled the samovar over to Natalia Cebotari's table.

Ma lit the candle beneath the pot and spooned tealeaves into the water. "Chef's making puppy boxes for take-home dining. First Minister, may I show you the menu?" [71]

----

[71] At a restaurant, if you have around half the meal left on your plate, the establishment may give you a 'doggy bag', which is code for 'let's pretend it's for the dog but it's really for me'.

"It's just Natalia," then she quirked a brow. "Puppy boxes?"

"Our version of a doggy bag," Ma said with a chuckle.

Although Ondine constantly felt the resistance's cover could be blown at any moment, it was also a massive relief to have customers again. When the restaurant was empty, people walked past, noted the empty dining room, then kept walking. Thanks to Natalia and her buddies, the people outside walked past, saw that others were enjoying themselves and came in. A classic case of success creating more success.

"Give me a hand with this out to the footpath will you love?" Ma said as she tottered over with an A-frame chalkboard. On one side she'd written, "Curfew special: A warm meal and a warm bed!" on the other side she'd added, "Come for dinner, stay for the duvet!" The two of them huffed as they lifted the heavy frame. "We have to try something for the evening crowd, the curfew is killing us! I can't believe it's still set at five o'clock when it's light now until six. And when daylight saving comes in, it will be light until eight."

"Careful," Ondine said as they shuffled the frame into position on the street outside. If someone overheard them, they might think her 'careful' was in the context of, 'be careful with the board, you might hurt your back,' but in fact she was hoping her mother would realise she really meant 'careful' in the, *'Be careful what you say, someone could easily report you to Lord Vincent for being unhappy'* kind of way.

Safely back in the dining room, Ondine noticed one of their patrons (not a member of the Brugelish Resistance as far as she could tell) sipping tea while working on a laptop.

"Plugged into our wall and using our electricity!" Ma said under her breath.

She had a point. Why would a person need to be

working on a portable computer in a restaurant? Sure, electricity supplies were unpredictable at the best of times, so that might explain it. Or the customer could be writing a novel (she'd heard that sometimes happened). But the really scary thought, which pushed all other thoughts aside, was that the woman with the laptop, drinking only tea and sucking their power out of the wall, might actually be a spy. Which meant she had to suspect there was something worth spying on, here at *The Duke and Ferret*.

Ma refused to confine herself to the kitchen and bustled about the tables, offering tempting samples of their most profitable items and pushing the puppy boxes. It was 'adapt or die' time, with a higher focus on take away items to counteract the lack of dinner crowds after curfew.

It must be how *On the Fang*, across the street, had survived the past year as well.

If Ondine's family didn't find new ways of bringing in customers earlier in the day, they'd go broke. It was getting close to that point, which was why Ma 'over bustled' in the dining room. You could smell the desperation on her.

Making herself useful, Melody now donned Ondine's old gloves and did the washing up. It had been a thankless task when Ondine did it, but 'the glasses had never been shinier' according to Ma. Ondine could do without the implied criticism, but she was nonetheless grateful that Melody was paying her way. It freed Ondine to wrap her arms around Hamish whenever she had the chance.

Which wasn't anywhere near as often as she'd hoped.

Taking a new tray of dirty teacups towards Melody, Ondine whispered, "I think we have a spy in the dining room. Is there any way you can find out?"

"Oh yes." Melody shifted her shoulders and clicked out the kinks. Then she held onto the edge of the sink, closed her eyes and breathed deeply. A hard line formed between her brows and her mouth tightened.

"Saturn's rings, she is a spy," Ondine gasped.

"It's not that," Melody said, her chin puckering with concentration.

"It's something else?"

"It's bad," Melody opened her eyes and shook her head. "I can't get through."

"She's blocking you then?" Only people with magic and something to hide would block astral projection.

Therefore she was a spy!

Melody kept her voice low, but the worry on her face spoke volumes. "Not just her, I can't get through to anyone. I can't astral at all."

"You haven't . . . lost your magic as well have you?"

"I hope not," she waggled her fingers over the hot water, it bubbled and frothed, the dirty teacups plonked themselves in and came out sparkling. "Nope. Still got magic! That's a relief. What do you mean 'as well'? Has someone else lost their magic?"

Quick, don't let on about Old Col, Ondine thought. "So why can't you astral?"

"It's like there's a blanket over me when I try to reach out astrally. It feels like it's made of lead and I can't lift it and I can't see through it."

"Has Mrs Howser put something on you?"

Melody rubbed her forehead, resulting in suds in her hairline. "I should have known they wouldn't let me go so easily."

"Ondine, out front please lovvie, we have more customers," Ma said, producing a new tray of dirty teacups and side plates for Melody.

A new couple had come in to the dining room.

Ma tended them while Ondine waited on/spied on their customer with the laptop.

Honestly, coming in with something that flashy was

bound to make her stand out.[72] With what she hoped sounded like chirpy tone, Ondine asked, "Working on a book?"

The woman stayed focused on the screen and said. "I come here for the solitude."

Point taken.

Ma fussed over the new customers, whom she'd seated at the table by the window.[73] They were two women dressed in dark suits, which reminded Ondine of the night last year when immigration inspectors had come into the pub and tried to deport Hamish. Shudder.

At Natalia's table, Ondine poured more tea and gave them two jam tarts to share between the four of them.

Over the next ten or so minutes, the suited 'window couple' spent the whole time looking at the menus. Ondine watched them from the safety of the kitchen doorway, wondering why someone should take so long to decide what kind of tea to have. Especially when they only had four types. Peppermint, Regular Black, Green and Brugelish Blend.[74] They needed to hurry up and get some food on the table so more people walking past could be lured in. It was already past three in the afternoon. By four, everyone would need to leave so they'd be home in time for five o'clock curfew.

"I can't seem to get them to order anything, they're saying everything looks so delicious they can't make up their minds," Ma said as she came back into the kitchen.

---

[72] As has been mentioned before, all of this took place at least a decade ago, so the laptop took up the space of two large coffee table books, and sucked electricity out of the wall like a vacuum aimed at a pile of confetti.

[73] Restaurants put attractive couples in the window, in an attempt to attract more attractive people.

[74] Brugelish Blend is a combination of Peppermint, Black and Green tea.

Ondine grabbed an empty plate and turned to Henrik. "Put a scone and a slice on it and we'll call it a sampler."

"Just one scone," Ma added.

"I'll cut it in half," Henrik said.

The result was a half-scone with a scraping of jam and a delicate drop of cream on top, next to a wafer thin slice of apricot delight. It had been apricot cake yesterday, but they'd had so much left over, Henrik had repurposed it into something closer to a brownie. Except it was apricot.

Ondine took the plate, added a red nasturtium flower as garnish and headed out to the dining room. With a warm smile, she approached the table and slid the platter between the two suited women. "Ma said you were having trouble deciding, so I brought you our house specials. Please enjoy."

The woman on the left asked, "Is this complimentary?"

Mercury's wings, cheapskates in suits? Maybe they *were* spies. Or maybe they were just city workers who'd ended up with too much month at the end of the money. "It's a sample platter, they're a schlipp each." Ondine beamed at how quickly she'd made that up.

The woman on the right said, "There weren't any sample platters on the menu."

"This is true," Ondine stalled for time, then inspiration struck. "There's a backlog with the printers and we have to wait." Of course there would be a backlog at the printers. They, like every other business, had to close early because of the curfew.

"Can I bring you some tea?"

Instead of answering, the woman on the left asked, "Why is that woman using a computer?"

Definitely a spy-like question. Best get them out of here as soon as possible. "Because the library doesn't let you eat at your desk. I'll be back in just a moment with the samovar."

It wasn't that unusual to take a portable computer out during the day. That was the point of them being portable. However, Brugelers were slow adopters to technology, so it was out of place.

Back in the kitchen, Ondine refilled the samovar with fresh boiling water and set the tea light candle underneath. The candle was an affectation really, keeping the water warm but hardly boiling. It wasn't even a proper samovar, just an enormous teapot with a faucet near the base, but that didn't matter either. With everything loaded on the trolley, including all four kinds of leaf tea ready to get spooned in, Ondine wheeled it towards the suited women. "Have you decided which blend? You only need pay for the first cup, refills are free." Ondine said.

"Then we'll share one cup of Brugelish Blend," the woman on the right said.

Ma bustled in with a plate of hot delicacies. They smelled divine; mushrooms and cheese wrapped in something bake-able. "I heard you couldn't decide, so I brought you our delicious mini savoury parcels. Resistance is futile!"

Resistance? Really bad word choice, Ma! Ondine felt like her heart would stop as she made her way back to the kitchen as fast as she could without looking like she was running. Stupid Vincent and his stupid curfew, ruining everyone's lives. If it wasn't for his mandatory home-time, the resistance would be able to meet anywhere they liked under cover of darkness.

Which, now that she thought about it, was obviously why he'd brought a curfew in.

"Eh lass, whatja gawpin' at?" Hamish said as he sidled up beside her.

Hamish was here. Everything would be all right now, wouldn't it? "The women on the window table. I think they're spies."

"Well, they'll be gone soon, it's nearly curfew."

Ma walked past and noticed Hamish. "Be an angel and dash over to *Fang's* for me. See if they have any potatoes? There's a good lad. We'll pay them back later."

"Hurry," Ondine said, giving him a quick kiss. "And be careful. There are cadets on every corner."

"Och, lass. I'm always careful," he said with a wink.

Staying busy so she wouldn't fret about Hamish, Ondine headed over to Natalia's table. As she stepped closer, the two suited women by the window took an increasing interest in everything going on. If they were spies, they sucked at it.

Keeping her voice bright, Ondine said, "More scones ma'am?"

"Thank you, yes, and tea," Natalia said, then she dropped her voice into conspiratorial range. "If those women on the other table think they're going to follow me home, they've got another thing coming."

"I'll freshen the samovar," Ondine said.

The light outside dimmed. Time marched on. Clearly Natalia wasn't leaving before the suited women left, but the suits were so slow they could have doubled as buskers dressed as statues.

Another ten minutes passed. Hamish came back from *Fang's* with a small bag of potatoes and presented them to Ma, who gave them straight to Henrik. "Soup for dinner again Henrik. Let's see how far we can stretch it."

The entire situation did Ondine's head in. The women in suits had to leave, right now, if Natalia had any hope of making it home before legal lights-out. "What are they doing?" She asked Hamish, "Playing curfew chicken?"

"I've given the suits by the window the bill," Ondine said. "But they're not moving. I think they're spying on us."

"Why would we have spies in here? Honestly!" Ma said

with a roll of her eyes. "Stop being a drama llama. Maybe they want to stay for dinner and a room?" Ma said.

That got Ondine's attention. "They'd be our first dinner guests in months."

Ma said, "It's about time we started having hotel guests again. We'll need to offer them a full Brugelish Continental breakfast in the morning." She rubbed her hands together in anticipation and headed over towards the women in suits, to suggest they stay the night.

Clearly, her mother didn't have a clue how serious this was. They had the leader of the Brugelish Resistance in their dining room, and two spies spying on her. Outside, there were cadets on street corners, watching everything. Natalia and her friends had to leave soon or they'd have to stay the night as well. Did they have enough food to feed everyone?

And another thing, where was everyone going to fit? They had plenty of rooms for family, of course, even the extended family plus Melody. But they only had one or two spare rooms and . . . uh oh, Ma returned with a gleam in her eye.

"Ondi love, you and Hamish get rooms ready. We're going to have overnighters again! Right, hand me the menu. Chef, Cybelle, tell me what we can offer them for dinner."

"Er, soup?" Cybelle said. "And their body weight in scones."

"Soup and scones?" Ma shrugged. "Eh, where are they gonna go at short notice anyway?"

"Weil, there is *Fangs* across the street," Hamish said.

Ondine gave him a nudge.

"Ahhhh, but they're only a restaurant, not a pub. If people stay too long at dinner, they'll have to sleep at the tables," Ma said, heading back out to the dining room. Her voice sounded two notches too loud, as if there were far more people than the measly handful. "My lovely guests, can I get anyone more tea? Apricot slice?"

The front door tinkled and three new people came in. Watching from the kitchen, Ondine could see them look directly to Natalia. A flicker of recognition flashed across their faces. The women on the other table cricked their necks back and forth to observe the exchange.

More people? Nobody would get home in time for curfew at this rate. Which meant things were going to be very crowded in the hotel tonight.

"Three more for the dinner special," Ma said as she came back into the kitchen. "Time for FHB."

Cybelle gave Ma a confused look.

"Family Hold Back. Paying guests first, us second."

"We don't have enough food?" Ondine didn't want to believe it.

"Not at the moment, but after they pay their bills, we'll re-stock," Ma said.

In protest, Ondine's stomach made the loudest gurgle heard this side of the Caucasus Mountains.

Da came in with extra fire-wood to keep the dining room warm. "If they're staying the night, how about we take their money up front? Then I can dash down to the market and restock now. I don't know about you Ondi, but I can't think straight on an empty stomach."

"But it's nearly curfew," Ma said.

"I'll be fine." Da headed into the dining room and built up the fire.

Ma said, "Hamish, you're good at getting people to part with money. Be a champ and collect deposits for the board and breakfast."

"Aye," he said.

Flustered, Ma shook her head. "We've never taken money from people up front before."

"We're doing lots of things we haven't done before,"

Ondine said.

A few minutes later, Hamish handed the deposit cash to Da.

"I'll be back before anyone has a chance to miss me," Da promised. He walked past Margi and kissed her on the head. She grabbed his hand and pressed it to her rotund belly.

"It kicked!" Da's face split with a smile. "Keep cooking little Berger. We'll see you when you're done!"

Ondine and Hamish followed Da towards the back door, Hamish asking the very question at the top of Ondine's list of worries: "I didnae think thae market was still open."

"It's not," Da said. "But I know a place."

"The cadets will see you, they're right out the front," Ondine said. Nerves pumped her heart, trembled her fingers and shortened her breath. Da was acting as if this were nothing more than a shopping trip, but if he was caught out after curfew he could be arrested. Or worse.

"I'll create a diversion, lass," Hamish said with a wink. "I like the look of their trousers!"

"Be –" Hamish vanished into his clothes, and Shambles the ferret crawled out of the crumpled sleeve on the ground. "– careful."

"Right, I'll head out the front door sharpish, Da can sneak out the back."

"Thank you Hamish," Da said.

"Awff we go then," Hamish as the Shambles ferret darted towards the door adjoining their private room behind the kitchen, only to pull up short. "Er, lass, I didnae think this through. Would ye mind opening the door for me? I cannae reach."

Reluctantly, Ondine turned the handle and opened the door enough to let the ferret out into the cool evening air. Through the gap, she saw the cadets sipping something from a hip flask.

While Shambles bounded out to the street, the door to the beer garden creaked open and Da slipped away. Please be safe, both of you, she silently begged.

***

Sleeping as a ferret at night in his safe, warm bed was one thing, but being a ferret out in the open, on the road, as the light faded for the day had Hamish feeling twenty kinds of nervous. Being so low to the ground made him vulnerable to the kind of heavy boots the Fort Kluff cadets liked to wear.

As a ferret, his adorably fuzzy little ears gave him excellent hearing. Da's footsteps faded off down the road, now was the time to act. Wailing like a banshee, Hamish leapt into the air and spun around on the spot, landing with a wet thud into a gutter puddle. Cold and wet, he wailed some more. A totally natural wail as it turned out.

"What?" One of the cadets noticed Shambles' efforts and walked across the street to get a closer look. "Hey Gregor, look at this funny cat!"

"I'm nae cat!" Shambles yelled. Standing on his hind legs brought him eye level with their kneecaps. Their tasty, vulnerable kneecaps.

The one called Gregor yelled and took a step back. "It talks!"

Diversion well and truly made, Shambles tapped his foot on the kerb. This was going so well he could barely believe his luck. "I can dance too, if ye want."

The other cadet said, "What's it saying?"

Gregor ran back to his post.

"Come back and play with me," Shambles called after him. As the cadet checked left and right to cross the street, he did a double take in the direction of the beer garden. Da should be long gone by now. Shouldn't he?

"Rav, get backup," Gregor said. "We've got an 'out after curfew'."

Desperate, Shambles leapt after Gregor, locking his claws into the cuffs of his cadet pants.

Gregor violently shook his leg. "Get off me!"

Dizzy and shaken, he clung on for his life, the fabric ripping where his claws dug through.

"What is that?" The other one said.

Shambles was in no position to tell who said what, as he clung on for his life. Being flung around like a rag doll, he focussed on survival.

"Don't worry about me, call it in!"

"But it's ripping your trousers!"

"Hurry up, he's getting away!"

The shaking stopped. Dazed and dizzy, Shambles clung on, took a second to get his breath back, then scarpered up Gregor's leg and on to his back. The cadet's arms flailed and whipped backwards, trying to grab him.

"Get this thing off me."

A hand clamped around his tail and pulled. Shambles let out a whelp of pain and dug his claws in to Gregor's uniform.

"He won't budge."

Shambles clamped his teeth down on something and locked his jaw. He was going nowhere.

"Unit three-seven-three reporting in, we have a citizen out after curfew. Has decamped in direction of unit three-seven-seven. Please advise."

A scratchy voice came in from a speaker somewhere. *"Advising unit three-seven-seven to apprehend."*

Shambles's hopes fell faster than a ferret dropping from a man's back. He scarpered to a safe distance and looked back. The cadets were checking the damage on Gregor's uniform and not chasing Da down the street. Which was a good thing. But no, it was bad, because the cadets stationed further down the street could already be in pursuit.

How could he be so stupid to think distracting the cadets on their corner would make a difference, when there were so many cadets stationed on street corners all over the city?

Dejected, he crept back to the pub and hoped that by some miracle, Da would be all right.

Naturally, Ondine was waiting for him. "How did it go?" She asked.

"Weil, ye Da got away at least," Shambles muttered, heading to his room to change back into human form and proper clothes.

"He'll be all right though, won't he?"

How could he answer that without crushing her spirits?

~ Chapter Seventeen ~

It was the first time they'd had overnight guests in
months. Ondine, Hamish, Thomas and Alexei madly
tidied five guest bedrooms, taking their own belongings
out and shoving them into other rooms for the mean time.
Alexei would share with his parents, Ondine, Melody and
Cybelle were with Old Col, and GrannyMa and GrandDa
were with with Ma and Da. That left Thomas and Margi
with a room of their own (seriously unfair as far as
Ondine was concerned) and Hamish would share with
Henrik.

Rooms sorted, Ondine hoped the two women in suits
would be happy to share a twin room. It was the darkest
room, with west-facing windows so the early morning
light from the east wouldn't wake the guests too early.
Ondine loved this room because it guaranteed a sleep-in,
especially in summer. With any luck, the two suited
women would sleep long into morning.

At the opposite end of the hotel, the early morning sun

ripped through the south-east facing windows. Natalia and her resistance friends could stay in this room, wake early and head out before the two suited spies had even opened their eyes.

A most excellent plan.

An hour dragged by. It was past curfew and growing dark outside. In the dining room, everybody stayed in their seats, sipping tea and dabbing at the crumbs of their afternoon tea. In the kitchen, things were getting crowded as GrannyMa, GrandDa and Old Col arrived for their dinner. Not that there was much to eat. The miserly soup would have to do. Where was Da with the food? Ondine looked out the back door again, willing her father to walk back in, arms aching with all the food he'd said he'd bring back.

"Looking isn't going to make Da come home any faster," Ma said.

"I'm getting worried." Ondine confessed.

"We all are, love."

The radio news came on in the kitchen.

"Duke Vincent has announced there will be no Brugel Daylight Saving Time. This means the clocks do not need to spring forward and nobody needs to be sleep deprived."

Everyone groaned amidst a chorus of "oh what?'s" and "come on's".

"Duke Vincent also announced there would be no need for the public holiday on the Monday the clocks used to go forward, which will be excellent news for productivity."

Henrik said the rudest word Ondine had ever heard.

"Can this night get any worse?" Ondine muttered to Old Col.

"You should know by now not to say things like that," Old Col said as she collected her soup and dinner roll.

Another hour dragged by. The oldies retired to the family room behind the kitchen and the rest of the DeGroots and Bergers prepared a thin dinner for the paying customers.

Margi, her pregnant belly bumping into everyone and everything, was relegated to the back corner of the kitchen where she sat at the bench and made dinner rolls out of flour and water (no yeast). She'd grown so large she had to sit side-on to the bench, but at least she was productive and contributing.

Where was Da? Ondine fretted. He had to come back soon.

Melody was up to her elbows in hot soapy water. Every few minutes she'd magic up more hot water and bubbles, saving the family money in heating and detergent costs. Unfortunately, using magic only made the girl hungrier, so she ate the raw dough from Margi's tray.

"Ooooh!" Margi sucked in her breath.

Everyone froze for a second, until Margi composed herself. "Kick in the kidneys, nothing to worry about."

Everyone sighed with relief. Margi's baby wasn't allowed to arrive early, not without Da home yet. Where *was* he?

As the minutes turned into hours and the evening wound down, Ma showed their assorted guests to their respective rooms for the night. Ondine dared open the gate to the beer garden to sneak a look down the alley.

"Where are ye awff tae?" Hamish gave Ondine a cuddle from behind.

"I wish I knew where Da was," she snuggled into Hamish. "He should have been back ages ago."

In the distance, sirens wailed and tyres screeched.

"I bet he's being extra careful coming home, that's all

lass," Hamish said. "He's probably spotted trouble and is laying low until it all blows over."

"I know you're trying to make me feel better, but I won't stop worrying until Da's home."

"Then I'll go find him meself."

"But then I'll have two people to worry about."

Ma came to the back door. "If you want something to do Ondi, I've got a list."

"I'm so worried about Da."

"We all are lovvie," Ma stepped forward and embraced Ondine.

"I'll find him," Hamish said.

"Don't you –" The word 'dare' hadn't even reached her mouth before Hamish shrank himself into ferret form.

He stood up on his furry hind legs. "It might be illegal for folks tae be oot in thae street, but nae ferrets."

"Please be careful," Ondine said.

"Aye, I'll be right back, and I'll bring Da with me."

Just like that, he was out the gate and down the street. Ondine's gaze fixed on his furry tail until it and the rest of him dissolved into the dark night.

Something crept into her side vision. A pair of urban foxes slinked around the corner. With a metallic clunk, they tipped over a rubbish bin and helped themselves to the contents. In the absence of people, animals now owned the night. Animals that wouldn't think twice about snapping a ferret in their jaws. The animals turned towards Shambles, their ears pricking, senses on alert as they detected his scent.

Fear charging through her body, Ondine ran out onto the street. "Shoo! Shoo!"

The foxes stopped but didn't back away.

Two cadets came around the corner. "Get back inside Miss, it's long past curfew," one of them said. She looked familiar. Ondine rummaged around in her brain until she remembered where she'd seen the girl before. It had been via Melody's astral projection. This was the cadet whose powers had mutated so much under Mrs Howser's tutelage that she was capable of anything.

Fear tied knots in her lungs as she struggled to breathe.

"Everything all right?" The cadet asked.

Silently, Ondine nodded.

The other cadet picked up some debris from the ground and hurled it at the foxes. "Go-on, get!"

The foxes took a few steps back. The cadet hurled something else and it shattered into pieces on the ground. The foxes slunk back into the shadows.

"Miss, you need to be back inside," that first cadet said.

The other said, "We'll take care of the foxes."

"You'd better," Ondine said, full of bluster to hide her terror. "They're sniffing around our chickens. They've scared them so much they've stopped laying."

They looked like they were trying not to laugh. Good, at least they weren't angry with Ondine or suspicious. "We'll do that Miss," the first one said. "And you get back inside."

****

At breakfast the next morning, food was scarce. Sleep had completely eluded the over-worried Ondine, who was none-too-gentle as she ruffled each hen's feathers in the laundry, looking for eggs. Four eggs, five eggs, six. Her elbow biffed the wall and she dropped one, tears spritzing her eyes as the gloop oozed out over the floor.

Back to five eggs. She used Henrik's swear word from the night before. It sounded good and purposeful, so she said it again. Cursing herself, her tiredness, the mess she'd made and the reduced food they'd have. For good measure she cursed Vincent a few times too. Even though he was

Duke, refusing to call him by his new title made her feel better.

Taking extra care, she took the eggs to the kitchen, saying nothing of the broken one because that would only make everyone upset, and they didn't need any more upset.

Ma said, "Only five eggs? We'll need to add a fair slosh of milk to make the scramble go further."

"I'll add bread crusts," Cybelle said.

"Curfew will be lifted in half an hour, we can send them across to Fang's if they're still hungry." Ma said.

Ondine peeked into the dining room, where the suited spies sat at their same table by the window. No sign of the novelist leeching their electricity out of the wall. That was a plus.

"Did Natalia leave early then?" She asked.

"No love, I don't think she's up yet."

What? Ondine wanted Natalia to get away early. Keeping her breathing steady, Ondine said, "I'd better wake her."

"You'll do nothing of the sort. I gave them the north room." Ma beamed. "The former First Minister deserves a dark room and a restful sleep."

Great. Not that she could tell Ma anything about the Brugelish Resistance and why Natalia should get away quickly. Best to change the subject. "Speaking of people sleeping in, what time did Da and Hamish get back last night?"

With a sigh and a chin wobble, Ma said, "They didn't."

"They're still out there?"

"Keep your voice down. Yes, they're still out there."

"We have to find them! What if . . ." Ondine couldn't comprehend the horrible possibilities facing the most important man in her life. And her dad.

"Go watch some telly. You're no good to me distracted."

Stomach rumbling with hunger, Ondine poured a cup of tea (not to the brim, because her nerves would slosh it out) and flicked on the set in their private lounge.

Huh? Brugel six had a static picture. "What's wrong with it?"

GrannyMa, sitting in the corner with her crochet and wool, looked up. "It's a test pattern, Belle. I mean, Margi."

"I'm Ondine."

"Course you are."

"What's a test pattern?" Ondine flicked channels, only to find all the regular stations had similar static pictures. "Why are they all on test patterns?" At last she found a station that was working.

"That will be the government broadcaster," GrannyMa said. "Takes me back to the old days, it does. One channel, one message. Isn't that right Col?"

Old Col had walked in and seated herself beside her sister, kissing her papery thin cheek. "Have they pulled the plug on the media?"

"It's Stalin one-oh-one all over again," Granny Ma said.

"Nothing if not predictable," Col said.

The two spoke in sister-speak, laughing about the old days. It wasn't a laughing matter as far as Ondine was concerned.

The only channel working was the government broadcaster, which had an exercise program.

"I knew they'd run that!" GrannyMa said. "Come on Col, up we get."

The two of them rose from their seats and imitated the action on screen. Young men and women in exercise gear bent and stretched and marched on the spot. "Gets the blood flowing, does the heart good," Col laughed as she spoke. "Oooh, eye candy. That's an improvement."

Grannyma and Great-Auntie acted like they were under hypnosis, moving their arms about and lifting their knees (not lifting them by much, but lifting them nonetheless). The world had officially gone mad. Twitchy with nerves and bored with only one channel to watch, Ondine went back to the kitchen and grabbed Melody by the arm. "Let's go to the market." The subtext being, "and find Hamish."

"I have to wash these dishes," Melody said, loudly enough for Ma to hear.

"The dishes can wait."

Just as they headed out of the kitchen, they came face to face with Natalia Cebotari.

"Quick, out the back," Ondine said, shoving them towards the rear door.

"Ahoy-hoy, going somewhere interesting?"

Uh oh. It was the two suited women.

"We're going to market," Natalia said to them, bright and cheery and as un-guilty as can be. "Would you like to come?"

Was she mad? They were supposed to be getting away from these spies, not entertaining them!

"What a splendid idea," and "lovely," the spies said.

Natalia, Ondine, Melody and the two spies headed for the back door. Natalia's friends were nowhere to be found. Which was when the twig snapped. If Natalia kept the spies pre-occupied, her friends could get home without being followed.

"Can I come too?" Alexei popped his head around the corner. "This place is so boring." Then he quickly added, "No offence."

***

The winds howled over Mount Verka Seduchka, sending petals and spring pollen through the air. Rugged up against the elements, Duke Vincent stood beside Birgit Howser, observing the team of Fort Kluff cadets dismantling the commercial broadcast towers.

"Don't bend it!" Birgit yelled. "You break, you pay!"

Such admirable people skills, Vincent thought.

"Once we move these towers to the old castle, they'll provide a huge boost to the dampening field," Mrs Howser said.

"Which will block Melody." It irked him how much he'd felt the young witch's absence. For one thing, it necessitated spending more time with Birgit Howser. Melody had been so easy to work with. He'd taken advantage of her desire to be near him. She'd been happy to do his bidding. At least, he'd thought she was. Mrs Howser on the other hand was a slippery fish. She'd become malleable since her time in the asylum, but would it last?

"It will block all witches, not just Melody," Mrs Howser said. "Can't have the resistance using astral projection to bypass curfew."

"There's a resistance group?" Vincent asked. "Already?"

"There's *always* a resistance group. Melody's in it, you know."

"She can't be." The moment the words left his lips, he knew it had to be true.

"You should have given her hope. Or at least the impression of it. A woman can only pine for so long before she eventually wakes up and smells the chicory."[75]

---

[75] An idiom peculiar to former Soviet Bloc countries. Because of supply shortages, local roasters regularly mixed coffee with higher and higher percentages of chicory until one day, at breakfast, the locals 'woke up' to the scam and could smell only the lie that was chicory.

"Who else is in the resistance?" Vincent asked.

"A couple of former politicians, of course. I've had my best witches keeping an eye on them. Melody tried to use astral projection to determine if they were spies. Oh don't worry, she failed. The short-range dampening field around *The Duke and Ferret* is holding, the cadets I've stationed on their corner are making sure of that. This tower will spread the net far wider. Once we get it running, it will cover half of Brugel."

~ Chapter Eighteen ~

Tension stretched to snapping point, Ondine followed Natalia for a walk to the morning market. The two women in suits – she still didn't know their names, which in ordinary circumstances would be considered extremely rude – followed a few steps behind. They wanted to visit the markets, which they'd 'heard so much about'. Melody had her arm linked with Alexei's; a sweet development for her friend and brother-in-law. Alas, it served to remind Ondine that she had nobody to link arms with because her beloved Hamish had not come home.

"We won't be too long, will we Natalia?" Ondine asked.

The former first minister muttered, "Just long enough to lose these two."

Ondine didn't feel right leaving the pub. "Because, I was thinking maybe you could stick with Alexei and Melody and . . . you know, I'm probably not needed."

"You want to be home in case your boyfriend returns

and you're not there?" Natalia said.

"If it's OK with you?"

"It's not. Stay with me, I'll need your help to make a distraction."

Perhaps the trip to the market would distract Ondine from her stomach-churning worries of Hamish's and Da's welfare. No, nothing could make her stop worrying. Instead, she carried her tight tummy and pained heart with her as they walked on.

They neared the markets, the smells and noises hitting them from across the street. Considering how much life had changed since Lord Vincent became Duke of Brugel, it was good to visit something comfortingly familiar. The same rows and rows of fresh produce, crowds of people, colourful banners, music, hot donut vans and yet more noise as people called out their special deals, fast and jarring.

"Apples, apples, apples! Get your bananas here."

It was the kind of call that dug into Ondine's brain, making her pay even more attention to the fruit on display. Especially the bananas. Tummies rumbling from a scant breakfast, Ondine and Natalia bought a banana each and walked amongst the teeming crowds.

Gee that Natalia was clever, Ondine realised. The market was heaving with people. Because of the curfew, the markets opened later and closed earlier. There was less time to shop, so people bought and traded with determination tinged with panic. In all the mayhem, it was seriously easy to lose sight of one another. The first to vanish from Ondine's notice were Melody and Alexei. One moment she could have sworn the two were haggling over the price of potatoes and the next they weren't. The two women in suits had halved, in that Ondine could only see one. The trouble was, they both looked so alike, she couldn't tell if she kept seeing the same one, or both of them at different times. But perhaps the suits had split up, one of them following Melody and Alexei, the other sticking close to Natalia.

"Apples, apples, apples. Get your bananas here."

A freshly crushed apple juice would go down nicely. Pushing against the flow of the crowds, Ondine guided Natalia towards a market stall selling juices and apple blinchikis.[76] Thankfully Natalia had a few schlips in her purse because Ondine's pockets were empty.

"Melody should be safely away by now," Natalia said, her neck craning back and forth as she checked for their none-too-subtle watcher.

Ondine looked around, "Has she gone back to the pub?"

"No, she's headed out of town to see how far the dampening field reaches."

The what?

"She hasn't been able to astral, has she?" Natalia said.

Ondine's eyes widened and things began to fall into place. "The spies weren't spying on you at all, were they? They were tracking Melody."

"They're not completely disinterested in me," Natalia said.

"Of course. No offense."

"None taken. Well, a little." Natalia leaned in low and conspiratorial-like. "We've been building the resistance, using astral projection to meet with people, but a week or so ago, astral stopped working. I knew Melody so some of us came to your pub. But then we couldn't even reach Melody in the next room and we knew there had to be some kind of dampening field."

---

[76] Thin and delicious crepes, which are excellent with all manner of savory or sweet fillings. Or both if you're pressed for time.

Ondine was seriously impressed. "You can do astral projection?"

"Course I can," Natalia said with a grin. "How do you think I lasted so long in politics?" Then she looked over her shoulder and spotted one of their suited women. "She can follow us back to the pub, then I'll head home. It doesn't matter if she follows me, we've got our answers, and we've got Melody on the case."

"But what about the other one in a suit?"

"If she is following Melody, good luck to her. Once they reach the edge of the dampening field, our suited friend won't stand a chance against Melody's skills. Come on, let's see if your father and Hamish are back."

Ondine sipped the last of her apple juice. "Can we get some blinchikis to go?"

***

The moment Ondine opened the back door, a streak of dirty wet fur charged past her. "Hamish! I've been worried sick. Wait a minute, where's Da? Where are you going?"

"I need tae get dressed lass. I'll not come home t'ye lookin' like this!"

The ferret bolted upstairs, his wee claws skittering on the floor.

Ma rushed in. "I heard Hamish. Where's Josef?"

Several minutes of confusion followed. "Da?" Ondine called out, walking to the back door again and checking the beer garden, on the off chance she'd walked in ahead of him and shut the door in his face.

GrannyMa and GranDa stuck their heads out of the caravan. "What's that love?"

"Did Da come through here?"

"No," they said in unison.

"I found him lass," Hamish said, catching up to them.

Relief flooded Ondine as she wrapped her arms around him. Proper Hamish, in his proper human form. Jupiter's moons she'd been so worried.

"I'm not following any of this," Natalia said.

"Neither am I," the woman in the suit said as she walked into the beer garden.

So she *had* followed them back to the pub. How predictable.

"Have you come to check out or will you be staying another night?" Ma asked.

Seriously, how did her mother stay so civil with a customer – and a poorly paying one at that – while Da was still missing?How admirably the rest of the family were keeping it together at a time when they wanted to run around screaming and wailing. If she ever went missing, she hoped the rest of her family would put on more of a show.

A hand wrapped around Ondine's elbow and pulled her inside the hallway. "Ye have tae keep it quiet lass, but I found ye Da."

Bells and clangs went off in her head, but she steadied her breath and asked, "Where?"

Clever Hamish disguised their conversation as a cuddle, so he could keep his voice low next to her ear. "He's in the lockup, *goat* arrested. They've charged him with being out after curfew."

"Arrested!" Her mind screamed but she said nothing out loud in response to the awful news. Instead, she hugged Hamish as tightly as she could, turning her fears and worries into muffled sobs.

"He's safe, lass, but it's no place for ye Da. I'm sure we can pay a fine or something and he'll be home in no time."

***

"We do not accept bribes," the constable said.

Ondine, Hamish and Ma had gone to the lockup. After Ma had (politely) cleared their guests out of the pub. The lockup wasn't a horrible building by modern standards, or even Brugelish ones, but it lacked anything resembling what Brugelers liked to call *bonhomie*. Built and decorated perhaps forty years earlier, the walls were covered in yellowing remnants of decades-old sticky tape. New posters declaring, "If you see something, say something," stood out for their bright colours against fading posters of missing people and road safety messages. The front door creaked and groaned each time somebody opened it, while the internal door behind the main desk had completely lost its hydraulics and banged like a gun every time a police officer came or went.

Ma drew in shocked breath. "Oh no! It's not a bribe. Not in the slightest. Oh goodness, what a terrible misunderstanding. We're here to pay his fine."

Ondine's hand curled tightly into Hamish's.

"Let me see," the officer checked a list of prisoners in the lockup. "Josef de Groot, no, his charge is too serious, he has to go to court."

Court? For being out after curfew? Ondine would have screamed at the officer in rage, but he'd probably arrest her on the spot.

"Can we at least see him? Bring him some food?" Ma lifted the lid on her basket and produced a wrapped tea towel.

With a sniff, the officer lifted the wrapping away, then grabbed a metal ruler from the side of his bench and slapped it through the crust. Chunks of pastry crashed and crumpled, the pie completely lost integrity, mashed into chunks of chicken and vegetables on the tea towel. Then the officer wiped the ruler on the towel and nodded. "That's fine, you may take it in. I'll get you an escort."

He walked through the internal door, which crashed shut, making Ondine jump.

With trembling hands, Ma wrapped the desecrated pie into something resembling its original shape and made for the connecting door to visit Da in the holding cells. Everyone lined up behind her.

The internal door opened and banged shut again as the officer came back to the desk. Then a second later, a woman followed him, opening the door and letting it bang shut. Could the first one not have held the door open for the second, thus reducing the bangage?

"Only one visitor per day, that's the rules." The officer said.

It was impossible not to roll her eyes, so Ondine hid them under her eyelids.

"Come on lass, let's go home," Hamish said as he wrapped his arm around her. He was a good man, that Hamish, leading her out of the police station before she completely lost her temper and ended up sharing a cell with Da instead of visiting. If only one of them was allowed to visit Da, it should be Ma.

For the entirety of the walk home, Ondine didn't have one single idea of what she could do next. Nothing came from Hamish either, which made her feel even more despondent. Hamish was brilliant at encouragement and ideas, but now their collective mood was so heavy, not even he could lift it.

Melody could, though. She was full of smiles as she met them at the door, with Alexei by her side. Ordinarily this would be an interesting romantic development in the private lives of the ever-growing number of folks living under the pub's roof, but now wasn't the time.

"We found out what's causing the dampening field," Melody said. "There's a new tower that's gone up, at the castle where we had Coven-Con. It's blocking all our astral projection signals." She sure knew how to deliver bad news with a smile. "And they're monitoring the phone lines, when they're working that is."

Alexei had drunk from the same 'happiness well' too. "Now we know what's causing it, all we have to do is pull it down."

"That's nice," Ondine said. *Outrage fatigue*, as her mother had called it, had left her completely fatigued.

"You could be a little more pleased," Melody said.

Ondine could only sigh pathetically.

"We've had a wee bit of bad news," Hamish said. "Da's in the lockup. They arrested him for being out after curfew."

"Do you need money to pay his fine?" Alexei asked. "I'm sure my parents have a little saved."

If only. Ondine sniffed, "We tried to pay his fine but they accused us of trying to bribe them. And they'd only let Ma go in and see him."

"And not for long either," Ma said, walking into the house and collapsing into a nearby chair. "They've set his trial for a week from today. They let me in long enough to give him the pureed pie, then they pushed me out. He said to give you all his love. They've told him he can ask Vincent for a pardon, but to get that he has to first plead guilty to treason."

"Treason!" Everyone yelled at once.

"Thank you, I didn't need that eardrum," Ma rubbed the side of her head. "Lord V– I mean, Duke Vincent can only give a pardon to a charge of treason, so Da has to plead guilty to that charge in order to qualify for a pardon."

"But he hasnae done it!" Hamish said.

"We know that, but you can't get a pardon for a crime unless you admit to it first."

Ondine threw her hands in the air. "The world has gone

whirlypits!"

"That's my line!" Hamish said.

"I've had enough," Ondine said. "Ma, Hamish, get everyone together, we're having a family meeting. We need a proper plan and we need it fast."

***

A year ago, if someone had told Ondine she'd be plotting to overthrow the government of Brugel, she would have laughed. A good derisory laugh too. Despite this, Ondine found herself sitting at the table in the family's private room, surrounded by family and friends, plotting to oust Duke Vincent.

He had it coming, really. If he hadn't made life so difficult, Ondine and her friends would have been up to their necks in college work and assignments. Instead, they had enough time on hands to gather plenty of supporters to plan a really good revolution.[77]

"Alexei, I need you to –" Ondine was about to say 'stay here and help Ma and Thomas' but Melody jumped in with:

"– Get the bicycles."

All heads turned Melody's way at whiplash speed.

"Thae what?" Hamish asked.

"Bicycles," Melody confirmed. "They're quiet and we'll cover more ground than walking or running. Plus, if anyone does spot us, we can bike away faster than they can run after us."

"What if they're in a car?" Hamish asked.

"Then we'll improvise."

____

[77] Closing universities during a coup d'état is a rookie mistake, and one I expect none of you to make.

Ondine smiled and embraced Melody in a hug. Then she pulled away and said to Alexei, "You heard her, get the bikes."

With a quick salute, Alexei headed toward the gate.

"I'll help," Melody said, taking off after him.

"Aww, so nice, they're in *loave*," Hamish said, giving Ondine a squishy squeeze.

Ondine couldn't help smiling. Melody deserved some 'nice' after everything she'd been through.

***

"May I enquire, where is *my* bike?" Old Col said as Alexei produced the fourth bicycle that afternoon.

"You're not serious?" Ondine looked at her great aunt, who, it had to be said, was looking frail these days. And the woman had dodgy magic; she'd admitted as much. What could she offer their young group, aside from a handbrake to slow them down?

Hamish, Melody and Alexei suddenly made themselves busy, dusting off cobwebs, oiling the chains and pumping up the tyres.

Old Col cleared her throat. "Birgit Howser's been the biggest thorn in my side since I can remember. I want to be there for her downfall."

"But Col . . ." Ondine searched her brain for an excuse, then found it. "The more of us there are, the more chance we'll be seen."

"I know her weaknesses," Old Col said.

"And she knows yours," Ondine shot back. "Please stay home. I don't want to be worrying about you, OK?"

Grumbling and muttering about 'missing out on all the fun,' Old Col turned back to the house. Only after she closed the door did Ondine sigh and get her thoughts back to tonight's task.

243

"Help me remove the reflectors," Alexei said. "Less chance of being seen."

"Good idea. But we'll also have to be extra careful of cars because they won't see us." Ondine said.

With a shrug, Alexei said, "The only cars out after curfew are police vans anyway."

"Backpacks everyone," Hamish said as he handed them out. "Careful with yours Alexei, it's full of explodey things."

"Melody's got the matches in her pack. Safe as houses."

"We travel in pairs," Ondine said, "no bunching up, otherwise we'll look like a mob. Alexei, Melody, you two go on ahead, we'll be right behind you."

"Yes sir," Alexei said, giving Ondine a salute.

****

It was way past curfew as the four of them cycled at a steady pace under cover of darkness. Stealth underpinned the success of this mission. If they were caught out, they'd share Da's predicament. The weather gave them no assistance. It may have been spring, but the chill rain coming in from the north spat in their eyes as they rode. Squinting made it harder for the rain to pelt her eyeballs, but didn't stop the icy drops from biting into Ondine's cheeks and neck, slipping down her clothes and chilling her body.

This had to be done tonight, weather be damned. If they waited until summer to assault the mountain, Da's fate would be sealed.

Up ahead, Melody and Alexei vanished around a corner. The side of the road hit an incline. Ondine had to pedal harder to keep moving. The bikes rattled as they hit cobblestone alleys, jangling Ondine's nerves. Putting her palm directly over the bell on the handlebar silenced the metallic dinging.

The night grew thick with darkness and rain as they pushed away from the last of the street lamps. They were heading out of the city towards the castle on the hill. Memories of last year's CovenCon came back to Ondine as she pedalled into the night. The crowds, the natty little funicular railway to get to the top, the way Mrs Howser had utterly creeped Ondine and Hamish out that time by the pool. And the other time with that oily shadow thing growing out of her. Plus all the other times Mrs Howser had made her skin crawl.

Beside her, Hamish too worked his bike faster. They couldn't see Melody at all now. A 'whoosh' sound came from behind. Ondine turned to Hamish to see if he was breathing hard or something.

'Woosh.' there it was again.

Then Old Col flew beside her. On a broomstick.

"Darn site quieter going over cobblestones let me tell you. And more comfortable." Old Col said.

Ondine nearly crashed her bike. "I thought you'd lost your magic?"

"I'm having a hot flash, dear. Might as well put it to good use."

~ Chapter Nineteen ~

As they neared their target, Ondine, Hamish, Alexei, Melody and Old Col stopped for a quick regroup. The castle was at the top of a nearby mountain, hidden aloft in the murky darkness. They'd have to go the rest of the way on foot, which meant leaving the bikes behind.

The five of them huddled together behind some bushes. Old Col calmed everyone by conjuring hot chocolates out of thin air. The hot drink gave Ondine a glimmer of hope that Old Col's magic might stabilise enough to help them in this mission.

After their drinks, they crept down a quiet path that was little more than a goat track. It followed the side of a stream that splashed over rocks, masking any noise they might be making but also splashing the track and turning it into mud. Shivers spread through Ondine. Were they doomed to perish in the elements before they'd even reached their target?

The river slipped into a culvert that went under a road.

The culvert was too small and tight to allow people through. The road looked promising, as was the paved driveway leading up the mountain.

Taking the driveway would make their mission so much easier, but of course there was a blockage – a security gatehouse. Floodlights around the outpost reached into the night, skirting the road and making a full circle of the area. Alexei drew a stopwatch from his backpack and timed the rotations.

"They're on a set loop," he said, "Once they go past us, we have thirty-four seconds to get over to that ledge over there," he pointed to the other side of the rain-slicked road. "There's another track on the other side, it goes past the pond and the waterfall. We can take the funicular railroad. Once we get over, we stay low."

In the darkness, everyone nodded. Well, Ondine nodded. She assumed the others did as well.

"I'll go first," Alexei said.

Ondine heard Melody say, "Be careful," and then heard something that sounded like a kiss.

A grin crept over her face as she needled Hamish in the side with her elbow. Hamish needled her back again. The blinding searchlight swung over their heads and moved on, giving Alexei his cue. With admirable stealth, he darted out and padded across the road, barely making a sound. He made it with time in reserve as the light swung over them again and they all ducked down.

"Me next," Melody said. Darting out, she tore across the road, her feet padding just like Alexei's. In the darkness, Ondine squinted to see how she did it.

Melody was safe with Alexei, thank goodness. Even if they stuffed up now, at least two of them were across the road and closer to their target.

Old Col touched Ondine's shoulder. "Run on your toes. Makes less noise."

The light swung over them again and Ondine whispered, "Go!"

"Nah, I'll wait for the next one," Col said, sounding incredibly calm. "Let's give Melody a moment with her beau."

Hamish quietly snorted.

"We're on a mission here," Ondine said as a fresh shiver rippled through her body.

The light swung over their heads again. This time Col darted out immediately after it cleared, her feet making no sound at all. At which point Ondine realised Col had used her broomstick again and could have flown above the searchlight anyway.

"You next, lass," Hamish said, then gave her a quick but thrilling kiss. "All this excitement is making me jumpy."

Waiting was killing her, but she had to time it perfectly or she'd miss her chance. The light moved over, Ondine shot out. Staying on her toes, she stepped lightly but quickly over the road. Every nerve on heightened alert as she raced to the other side. Lungs burning from exertion, face freezing from the rain, she pushed hard while being as silent as she dared.

Safe!

It felt like forever for her breath to settle down. Making noisy gasps for breath could alert the people in the gatehouse. Would she doom them all because of her noisy breathing? Oh why had they not trained for this? When Ondine finally felt able to look back towards Hamish, her heart thumped even harder and her whole body fizzed with nerves. The light swooped, Hamish crept out, sneaking over the road with his body low. Just as a car came hurtling around the corner.

Ondine opened her mouth to scream. Old Col slapped her hand over her to keep her silent. The car headed straight for Hamish. The driver of said car opened his mouth in shock, then lifted his arm to cover his eyes. Hamish stood there in the middle of the road, until suddenly he wasn't. His clothes, previously filled out by a human, crumpled away, folding in on themselves. The car motored right over him, catching Hamish's shirt onto the radiator, carrying it off for several metres before it fluttered away.

But no Hamish. No hideous thump and crunch of bone and muscle on the bonnet. Hamish simply slipped under the car as it kept right on going.

The car stopped in a screech of brakes. Ondine, Melody, Col and Alexei squished themselves as low as they could, all while saying nothing and keeping their breaths as quiet as possible. Desperate to see what had happened, and desperately worried about her beloved Hamish, Ondine parted a bush limb aside and dared to peek.

The driver got out, torch in hand, searching the road looking for whatever he'd hit. Or missed. Had Hamish ferretised in time or not? If so, was he becoming human again and reclaiming his clothes, or was he out cold or . . . no, don't even think of the worse thing. The spotlight from the security gate rolled over the road on its regular sweep, blinding the driver and exposing his car.

"State your business!" a voice said over a megaphone.

Was that for Ondine or for the driver?

"It's all right, I'm just doing a milk run. I have papers allowing me to be out after curfew," the man shouted back. "I think I ran over something."

"Approach the checkpoint." Megaphone said.

"Fine." The man sounded disappointed.

This could be their chance to get away. At the sound of his car starting and reversing towards the checkpoint, Ondine felt a tap on her shoulder. It was Alexei, showing that he, Melody and Col were heading towards the funicular tracks.

They couldn't leave Hamish behind, could they?

"If we stay here, we'll be seen," Alexei said in a low murmur.

"I'm waiting for Hamish," Ondine said.

"But we have to go," Alexei said.

"Would you leave Melody behind?" The defeated look on Alexei's face proved Ondine right, so she added, "You go on, I'll catch up."

Which he did. The rotter! Not that she could blame him. They had to get the dampening transmitter down so Melody could get the astral word out. Or the *thought* out.

Sitting alone, Ondine shivered with fear as she looked for signs of Hamish on the road. The car was now up near the checkpoint, but too far away to hear what they were talking about. When the searchlight crossed the road again, her heart could have stopped. No sign of anything at all. No clothes and no ferret. On the up side, no wiped out boyfriend splattered on the bitumen either.

A whoosh of air blew hair across her eyes. In a rush of breath, Hamish landed on the ground beside her. Disregarding their need for stealth, Ondine threw herself onto him. "Oh my darling! I was so worried."

"Not half as worried as me, lass. Hush now, let's get to the others, sharpish."

He had far too much bare skin where there should be fabric. Which ordinarily would be a lovely thing, but not when they were in the middle of a dangerous mission on a cold spring night. "Where's your shirt?"

"In me hands, along with me pants. I had tae leave me shoes behind. Give me a second to get dressed."

No shoes? "You'll get frostbite," Ondine said.

"I'll worry about that when it happens."

The moment he donned his clothes, they scarpered towards the beginning of the funicular track, ready to climb the sleepers up the side of the mountain so they could reach the castle and the transmitter at the top. Silently, everyone gave Hamish hugs of support and relief, but these were soon over because they had a climb to make.

At least, they'd *planned* to climb up the sleepers. Because the funicular railway, one of the steepest in all Europe, and certainly steeper than anything Slaegal had to offer, was not switched off as they'd assumed. If it had been switched off, with the two carriages stored safely in their homes at the top and bottom of the mountain respectively, they could have made the cold, slippery climb unencumbered. Now they would be massively encumbered as the carriage descended towards the bottom station, leaving them no climbing room or time.

"We need plan B," Alexei said to Ondine.

Luckily they were from Eastern Europe, where the old alphabets were still in use. If plan B failed, they had another 34 letters to go.

"If the train is switched on, we use it," Ondine said, with more confidence than she felt. "Climb on as the carriage goes past."

Hamish grabbed Ondine by the shoulder. "Get back!" he whispered, at the same time dragging Melody down with him. Old Col and Alexei followed suit. A group of guards were sitting inside the descending carriage. Another group heading into the lower station, ready to switch over with them for the next shift. How would they make it to the top unseen now?

Utterly trapped, they waited until the groups changed over. The only good thing coming from this very near disaster was that the guards' heavy boots drowned out the noise of Ondine's panicked breathing. "OK, here's what we do now," Ondine said. "As it goes past, we climb on the back of the carriage and hold on."

"Not all of us will be strong enough to do that, dear."
Old Col said.

"We'll all hold on to each other," Ondine said.

"I have an idea," Alexei said. "Melody and Old Col go up first, the rest of us get the next one."

"You and me go first Alexei," Melody said. "We can –"

"Don't argue, the carriage is right here and you two need to be at the top first." Alexei grabbed Melody by one hand, Old Col with the other and darted to the carriage. With a solid grunt he lifted Old Col onto the back, where a narrow fender gave her a foothold, and the rear light mount provided a welcome seat. Next he pushed Melody into position and saluted her.

The whole time Ondine's heart was virtually in her throat as Alexei managed the impossible. Now all she and Hamish had to do was wait for the corresponding returning carriage to come past them and they'd get their ride. Worst luck, when the return carriage reached the bottom and Melody and Old Col's carriage reached the top, the guards climbed out and the entire railway shut down.

Alexei, Hamish and Ondine looked at each other, sighed at the job ahead of them and started the arduous climb to the top. For the next twenty minutes they did nothing but put one foot ahead of the other on the next sleeper, one arm reaching ahead of the other, scaling the steep incline. Naturally the rain became heavier, because nothing in life was allowed to be easy.

Every few minutes a searchlight would swing over the tracks, making them flatten down between the rails. Ondine didn't dare move until it was completely dark again, but she'd only have a few minutes until the next sweep of lights.

Wet, cold and sore, they finally reached the top and sat there, gathering their breaths and their bearings for the next stage of the plan.

"OK, where are Melody and Old Col?"

"Psst!" they heard from behind some huge rocks.

Good. They were all together. Sure, Ondine was aching from the exertion and shivering uncontrollably from cold and adrenaline, but the plan was still holding.

"Let's get to the tower," Ondine said. "Col, we're going to put roman candles all over the tower legs. I don't suppose you have a some magic to make them burn hotter?"

"Once they're in position, I'll see what I can do." Old Col said. "You lot take on the tower, I'll keep a lookout. If anyone comes, I'll hoot like an owl."

"There are no owls up here," Ondine said.

"Exactly, so you'll know it's me." Auntie Col said.

From his backpack, Alexei took out a grappling hook and cables, then handed them to Hamish. The rest of his pack held what could only be described as a firebug's dream arsenal. Pinwheels, Roman candles, small rockets and crackers. The noise was going to be intense. They'd have to get this done in one shot or it would all be over for them.

"Wish me luck, lass." Hamish gave Ondine a quick kiss before turning into a ferret again.

Hook in mouth, Shambles scrambled up the transmitter tower, Ondine and Alexei fed the cable after him. Melody rolled her shoulders and made herself ready with whatever she needed so she could astrally project their revolutionary message.

The cable in Ondine's hand tugged three times. All set. Shambles shimmied down the struts and landed at Ondine's feet. Then it was time to take Alexei's fireworks up there. Being a ferret, he could scarper up and down quickly, but being so small and lacking opposable thumbs meant he had to repeat the climb and descent so many times.

Then it was time to take the last of the big bangers up the tower. Old Col came over, twirled her hands above the giant cracker and showered it with sparkly white magic. The air felt hot, Ondine took a step back.

"No need to fret," Old Col said, "It won't blow up in our faces."

"Nor mine, eh?" Shambles said as he grabbed the firework carefully between his teeth and scrambled up the metal once more.

This firework had a particularly long fuse, which dangled all the way to the ground. Shambles scurried down for the last time.

"One more thing," Old Col said, stepping up to the tower leg. She pressed her hands against the metal. Light beamed from her palms and the rivets on one side popped free. "Now!" She yelled.

Alexei struck a match and lit the fuse. The tiny flame raced up the tower leg. For the tiniest of semi-seconds nothing happened, then the most thunderous racket broke out as the fireworks exploded in a brilliant chain reaction. Had this been any normal celebratory night, it would have been gorgeous to gaze upon the sparkles in the sky. Red, green, orange and yellow clusters burst out from the tower, looking impossibly pretty. The structure began to sag and bend a little.

"Heave now!" Hamish cried out in his Shambles form. (He hadn't yet changed back.)

Ondine, and Alexei pulled together on the cables. As they hauled and strained, Ondine was stricken with panic that the noise and sight of the incandescent colours in the sky would bring all the guards down on their heads. Suddenly Hamish was beside them, dressed again, pulling on the cables as well. Everything shuddered and groaned, until, like a statue of a deposed tyrant, the tower came down in a sudden rush of creaking, twisted metal. It tumbled over the edge of the platform and dropped down the side of the cliff. It came to rest in a mangled heap at the foot of the mountain, next to the base of the waterfall.

"Now Melody!" Old Col said.

"On it!" Melody said, standing tall and holding her hands wide as she looked over Venzelemma.

The rest of them stood in frightened silence while Melody projected her message. Inside her head, Ondine could hear Melody pleading with all good people of Brugel to take to the streets and gather in Savo Plaza. "Turn the lights on in your homes to show you heard the message. Join the revolution!"

Please let this work, please let this work, and hurry up and work because we made so much noise people will be here any second.

Slowly – so slowly Ondine thought she was imagining it – lights came on across the city. Neighbourhoods brightened as homes lit from within, chasing away the gloom. Venzelemma shone brightly.

"It's done," Melody said, her hands falling to her sides. "I gave the message. Savo Plaza, nine tonight."

"Nine?" Everyone else said.

"Doesn't give us much time to get there ourselves," Old Col said. "Can't have a revolution if there's no-one to lead it."

Filled with excitement and adrenaline, the five of them made for the railway to scramble back down and get away.

A familiar, haughty voice said from the darkness, "You won't be going anywhere."

Ondine should have known things had gone far too well for them, as she turned to face her nemesis, Mrs Howser. "You've lost!" She said. "You're too late! We got the message out!"

"I don't think so." Mrs Howser raised her hands and

shot a bolt of cold light straight into Ondine.

The magic lifted Ondine off the ground, spinning her in the air. Ondine screamed as she tumbled and tipped. Hamish leapt at Mrs Howser. Mid leap, she blasted him sideways. Ondine kept spinning, tumbling and turning and flipping and flopping, nausea threatening to spill out at any moment.

A bolt of green magic shone in the sky. It hit Howser hard on her side; she screamed and fell on the ground. Ondine dropped with a sickening lurch, falling not on rocky ground but into Hamish's waiting arms. "I've got you lass."

"Get out of here, kids!" Old Col shouted, her stance ready for battle.

Old Col? Firing bolts of witchcraft? What a brilliant time to have a magical hot flash!

"I'm going to enjoy this," Mrs Howser said as she righted herself, seemingly unharmed. "The young ones should stay." Howser summoned purple orbs of magic, growing them in her palm. "They can watch me destroy you!"

Hamish grabbed Ondine and pulled her towards the funicular. Melody and Alexei were right behind them. Troops marched into position near the top of the railway, blocking their exit.

"Jupiter's moons, now what?" Panic raced through Ondine.

"This way," Melody yelled.

Melody darted off. Old Col kept trading magic blasts with Howser. One incendiary flash after another.

"Get out of here!" Old Col yelled at them.

On the four ran, slipping and tripping over the wet and rocky ground.

"Where are we going?" Ondine asked, then saw the answer. The waterfall, straight ahead.

"There's a path behind it, over this way," Melody yelled back.

Boom! A blue flash from Mrs Howser transformed the waterfall into solid ice, blocking their escape. The freeze extended to everything damp, spreading like an ice-fire, freezing grass, mud and Ondine's feet. Stamping hard on the ground, chunks of ice fell off her shoes, but she couldn't feel her frozen toes.

They were trapped. They had troops behind them, a wall of ice in front, a steep hill to one side and a vertiginous drop to the other. Panicking, Ondine looked to Old Col, still trading magic blasts with Howser. In a crackle of light and boom of thunder, Col split a green ball of magic in two. One headed to Howser, the other straight to Ondine.

Ondine threw herself down. What a time for Col's magic to wonk out! But no, the wayward ball of light was deliberate. It flew over her head and hit the waterfall, carving a slalom-style slide across the face of the vertical drop. Melody and Alexei ran for it. Hamish hauled Ondine up and ran towards their icy escape route.

Ratttatatatatata! Bullets fired over their heads.

Melody and Alexei leapt onto the slide. In a swoosh, they vanished down the slope, twisting and flailing around a hairpin bends Col had magically carved out of the ice.

"Col! Hurry!" Ondine yelled as Hamish dragged her to the slide.

"Get going!" Col yelled back.

It was all the distraction Howser needed. The evil witch threw an enormous bolt of deepest purple straight into Old Col's chest, sending her sprawling.

"No!" Ondine cried out, clawing at Hamish to let her go.

"We havetae go!" Hamish yelled back, pulling her onto the slide and away from the mayhem.

Down they went, sliding and twisting out of control.

Ondine could see the mountain, the purple glowing sparks from Howser as she aimed both hands towards Old Col and blasted her. Col screamed. Ondine screamed; her skin froze as she slipped further away from Col.

"Get up, Col! Get up!" Ondine begged as they dropped away from the battle. Twisting around, she fought to get a clear view, but Hamish was barrelling after her, his body in the way. Another bend, other sickening lurch and she twisted around again. No more green sparks flew on the mountain. Only that horrible purple, all raining down on her great aunt, who wasn't moving any more.

A guttural sob came from Ondine at the thought Old Col was dead. That Mrs Howser had killed her. By staying behind, Col had saved Ondine and her friends, but not herself. Then a sickening crash smacked into her as the slide ended and the road came up to meet them.

Hamish dragged her to her feet. "Come on, Ondi, we havetae get away."

A bolt of cold light slammed the ground, sending dirt and ice exploding into the air. Another soon followed, shattering the ice slide. At least Mrs Howser wouldn't be able to follow them down that way.

Dodging magic, live bullets and icy debris, the four of them ran off to the shrubbery, to the place where they'd parked their bicycles.

Melody was the one with a clear head, she found the bikes first.

Crying while riding, Ondine gulped for air and sobbed every breath. On she rode, with blurry vision and runny nose. Grief had her in its grip and she couldn't stop it. Great Auntie Col was dead.

Ahead of her, Alexei and Melody kept up a punishing pace. A shirtless Hamish pedalled alongside, urging her to keep going. The next long while passed in a blur of narrow bike paths and alleys, Alexei choosing the routes where cars couldn't follow. Ondine lost all track of time and purpose as a single thought beat the drum of her heart.

Old Col is dead.

Old Col is dead.

Who knew how much time passed as they rode into the city outskirts?

"Let's split up, we'll go on ahead." It was Melody's voice inside Ondine's mind. Good, if Melody could still astrally project into Ondine's head, it meant Mrs Howser hadn't switched the dampening field back on.

But for how much longer?

"Howser's trying to get into my head, but it's my turn to block her now." Was the next message Melody sent through.

Good. Give the old witch a taste of her own medicine, Ondine thought. At which point her legs finally ran out of puff and she had to pull up beside a closed convenience store and slump to the ground.

"Eh lass, we have tae keep going," Hamish said, shivering.

They should have brought extra clothes.

They should have had a better plan.

"I can't. I just can't go one more block. Col's up on that mountain and we just left her there and I just can't . . ." Breaths came in big ugly gulps.

Warm arms wrapped around her. She pressed into Hamish's chest, seeking the security he offered. "Dinnae cry lass, or I'll come undone meself."

Which only set Ondine crying even more. "She shouldn't have come. I should have made her stay home."

"Aye, and then we might all four be dead on that hill instead of safely on our way to the city."

A howling noise came from somewhere deep inside as she gave into her grief.

"Please, please, Ondi love," Hamish begged, tucking her lank hair behind an ear. "I don't mean tae be callous, but we must keep going. Col stood up to Howser so that we could get away. It will all come tae naught if we don't get tae the plaza in time."

"I know, I know." He was right, of course. But her emotions were out of control and her brain couldn't see reason. She dragged her sleeve over her face. "I can't stop bawling my eyes out."

"I'll give ye a backie. Up ye get on thae handlebars."[78]

The cobblestone streets were so jarring Ondine felt each bump and jolt. But she held on and endured, taking the punishment for wasting time indulging in an emotional meltdown. At least the physical pain took her mind off her emotions. Maybe, just maybe, Old Col had somehow eluded Mrs Howser and they'd all meet up at the family pub, regaling each other with stories of daring and skill.

On Hamish pedalled, his breaths louder with the effort of carrying an extra person.

"I should never have helped Vincent," Ondine said. "That night at the BrugelMelody competition. We should have gone straight home and had nothing to do with him. Then he would have had to present Ruslana as his orange from Norange and people would have laughed him out of town."

"Aye, it's been playing on me mind as well," Hamish said through several grunts. His voice sounded scratchy, as if he were coming down with laryngitis. "I should have spoken up."

"I should have kicked him in the shins," Ondine said.

---

[78] A 'backie' is a passenger on a bicycle, who is not always at the back, as the handlebars are often more comfortable. It is, however, dangerous and often illegal.

"I should have held him while ye did so."

If felt good to share their regrets, neither blaming the other, just wishing they'd done things differently.

The puffing and straining from Hamish became too much for Ondine. "I can walk from here, let me off." As she set down from the handlebars, she looked back to Hamish.

A gasp leapt out of her throat. "Saturn's ring! You're white!"

"Eh?" he said, with a phlegmatic rattle usually reserved for nursing homes.

"Your hair, your face, oh Hamish, what happened?" Ondine took in his face, the tissue-paper-thin skin, the deep lines, the gravity-sag. His neck displayed the ravages of encroaching jowls, his eyes drooped with age. And his hair, his rich, dark hair had turned completely white, gathered in a horseshoe of tufts around his scalp.

Putting a hand to his head, Hamish cried out, "I'm bald!"

Ondine held him close, pressing her ear to his chest, hearing the crackle in his breaths. "You're ageing so fast, you have to change into a ferret, right now."

"Aye, I'll do that sharpish," Hamish said, bracing himself for the pain.

Which didn't come.

"We're running out of time," Ondine said, wiping frustration-tears away.

Hamish stood there, slack-jawed and unchanging. "I cannae do it. It's nae happening."

"Why not?" Ondine sounded so whiny. Tired, cold and aching all over, she petulantly stamped her foot on the cobblestones, sending jarring pain up her leg. "Just do it, will you?"

"I want tae, lass, I honestly do, but the spell's gone and I dinnae ken how tae get it back."

The abyss of despair pulled Ondine onto the cold ground. "Then she's really gone," it came out as barely a squeak. "Old Col. The curse she put on you was, 'you can stay like that for all I care'. So if she really is d–, if she's not with us, then she's not here to *care* any more and keep the curse alive."

"Oh dear," Hamish said, reaching for Ondine and noticing the liver spots on the back of his hand. "Ondi love, I'm so sorry. About everything."

Choking back a fresh bout of crying, Ondine stood up. "Hamish, don't get me wrong, but we have a job to do and I can cry later. We need to get to Melody."

"Aye?"

"Yes. You're in no shape to start a revolution. The first bump and you'll break a hip. We'll get Melody you get your youth back and when all this is over I can fall to bits at my leisure."

"I loave you so much," he said, leaning in for a kiss.

She ducked her head and turned it into a hug instead, not wanting to offend him. "We're going to fix you," she said, the unspoken part of that being, "I'm not losing two people I love in the one day."

On they walked, past the shops and houses, Hamish making quiet little grunts and complaints about his knee giving him trouble.

Thanks to the message Melody had sent out on the mountain, every single streetlight was on. Behind every window, lights glowed with golden warmth.

"You know what I really should have done?" Ondine asked as Hamish brought them to the edge of the plaza. "I should have realised Vincent was hell bent on becoming Duke. Whether we helped him or not, nothing would have changed the outcome."

"I love ye Ondi," Hamish said. "I've been laid low with guilt for so long about all this. Wishing I'd done more, wishing things were different. Wishing I hadnae been so selfish. But ye just hit the nail on the head, so ye did. Nothing we could have done would have stopped Vincent from becoming Duke."

Hands on hips, Ondine took a deep breath. "And now, we are going to make sure he's not Duke for much longer."

Melody and Alexei appeared from a shadowed doorway. Alexei examined his feet, looking bashful. Melody stepped forward. "Oh, there you are!" Her lips looked chaffed, her hair mussed. Her mouth dropped as she saw Hamish. "Oh dear! You won't last a minute in the plaza."

"So it seems. Ye wouldn't happen to have an elixir of youth on ye perchance?"

Melody chewed her bottom lip in thought. "I have an idea. Hold hands."

The four of them stood in a circle, holding hands. Slowly, a warm energy began to radiate from their hearts, spread through their hands and moved from Melody, Alexei and Ondine into Hamish. Glowing, Hamish's hair grew back and turned a youthful black, the skin on his neck tightened and the curve in his back straightened.

"I feel *wonderful.*" Hamish said. "What are ye doing?"

"I'm transferring some of our energy to you," Melody said.

"How much energy?" Ondine asked.

"Enough to get us through tonight," Melody said.

"And then what?" Ondine asked. "One night isn't much help."

Melody let out a sigh. "If we get through tonight, I'll work on a more permanent solution."

"Don't you mean *when* we get through tonight?" Ondine asked.

Melody nodded her head. "Let's stop internalising this and face the music."

Still holding hands, the four of them walked the final few metres into Savo Plaza, ready to meet their fate.

~ Chapter Twenty ~

So many lights shone in Savo Plaza Ondine virtually needed sunglasses. The best kind of festival vibe filled the air. Such an enormous crowd had gathered it was hard to see much of the plaza itself, and getting through it involved a lot of squishing and 'Excuse me's.

Hamish jumped to get a better view and then smiled to Ondine. "Lass, you're gonna *loave* this." He lowered his cupped hands to help her step up and lean on his shoulder.

There, on a makeshift stage, stood Cybelle and Margi. Singing and dancing and encouraging the crowd. Cybelle swayed her arm above her head to the beat of the music. The crowd followed her lead. Margi, her belly protruding like a second floor balcony, merely swayed a little from side to side. Thomas drummed wooden spatulas onto an upturned catering bucket. Henrik played metal spoons on his knee. A palpable sense of goodwill filled the plaza. They had safety in numbers. After all, the government couldn't arrest everyone for being out after curfew, could they? The numbers would show how many people disapproved of Vincent. How much they wanted change. Vincent would have to listen to them now.

"People Power!" Cybelle called out.

The crowd threw cheeseballs into the air and cheered.

"Come on," Melody grabbed Ondine by the hand and hauled her through the crush towards the stage.

Cybelle told the gathering, "Thank you everybody for hearing and answering the call. Tonight, we take Brugel back! Brugel for the people!"

The crowds went crazy. It had been a year since the coup in this same plaza, but the mood tonight was completely different. Melody pulled Ondine onto the stage, blinking like a stunned deer. Cybelle thrust the microphone into Melody's hands.

"Thank you, everybody, for coming out tonight," Melody said. "No doubt all of you have suffered terribly this past year as Vincent has done whatever he liked with Brugel. We're here to say 'Time's up' for Vincent. He has to give Brugel back!"

The crowd went insane with joy and began chanting, "Give back Brugel! Give back Brugel!"

"Ondine," Melody pushed the microphone into her hand, "Tell them what your family has been through."

Dry of mouth and trembling of knees, Ondine tried to swallow past the boulder in her throat. "Hello, everyone. This is an amazing turn out," she said.

The crowd murmured and gave a little clap, but not much.

"My name is Ondine, and my family, just like yours has been hit hard. My family runs a hotel, but we've gone broke because of the curfew. Vincent has made our lives impossible. As he's made yours."

The crowd clapped a little more, warming to her subject.

"We've taken in all our relatives, and some friends, because everyone's doing it hard. But then we ran out of food, so Da, I mean, my father, he set out to get us some food, but it was past curfew and they arrested him. Just because he was trying to get us some food! Now he's being told he has to plead guilty to treason by next week. We don't know if we're ever going to see him again! Since when was it treason to try and feed your family?"

More sympathetic clapping.

"My sister," Ondine looked behind her, to see Margi standing nearby. She and Cybelle had clearly been entertaining the crowds with their music. Despite the cold, performance-sweat shone on Margi's face. "My sister is having a baby any day now, and our Da won't even be there to see his first grandchild!"

The heavy sound of 'boo' and disappointment rippled like a wave through the crowd.

"But the worst thing is my great aunt –" a sob caught in Ondine's throat and she couldn't go on. It didn't stop her from trying though. "Her name was Colette Romano, and she was batty and funny and cranky and wonderful, and she was up on the mountain with us and –" Instead of words, sobs fell out. Ondine had to hand the microphone over to Melody.

Melody wrapped Ondine in a warm embrace. "I'll tell them," she said, assuring Ondine.

Margi and Cybelle both moved closer to Ondine, worry writ large on their faces.

"What happened to Old Col?" Cybelle asked.

"It's too horrible," Ondine cried.

Stepping away from the tearsome huddle, Melody faced the thousands-strong crowd and said, "We lost a great woman tonight, and a brilliant witch. She battled Mrs Birgit Howser, Vincent's right-hand-witch. Colette Romano sacrificed herself so that we could escape and get here to the plaza, to tell you what's going on. And we're here to tell you that tonight, Vincent's reign ends. Tonight, we take back Brugel!"

The crowd went insane, cheering and whooping.

"We don't need some pushy little lord telling us what we're allowed to say and when, what time to go to bed, when we're allowed to get up."

Wow, she really had fallen out of love with Vincent. And hard!

"And you definitely don't need one precious little prince doing all this when we used to have an elected government."

The crowd brayed and cheered so loudly they could have lifted the cobbles from the street. Ondine's heart grew so big her ribs might crack.

"We want our country back!" Melody shouted.

The girl was born to control a crowd. A genius behind the microphone, she knew just what to say to get the people on side. Perhaps Melody was using a little extra witchcraft to help her along?

This time Melody waited for the crowd to settle down. Then she lowered her voice and spoke clearly, making sure her words were understood. "What we need is a massive show of people power. Good people, using good power. And here's what we're going to do. We are going to take back Savo Plaza as a place *for* the people." Now her voice rose, along with her passion. "We are going to show that love and hope can overcome. We will show Lord Vincent the door. He has no power over us."

The crowd went insane with joy and threw even more cheeseballs high in the air.

Melody turned quickly to face Ondine and Hamish, "Hurry up and smooch, will ya!"

Huh?

"Kiss already!" Melody twirled her finger in the air and

sparks flew, twining Ondine and Hamish into a squishy embrace.

Of course! The magic curse! They had a plaza full of people making good wishes for Brugel, and here's where it could all come true. Because Mrs Howser had never lifted the curse on them, so when they kissed, Ondine could make other people's wishes come true. A whole plaza full of people who wished to get rid of Lord Vincent and Mrs Howser.

Wrapped in her love for Hamish and her country, she pressed her lips to his for a beautiful kiss for the ages. Her hands fastening to his bare chest, because he still hadn't managed to get another shirt in all this time.

And oh how they kissed.

For freedom.

For Brugel.

On they smooched, forgetting the outside world and luxuriating in this most wonderful moment of love. Ears ringing from the cacophonous crowds and stomping feet, she closed her eyes and immersed herself into her love for Hamish. The rumbling grew louder. The crowd wild with delight. No, wait, the noises didn't sound the same. Fear spiked Ondine and she pulled away in time to see tanks rumbling into Sava Plaza.

Heavy boots thumped on the cobbled streets. Grinding metal shrieked from the tanks' caterpillar wheels. With a burst of white, the invaders fired water canon on the crowd. People fled but couldn't get out. Screaming filled the skies as panic set in. The blast of water sent people slipping and smashing into each other. But instead of fleeing, the good people who'd come to protest against Vincent got to their feet and stood tall. United.

Melody sent magical sparks into the crowd to protect them against attack as the battle between good citizens and a dark army of cadets kicked off. If Ondine wasn't afraid for her life, she could have revelled in the epic nature of the battle.

People linked arms and shouted, "Hey no, we won't go!"

Blasts of magic crashed through the air. Weapons fired. Smoke and gas rained down from the skies. The screaming rose by 20 decibels as confusion gripped everyone in the plaza. Small bottles with burning rags jammed in the top hurled through the air, crashing and splattering flames and flares all around. These *Ribbentrop cocktails* didn't do much damage, but they burned everything they crashed into, including clothes.[79]

In all the chaos and open warfare, Ondine forgot about Margi. Where was her pregnant sister? This was no place for her; they had to get her out. But the battle had blocked every lane and road leading out of the plaza. From the corner of her vision, a bubble floated past.

A bubble?

Time to take cover, as Ondine raced to the back of the stage and found Margi and Cybelle, crouching behind some potted plants. Bangs, crashes and explosions filled the air. They were coming closer. Ondine poked her head out and saw a shiny, rainbow globule, wobbling and bobbling in the air. Then it exploded on the side of a statue of Lord Vincent.

Wait, what? *A statue?*

Since when had there ever been a statue of Lord Vincent in Savo Plaza? By all means, put a reminder of Savo himself, after whom the plaza was named, but Vincent?

Nope.

---

[79] Ribbentrop cocktails are named after Joachim von Ribbentrop, who signed the Molotov–Ribbentrop Pact in August between Nazi Germany and Soviet Russia in 1939.

More bubbles popped against the statue, giving Ondine the best idea she'd had in minutes.

"Look after Margi," she said, putting her sister's hands into Thomas and Hamish's care. (They were also sheltering at the back of the stage) Then she ran to where the bubbles were coming from. Sure enough, there was a bubble machine at the side of the stage, always a welcome addition at a party, but a total distraction in a revolution. Sneaking between the fighting crowds and the closed vans of the hot cheeseball vendors, Ondine made her way to a Fort Kluff water canon. No time to second guess the craziness, she climbed on top and opened the hatch. Only to find a person inside it, but no water.

"Don't mind me," she called out, slamming the hatch shut.

Yikes. Where exactly was the hatch for the water to go in?

Ooops, wrong type of canon. This was just an every day tank. The water canon was several meters away, and guarded as well.

"Melody! Help me out here!" Ondine screamed.

"Hey, what are you doing?" A group of cadets turned on Ondine.

Her belly lurched. Time to sound important. "They sent me over to put an additive in the water. Purple dye so you can find people later to make arrests." *I'm so impressed with me, I can't wait to tell Hamish later.*

"You think we're stupid?"

Maybe not. Gears and cogs clicked in her brain. Something rumbled over the cobbles, coming closer. Hamish poked his head out the top hatch.

"You want to know what I have?" Ondine said. "I have a tank right behind me."

The cadets combined their dark magic to hold the tank at bay. The lid shut down hard on Hamish's head, muffling a yelp from inside.

Jupiter's moons, this wasn't supposed to happen.

To Ondine's relief, another group of protestors turned up, their focus not on the tank, but the cadets.

"They've got your good magic," Melody said inside Ondine's head. *"We're going to win!"*

The display of good magic was simplicity itself. Every single rivet popped out of the tank behind the cadets. The machine fell apart like a rusty bucket. A puff of glittering yellow magic dust blew all the components into the air, leaving a shivering cadet sitting in the driver's seat, control knobs in his hand.

Another cloud of magic swept the cadets from their feet, sending them wafting through the air like a swirl of snow. The crowd of revolutionaries cheered and jeered at their defeated foes.

No time to rejoice, they still had a revolution to win and Mrs Howser would be here soon with her henchmen and women. Or hench-cadets. Hurrying, Ondine found the water canon's inlet cover and poured the bubble mix into the reservoir. Then she cranked the nozzle high into the sky and hunted for a switch. They all looked round and green. Nothing so simple as a big red lever.

Silently she reached out to Melody, hoping the clever witch was somehow keeping track of her, despite the chaotic battles surrounding them. *Please help me?I need superconcentrated good magic and I need it now.*

In three heartbeats, nothing at all happened, then suddenly a burst of magic entered Ondine's body, swirled in her brain and poured through her hands. She pressed a small green button and a water fountain charged into the sky, spreading bubbles through the air.

"Are ye right lass?" Hamish said as he came over and stood beside her.

Bubbles continued to spray into the sky, falling in

snowy drifts all through the plaza. As each feather-light bubble landed on a cadet, it's popped and showered them with good magic, putting love back in their hearts instead of anger.

The fighting continued, but bubbles kept landing on the cadets, confusing them momentarily, before they dropped their weapons and started playing with the bubbles instead of fighting.

Good magic was winning against evil. People slipped and giggled and laughed as the ground became slick with detergent.

Clomp, clomp, clomp. A new threat marched into Savo Plaza.

Leading a platoon of cadets, Mrs Howser hovered on a broomstick. Just to pick over that fresh emotional scab, Ondine noticed that broomstick was Old Col's.

Everyone froze. The water canon switched off. People turned to Mrs Howser as she hovered above the melée and aimed her finger directly at Ondine. A blast of magic hurtled through the air. Ondine leapt behind the water canon as Howser's magic crashed against the machine, instantly freezing the metal. Being wet, Ondine stuck fast to the frigid surface. She ripped hard and tore her sleeves off, but at least she was free. A huge boom echoed around the plaza as the water canon exploded into icy powder. *Run!* A voice yelled inside her head. It didn't matter whose, she heard it and she ran, ducking and zigzagging to get away from Mrs Howser and her magic bolts of frozen death. Running for her life, Ondine's face burned red with panic. Her heart hammered so hard it blocked the sound of her boots on the cobbled stones. A laneway came up, already blocked with fleeing protestors. Ondine shoved into the panic, carried along with the flow of people until she fell out into an open street.

Screams came from the plaza, from the innocent people

she and Melody had summoned here. The people who'd risked being out after curfew to show their support – except Ondine had run like a coward and abandoned the very people she needed.

Stopping, she turned back to the plaza, but her feet wouldn't obey. Nerves had taken hold, she couldn't move. "Get back in there!" she yelled at herself. But her feet weren't listening. Stupid feet. And the flow of people squeezing out that one small laneway meant she couldn't get back in if she tried. The crowd were coming to her, pouring through the bottleneck of the lane and out towards the next major open area only a block away.

On she ran, ahead to the clear space, which just happened to be the steps of Brugel's Dentate.

In the old days these steps would be teeming with night markets and festivals, assemblies and general tourism. Tonight those steps were bare and glittery wet in the cold night air. Ondine's feet raced towards those steps, where an enormous, permanent screen featuring images of a beaming Lord Vincent mocked her approach. The urge to rip off her boot and hurl it at the screen had never been so strong. Unfortunately, her hands were so stiff with cold she couldn't manage the laces.

"Stop running, girl," Mrs Howser said from behind her.

Only her last reserves of courage held her up. It took a few breaths but eventually she turned to face her nemesis. Mrs Howser was sitting on that broomstick, floating in the air. No doubt she'd ridden over everyone through the lane to get here.

Meanwhile, people kept teeming out of the plaza, into the open streets.

The enormous screen flickered and crackled, making Ondine turn around. Lord Vincent's face was gone – hoorah! – but now it showed the back of Ondine's head. It took a few double-takes, but somewhere on the top of a car, or up high, somebody had a camera aimed at her. And Mrs Howser. Aha! There on the walls of a building were several cameras and projectors, capturing everything and beaming it onto the screen for all to see. Ondine's showdown with her arch enemy would be massively public.

And massively humiliating for one of them as well. Ondine hoped it wasn't her, but with the way her luck was going, she couldn't be sure. Clever words and speeches deserted her as she trembled on the steps.

Mrs Howser advanced on Ondine and growled, "This ends here, girl." Then the witch turned around to face the crowd now gathering at the base of the steps. The people should have fled. Nope, they were hanging around to see what happened next.

Clomping feet and rattling metal brought the rest of Mrs Howser's dark army to the edges of the crowd, creating a new barrier to escape. At the head of this dark army, Ondine recognised that powerful cadet, the one she'd seen in her street the night Da had been arrested. The same one from the shared visions with Melody, who had trained under Mrs Howser at Fort Kluff. Looking at her now, Ondine could see rips and tears in her uniform, where she'd engaged in direct combat. Her face had no bruises at all, showing just how one-sided the cadet's battles had been.

At that moment Lord Vincent himself stepped out – of where, Ondine couldn't tell – and quietly walked up the steps to the top, as if taking control of proceedings. But he wasn't in control. Neither was Ondine. Mrs Howser was the one in control as she raised her hand and sent a hideous dark shadow flying out from her fingers. The shadow arched in the air like a net over a school of fish.

"Kill them!" Mrs Howser cried out to her dark army.

"Kill them all!"

"No!" Ondine leapt towards Mrs Howser.

"Arrrrrrggggggghhhhh!" Hamish's familiar cry carried up the steps as he ran towards Ondine, making her heart soar.

Dripping with sarcasm, Mrs Howser shouted, "Oh come on!" She threw a fresh bolt of magic and caught Hamish straight in the chest.

He absorbed the impact but it didn't stop him taking those last steps to be closer to Ondine.

Mrs Howser glared at Ondine and Hamish as a fresh ball of darkest green magic built in the palm of her hand. "This ends. Now."

The ball rocketed towards Ondine. Hamish leapt out to take the blow. The sound of crunching gravel filled the air. Hamish's entire body froze in mid-leap.

"No!" Ondine screamed as she grabbed him, her hot skin pressed against his marble-cold form. Beneath her arms, his flesh turned to stone. She pressed herself against his chest, feeling the last thuds of his heart as his body fossilised in her arms. Blubbering now, she held on, as if her softness and warmth could transfer to his body through sheer force of will. "No, no, no. Hamish. Oh Hamish. It wasn't meant to happen like this."

Mrs Howser, her voice low and deadly, said, "Yes it was. It's exactly how it was meant to happen. This was how it was always going to end, right from the start."

"Not like this. Never like this. Even you can't be this cruel."

"Yes, I can. This is *my* magic. I designed it so everything would come to this point. And beyond." The witch stood closer, gloating her victory. "I made it so that once he bonded with someone, their affections would make other people's wishes come true. That's how the magic spread so beautifully in the first place. As each wish came true, people absorbed the magic and passed it on. Such a marvellous virus."

"Shut up!" Hot tears blurred Ondine's vision. They ran down her cheeks and fell with a splatter on Hamish's granite form. He was heavy in her arms. So heavy. So solid and cold. Too heavy to lift, she lay him along the step.

"It's my best spell ever, even if I do say so myself." Mrs Howser smirked. "Contagious magic that everyday normals can catch! Don't mean to brag. Well, actually I do, because it was so, so clever and you never even worked it out."

Hamish's body wasn't getting any warmer, or lighter. Ondine couldn't move for the weight of him, or the sheer terror of being fixed in Mrs Howser's glare.

"I designed it so the first normals to catch it would be ever-so-sweet and lovely and *good*," Mrs Howser shuddered, "that you wouldn't be able to help yourself spreading even more. And then, and see, this is the bit I'm really proud of, then the good ones would keep spreading magic to even more people, like ripples in a pond, and then it would mutate and get darker, and so many more people would catch it. Enough to fill a whole army with dark magic."

Frustrated and sick with fear, Ondine yelled, "I don't believe you!" Even though in her heart, she knew it was true.

Mrs Howser cackled and wafted her arm out. "Look around you, gaze upon my magnificent dark army. They are here because of you, Ondine. In a way, this is all your fault."

The dark army filled the streets, standing to attention, waiting for their next directive.

"Don't you dare blame me!" Ondine said through gritted teeth. "This is your horrible magic, not mine!"

"Let me show you, my dear." Mrs Howser tapped her

wrinkled hand on the top of Ondine's head and her vision filled with images and memories.

Disgusted with the images filling her head, Ondine turned away from Howser. Yet those same images now played on the big screen at the top of the steps, for everyone to see.

Pain lanced Ondine as she looked at her beloved and batty great auntie, dancing at a debutante ball with Hamish. It wasn't recent Old Col, it was a much younger version. On the sidelines, a youthful Birgit Howser was glaring at Col and Hamish waltzing past. Ondine almost didn't recognise Howser, because she looked so wholesome. On the screen and inside her head, images bounced around.

Near the drinks table a furious Howser was now yelling at Col. "You knew I wanted to partner with Hamish. So you cast a spell on him so he'd choose you over me! I'll never forgive you for this Col!"

Later, after having too much alcohol to drink, Hamish slurred "You tricked me you witch!" He then accidentally stepped on Col's feet, falling over and ripping her dress. Looking embarrassed, Col waved her hands casting a spell on him, "You revolting little weasel. How dare you break my heart? You can stay like that for all I care. You're all the same, you lot."

Up on the screen, for all to see, Hamish the handsome lad screamed as he transformed into Shambles the ferret for the very first time.

Then the image flickered to a new scene, with Mrs Howser taking in Shambles after Col had spurned him. Time then flew forward again, to a moonlit night at the Psychic Summer Camp. As Shambles slept, a now middle-aged Howser stood over him. She chanted and waved her hands, casting another spell on Shambles.

"A girl of whom you are fond,
the two of you will form a bond.
You'll make other's wishes come true,
When she becomes closest to you.
Those wishes will turn dark and loyal,
To make an army for one who is royal.
A new Brugelish ruler to be adored,
And I shall finally get my reward."

In the next image, Mrs Howser was at the Autumn Palace, placing her curse over the stones at the gatehouse, which she knew Shambles would one day cross over, therefore setting all her twisted magic into motion.

Then a memory played out of Ondine, from nearly two years ago, at Psychic Summer Camp, where she found Shambles face-deep in her Brugelwürst sausage.

"And now we've come to the end of the memories. For you at any rate," Mrs Howser said.

Footsteps sounded. Melody charged up the stairs. "What have you done?" She was out of breath. "Tell me I'm not too late?"

"Oh dear," Mrs Howser said. "My protégée is here, and she is too late. He's already dead."

Vincent, who had said nothing all this time, interrupted. "Won't Hamish's death mean the end of your curse that made the dark army?"

Ondine inwardly swore. *Vincent's such a selfish basket.*

"You are especially thick tonight," Mrs Howser said. "His death means nothing. I made the curse, the curse lives on as long as I do."

Melody's eyes rounded like saucers. Ondine's breath staggered in her lungs. Mrs Howser's showboating had just given them the key to ending this. If the old witch died, the curse would die with her.

"Kiss him," Melody urgently whispered to Ondine.

"One more make-a-wish kiss."

"No you don't!" Mrs Howser said, delivering a nasty blast of magic towards Hamish.

In Ondine's arms, Hamish the man shrivelled into a cold, stone ferret.

Tears poured from Ondine as she looked at Howser, standing over them. "Only you could be so cruel!"

"Kiss him anyway!" Melody said.

The deepest sorrow from losing her one true love welled inside Ondine. Her dry lips met his stone head, the only warmth came from the tears running from her face onto his icy body, begging him to come back to her. Then Melody's voice rang inside her head. She was sending out another message, to every magically-receptive mind in the crowd: "Wish that Ondine becomes more powerful than Howser."

Ondine held Shambles, willing his stone ferrety body to warm. "Come back to me. Please, please come back to me. Hamish I love you with all my heart and my being. You are mine, you hear me? Mine. Now come back to me. Please." Another soft kiss on his hard little head, then a sob of pain as she stroked his cold ears and felt as if she too would rather turn to stone than live without him. Nose pressed to the tip of his, she cried and sniffed and made a mess of his face. Reverently she wiped the slick with her sleeve and kissed him afresh.

He felt warmer this time. Probably a trick of her hot tears warming his stone skin. "I'm not done with you," she said, her voice choking with emotion. "You have to come back. I love you Hamish. Pure and simple. I love you and you love me."

Something magical stirred in her chest and her belly as she kissed him again. A tinge of golden mist came from her lips this time. Magic. Coming from *inside* Ondine.

The people in the streets were holding hands and

wishing for stronger, kinder magic.

Thank you Melody. Hope surged within. "Come back to me, my love." Ondine caressed Shambles's stony forehead.

"Right well. Busy schedule," Mrs Howser said, turning her hand left and right, building a new ball of magic in her palm. "This has been fascinating to watch, but time's a'wasting."

"Stop!" Still holding Shambles's prone form, Ondine stared at Mrs Howser. "Stop now."

Wisps of gold traced through the air, from Ondine's lips towards Mrs Howser. The woman did indeed stop, her body slowly curved inwards, as if her entire being formed a scowl. "How are you doing this? You have no magic!"

"I do now, thanks to yours," Ondine said, putting the pieces together. "Hamish is alive. He's coming back to me right now. And I have your curse to thank for it."

"But . . . you can't!" Crumpling now, as if her body was imploding, Mrs Howser curled around her ball of magic, unable to fling it away.

"I can." Boldness filled Ondine. Something magical and calming settled inside her. Fear lost all meaning as Shambles's body warmed in her lap. In a few seconds, his ferrety head grew back into his lovely humanly Hamish face, gold sprites played about his head as his hair changing from a carved solid into the lush strands she loved playing with so much. All the while, Mrs Howser stood there, curling into herself.

"It's all your magic, Birgit. The people wished me to have it, and so I have. You shouldn't have bragged. Only the witch that created the curse can take it off. The curse doesn't die until the witch that made it dies. When you're dead, your curse will lift and life will return to normal."

"I'm not going anywhere," Mrs Howser said. With a gasp and a grunt, Mrs Howser threw her ball of magic towards Ondine.

"No!" Ondine held her palm out to protect Hamish from the blast. Mrs Howser's ball of power ricocheted off Ondine's hand and barrelled back towards its maker, crashing straight into her heart.

For a moment Mrs Howser sat there, looking stunned and shocked that events should have come to this. For a moment. In the next, her body shook as she desiccated on the steps of the Dentate. Howser's body capsized like a vacuum-sealed bag, sucking her ever inward as her cheeks hollowed, her eyes sank and her body shrivelled. Accelerated ageing turned her limbs into virtual sticks, clothes merely hanging in place, wafting in the breeze. Her lifeless body collapsed, her skeleton no longer supported with life-giving muscle. All that remained was a pile of powder and crumpled clothes.

A breeze picked up the bone dust, swirling it into the sky, leaving nothing but a few clothes and a smear of ash on the Dentate steps.

"And I love ye lass," Hamish said from where he lay on the steps, breathing hard and holding his hand out to her.

Melody quickly draped Mrs Howser's abandoned cloak over him for modesty.

Ondine and Hamish celebrated with lush kisses and more tears, but these were tears of happiness. The cheers from the crowd lifted their spirits as high as the stars.

When they stopped kissing – this took a few minutes – Ondine looked out at the crowds before them. People were hugging and kissing each other with victory, cheering and yelling and throwing cold cheeseballs into the air.

The cadets who had formed Mrs Howser's dark army were not as cheery. If anything, they looked confused and upset, as if they'd woken from a particularly hideous dream. Ondine's gaze alighted on a familiar female cadet. Previously she'd appeared battle-hardened and strong.

Now she stood, leaning against the wall, her arms wrapped around her torso, weeping copiously. "I tried to resist, but it was so strong, I couldn't fight it!"

"Melody, I think she'll need your help," Ondine said.

"Aye," Hamish added, as he took in the scene of celebrating citizens and confused cadets. "We have a lot of people affected by magic who won't know what to do with it."

"Too right," Melody jogged down the stairs towards the upset cadets, holding her arms out for an embrace. To let them know they too had been under a curse, but there was a way back.

From the corner of her eye, Ondine saw Vincent stepping away from them. Quick as a flash she blocked him. "Where do you think you're going?"

~ Chapter Twenty-One ~

A hush fell over the crowd. Those in cadet uniforms sat down, exhausted. They took their helmets off and rubbed their heads or necks, trying to make sense of the world.

The dark army Mrs Howser had created stood (or more accurately, sat) defeated. Demoralised.

Vincent stood nearby on the Dentate steps, unmoving. "Thank you. Howser was becoming a liability."

Panic flooded Ondine. Would he make a run for it? Would he escape the punishment he so sorely needed? Wait, *what*? "I don't want you thanking me," Ondine said.

"We are not on your side!" Melody spun around, hands balling into fists.

"Of course you are." Vincent took a step closer, his palms up in what could look like surrender. *As if.* "You're my main witch. We're going to rule Brugel, we're going to form an alliance with Slaegal and become the most powerful nation in Eastern Europe.

"I'm not your *anything*," Melody said. "You used me. And against my better judgement I let you."

It all sounded far too personal to be discussed in such a public theatre, but Ondine was in no position to interfere. Yes, she wanted to smack Vincent on the head, but Hamish needed her. He'd nearly died and although he'd come around, his skin had a grey marbled sheen to it instead of healthy pink.

"Oh lass, I'm so sorry. I wish things had turned out different."

She pulled her sleeve down over her wrist so she could wipe his perspiring brow. He needed to go home and rest, but she lacked the strength herself to get him feet-wards. Plus Melody had come back to face-off with Vincent. Ondine wanted to see how things would turn out between them.

"Without Howser, you're nothing," Melody said.

"I still have you," he said, getting close enough to gently tuck a stray lock of her hair over her ear.

"No, you don't." Melody pushed his hand away. "You're finished."

The image on the big screen flickered to life again. The video was from events that took place almost a year ago. There were three men in the picture. One was handed an envelope bulging with cash, then they all shook hands. One of them had a blue hand.

"My camera!" Ondine leapt to her feet in delight.

"Boak!" Hamish's head tumbled from her lap and he splayed out on the steps.

"Oh my darling, I'm so sorry!" She rushed to cradle him. "But look, look what's playing on the big screen. It's from when Vincent and Babak were bribing Valentin to distract Anathea into giving up the throne! Isn't that wonderful?"

"Yes hen."

Wait a second. "Who is doing that?" Ondine asked Melody.

"Alexei," Melody said with a too-wide grin.

"Aye, he's a good lad that one," Hamish muttered.

"I'll say," Melody beamed.

As the crowd watched the image play and replay, they began to boo and heckle.

"You've got a lot of grovelling to do Vincent," Melody said.

"I'm sorry. Is that what you want? An apology? OK then." Vincent said, "I'm sorry that I knew I was the only one who could give Brugel stability and was brave enough to step up."

"Oh come on!" Melody said.

Vincent's face puffed red. Bits of spittle flew from his mouth. "I'm sorry you got hurt along the way, but that's just how things turned out. Without me, Brugel is nothing."

"You really suck at apologies," Melody said, stirring up a ball of magic out of thin air, then flinging it at him. A strap of blue plaster slapped over his mouth, leaving a small breathing hole so he didn't suffocate.

Ondine couldn't believe her friend's restraint. "If I had your power, it would involve a hedgehog going somewhere tender. Sideways."

"That would be unkind to hedgehogs," Melody said, sending another blast of magic Vincent-wards.

He ducked and the ball of energy exploded, showering sparks over him and setting fire to his hair. Frantically he slapped at his scalp to put it out, but there was so much gel in there it only fanned the flames. He ripped the tape off his mouth. "Get it out!" He screamed in panic.

A flick of Melody's wrist and a bathload of icy water tipped over his head.

The crowd cheered and hooted their applause.

Shivering from cold and fury, Vincent rounded on Melody. "Seize her!" He yelled.

To whom?

Anyone, anyone?

Looking around, Ondine couldn't see a single person leaping to Vincent's rescue. There were a few cadets still hanging around. Sad, dejected cadets who had marched with Mrs Howser. Now that her spell over them was gone, they were creasing their foreheads and wondering what they were doing out in the streets at night.

"It's over Vincent," Melody stood toe to toe with him. "I don't know what I ever saw in you."

"Same here sista," Ondine said.

A shuddering sound came through on the wind. Staccato and rhythmic, like a ceiling fan cutting through the air. It grew louder and closer. A fresh spotlight fell on Vincent, from a helicopter, hovering into view. A rope ladder unfurled beside Vincent. He wrapped his arms around it and stepped up, climbing higher.

The crowd surged towards him, darting past Hamish and Ondine on the steps, pushing Melody aside in their efforts to grab Vincent. They were too late. The helicopter lifted Vincent above their grasping hands.

A woman with orange skin looked down at them through the open helicopter door. Her blonde wig flew off and fluttered to the ground.

The crowd burst into song, which involved a lot of 'na-na-nanas' and ended with 'goodbye.' Nobody was sad to see Vincent go.

"You didn't finish him awff?" Hamish groaned as he got to his feet.

"Oh, he's finished. Utterly," Melody said. "He's stuck with Babak and Ruslana in the heli. They'll probably take him to exile in Haute Montagne."

"Where's that?" Ondine scratched her head for a mental

Atlas.

"In the mountains." Melody shrugged, but her smile betrayed a secret delight. "It snows a lot. When it's not snowing, it's raining."

The crowds were still here, staggering about, aimless. Like the born leader she was, Melody set off sparks into the sky like fireworks. Showering the air with goodwill and love. The revolutionaries had a new focus: celebrations.

"Lord Vincent and Mrs Howser are gone. Brugel is once again free." Natalia Cebotari appeared with a microphone. Ondine hadn't seen any speakers located anywhere, but the former First Minister's voice rang out anyway. "Good magic has prevailed. Brugel belongs to the Brugelese!"

Politicians eh? Ondine thought. So keen to step into the spotlight the moment they got a chance. Quietly she turned to Hamish. "If I never see another politician or duke or duchess again, it will be too soon."

"As of this moment," Natalia declared, "All political prisoners or those charged with being out after curfew will be set free!"

The crowd erupted with cheers and began to chant, "No more Vincent, no more Vincent!"

"And another thing. The curfew is rescinded!" Natalia yelled over the screaming.

People hooted, clapped, stamped their feet, whistled, yelled and hollered.

Alexei appeared, racing up the steps towards Melody. They locked together, Melody kissed him all over his face.

Hamish looked at Ondine and winked.

Ondine nodded her assent. "Melody deserves a happy ending."

"As do we lass. Now, what's a lad got tae do around here tae get a lift home?"

An impromptu party erupted around them. Sensing a profit, fried cheeseball traders pulled their vans into the street, along with people selling all sorts of drinks by the cup. Euphoria filled the streets and people burst into song, turning Battlefront's *Anthem* into a song for the people. Refuse bins were piled together to make a bonfire. Cadets, now free from their dark magic spell, emptied their weapons and threw them onto the flames.

None too steady on his feet, Hamish leaned against Ondine for support. "Thank ye lass."

"We'd best get home, yeah?" Ondine beamed. "A good meal and a solid sleep is just what you need. And maybe some of Melody's magic."

Melody and Alexei were so busy kissing they probably didn't even notice the chaos around them.

"Awww so nice," Hamish said.

"Yeah. Let's leave them to it. They'll come home when they're ready."

They shuffle-walked down a laneway into Savo Plaza, stopping from time to time for Hamish to get his breath back. "Naw lass, I'm fine, let's keep going."

"I can barely support you as it is. If we keep going and you pass out on me, neither of us will get home."

Home, where Ondine could deliver the good news tinged with bad.

"I'm nawt likely to pass out," Hamish said.

Oh really? Ondine moved towards a bench, then shifted her weight just enough to make Hamish support himself. His knees immediately buckled and he slipped into the seat.

"That was uncalled for, lass," Hamish said.

A current of people moved around them, spreading the festive spirit through the streets of Savo Plaza and the steps of the Dentate. Getting Hamish through them would be tricky at best.

"Rest right here, I'll get you cheeseballs and something to drink."

He obeyed her to the letter, his eyes fluttering shut as the rest of him slumped onto the bench. Any moment now he'd be snoring. Good. Checking the crowd, she found people towards the right side of the street were moving towards Savo Plaza, while on the left they were heading out to the Dentate. She stepped into the current and made her way into the Plaza, where she scanned the crowds, the shops and the stage for her sisters and their men. She'd last seen Margi and Belle just behind the stage.

People were pelting the statue of Vincent with eggs, while other more sensible folk had set up a first-aid station and a makeshift treatment area. *Jupiter's moons, please let them all be all right.*

Scanning the patients, Ondine staggered in shock. Four patients, all very familiar. Thomas, Henrik, Cybelle and Marguerite sat on a blanket. Racing to them, her heart beating faster than her ears could hear it, she screamed out, "Are you all right?" She reached them, relieved to find them unbloodied and otherwise healthy. "Why are you here in the –" the rest of Ondine's words vanished on the breeze as Margi sucked a fast breath through closed teeth.

"It's not coming now, is it?" Ondine felt sick with fear at the thought. Out here, in Savo plaza, on the cold cobblestones! That's no place to give birth!

Pale face, dark hair sticking to her forehead with perspiration, Margi looked up and nodded.

"No. You're not having it here," Ondine said. "I'll get help. Stay here."

"You just said she's not having it here," Belle said.

"Not *right* now. I'll be back in a minute with Melody, Alexei and Hamish."

Turning around, who should she run into but Hamish, one arm over Melody, the other over Alexei. "How did you kn –”

"You were screaming loud enough in your head." Melody grinned.

"Right." Ondine went into organising mode. There was a baby coming! "OK, Henrik and Alexei, you get Hamish back home. Melody, stay with me and put some magic on Margi so she doesn't deliver in the street. Belle, keep Margi calm. Thomas, you and I are going to cross arms and make a seat so we can carry Margi back home."

Melody yanked Ondine by the collar and pulled her in closely, then dropped her voice. "I don't have magic to stop a baby coming."

"That's OK," Ondine kept her voice doubly low. "She just needs to think you do."

"Gotcha." Melody suffused the air with gold and blue glitter and sparkles that smelled vaguely of oranges and vanilla. It had a calming effect as Cybelle helped Margi to her feet, then into the makeshift seat Ondine and Thomas created with their linked hands.

"Keep that magic coming, it's lovely," Margi said, leaning on to Thomas's shoulder. She sucked in another breath and curled into the pain. As much as she could curl into that enormous stomach of hers.

Ondine said, "You're going to be fine, Margi." The lie came so easily she nearly believed it. "I doubt an ambulance can get through this crowd. We'll be home in a minute and we'll call an ambulance from there. Tell you what, Belle, why don't you run on ahead and make the call?"

"On it," Cybelle gave Ondine a salute and raced on ahead.

"Keep that wonderful magic coming," Ondine urged Melody.

Curlicues of pink smoke filled her vision as something seeped into her brain. It made Ondine calmer, her heart rate steadied. Her arms, on the other hand, burned from the strain. "Hey Melody, have you got anything up your magic sleeves to make me stronger? Sister here is heavy!"

"Got an extra life-form on board." Margi protested.

"You're doing great and I love you to pieces," Thomas said, giving her a messy kiss on the forehead as they marched over the cobbled streets towards the family pub.

From Melody's twirling hands and wiggling fingers came a ribbon of gold, sparkling around everybody, infusing Ondine with a cool sense of recovery. Her muscles had turned to hot blocks of wood, but the magic flowed through and big Margi miraculously lightened in her arms.

"We're nearly there," Melody said, spritzing them with fresh magic. "Almost home."

The sight of *The Duke and Ferret* hotel was like a refreshing drink. Arms and legs burning with the strain, Ondine couldn't wait to put her sister down.

A spasm clutched at Margi just as they reached the door to the pub.

Ma came charging out the front. "Oh my baby, my baby! You're having a baby!"

How clever, Ondine thought, for her mother to state the obvious. At least now they had extra people to help. In fact, there were people everywhere, holding the doors open, holding Margi's hand, making soothing noises and promising that an ambulance would arrive.

Arms aching from all the effort, Ondine stayed out on the footpath for a moment, rubbing her tired arms and catching her breath after all the excitement. So much had happened tonight, so much adrenaline had coursed through her veins she was likely to fall down if she didn't lean against the wall for support.

Her stomach plummeted when a police car pulled up to the kerb and two Fort Kluff cadets got out of the car.

"Ondine de Groot?" The female cadet asked, walking closer.

Ondine was about to say "Now what?" When she suddenly recognised the cadet. The scary-fit woman who could destroy all she encountered. The one who, perhaps a half-hour ago, had looked so distraught after Mrs Howser's dark magic spell wore off.

"My name's Raluca Pflugg. I wanted to help. This is the only way I know how. And I want to say sorry," she said, extending a hand to Ondine.

Scared of potential reprisals, Ondine extended her hand. But then her attention moved to the other cadet, who opened the passenger door.

Da stepped out. He made a few grunts as he did so, but he was able to step out of the car unassisted.

"Da!" Ondine cried. She pushed Raluca aside and ran to her father, grabbing him in a firm hug.

"Ooof, gentle," Da said.

There wasn't as much of him as she remembered. Less padding around the middle, more gristle, but it was her wonderful Da in her arms nevertheless. In one piece. Otherwise healthy. Tears blurred her vision. "I'm so glad you're out. And you're safe."

"We came as soon as we could," Raluca said from somewhere behind Ondine. "When Ms Cebotari said all curfew prisoners were to be freed, I remembered your speech. About how your Dad had been charged and, um, we went and brought him home."

Stepping back to take in her father's face – grey whiskers had infiltrated his marvellous black eyebrows – Ondine smiled anew. "I missed you so much."

"Me too baby girl. And I missed Henrik's cooking as well. Don't suppose there's anything to eat?"

His attempt at nonchalance had Ondine cry-smiling. "We never gave up on you Da. We did everything we could. We kept fighting."

Da said, "I know you did. It's why I'm out. Raluca filled me in on everything you did tonight. My brave baby girl, I love you so much."

Ondine was happy to surrender to Da's suffocating hug.

"Let's leave them alone," Raluca said to the other cadet in the car.

Ondine stopped the hug and turned to face the cadets. "Thank you for bringing Da home so quickly."

"Let me know if I can ever be of help," Raluca said. "If it wasn't for you and the Brugelish Resistance, I'd still be under Birgit Howser's spell. I did some horrible things under that spell, things I'm not proud of. If it wasn't for you, I'd still be doing them. Or maybe I'd be doing even worse things. Thank you for setting me free."

They nodded, a simple gesture acknowledging so much. Then Ondine held Da firmly by the arm and took him into the family pub. A cheer went up as they walked in, nearly blowing out the windows. Suddenly everyone converged around them, all talking at once. Crying, kissing, hugging, laughing, crying some more, sniffing, laughing and sighing in general exhaustion, happiness and amazement.

"Hey! Having a baby over here!" Margi yelled.

"You got back just in time," Ma said, kissing Da all over his face. "Everyone's home safe."

Resting on a nearby sofa was Hamish, a bowl of soup and bread roll at the ready.

Da looked around the crowded room. "Where's Old Col?"

Concrete poured into Ondine's stomach. Memories flooded back and fresh tears flowed. "Auntie Col was so brave. She . . . took on Mrs Howser so we could get away and start the revolution."

Da opened his mouth to say something. He and Ma looked at each other in shock.

Cybelle bustled past with the phone stuck to the side of her face. "She's just here. Yes. Right. OK, she's sitting on the floor. No I don't think she can get up into a chair at the moment. Right, I'll do that." Then Cybelle shouted to the room, "We need towels and blankets."

Margi grimaced through another contraction. Melody stayed close by, summoning more of her glittery gold to swirl around the scene. Ondine didn't know what the magic Melody was using, but even if it was just some pretty sparkles, it was having a calming effect on Margi, so she may as well keep doing it.

"We need to time them?" Cybelle said to the phone. "OK, that one lasted for about ten seconds . . . oh, you mean the time *between* them? How long since the last one Margi?"

Margi growled like a demon and spoke several swears into one long string of agony.

"OK, Thomas, you need to time the cont –"

Margi cried out in pain.

"That was another one," Cybelle said.

Ma turned to Ondine, her expression torn between wanting to know about her aunt and wanting to help her labouring daughter.

GrannyMa stepped in to the fold. "What's my crazy sister gone and done now?"

"She was so brave," Ondine said. She couldn't say the words past the knot in her throat.

In the background, Margi's moans turned into a full scale roar of pain. Melody swirled the magic sparkles so thickly it was a wonder anyone could see Margi underneath them.

Ma stepped away from her eldest daughter and came to Ondine's side. "Tell us the quick version then."

Like ripping off a bandage, Ondine blurted out, "She and Mrs Howser had a magical battle on the mountain. She sacrificed herself so the rest of us could get away."

Ma pulled Ondine into a tight hug, then kissed her on the forehead. "We'll mourn her properly when we have time. You've been so brave tonight, all of you." Then she let go and raced back to Margi's side. "I'm here my darling. Yes, you're being very brave as well."

Henrik and Alexei brought towels. Thomas was by Margi's other side, letting her crush his hand with each contraction.

"Everything's going to be fine," Ma said. "The ambulance is coming lovvie. Oooh, I'm going to be a GrannyMa!" Then she looked around and barked orders. "Henrik, grab me a tablecloth for modesty please. Margi, pants off, get ready." Then she grabbed the phone off Cybelle and spoke to the ambulance dispatcher. "This is Margi's mother, tell me what to do and I'll do it. Yes. Uh-huh. Dilated? How much? I'll have a look. Let me have a look Margi. Oh for goodness sake, I changed your nappies, it's nothing I haven't seen before. Oh great heavens, she's crowning already!"

Unable to look away, but not wanting to pry, Ondine crept towards Hamish on the couch to check in on him. He too had that expression of mild nausea mixed with excited anticipation. A new baby was coming into the world. But they really didn't want to watch it because it was kind of disgusting. And noisy. Maybe if it was their baby it would be a different story.

For now, it was best to keep out of the way, rest up from an insanely crazy night and let her body come back from the extremes she'd put it under.

"We're going to be SuperMa and SuperDa," GrannyMa said, giving GrannyDa a gentle squeeze.

Da knelt beside his Margi, holding her free hand now

that Ma was busy at the business end of things. Thomas kept making lovely reassuring noises, even though every bone in his hand must be crushed to powder by now.

Meanwhile, Ondine suddenly remembered something about washing hands and cleanliness, so she leapt up and grabbed a box of food handling gloves from the kitchen and started passing them around. When she came back out, Ma was under the tablecloth, Belle was reaching under it with one hand, holding the phone to Ma's ear. "Right, the cord's fine, it's not around the neck."

Margi cried out in agony. The wail of the ambulance matched the wailing of the purple (and pretty slimy) baby that rushed into the world with a ripe little cry.

"It's a strong little girl," Ma said, tears of happiness pouring down her cheeks.

"You did it!" Thomas cried in astonishment.

Da grabbed Thomas by the face kissed him.

"In through here," Alexei led the paramedics into the dining room, where they set about taking measurements and readings of both mother and baby.

"My little girl," Margi said as her baby daughter squawked like a bird. "Good set of lungs."

"Awwwww," everyone said.

"Have you thought of a name yet?" Ma asked?

Margi smiled up at Thomas, then back to their daughter and said, "She's our little Colette."

Da said, "That's beautiful. Hello little New Col!"

New Col. Ondine wiped tears away. She hugged Hamish and cried out her happiness and relief right along with everyone else.

"She can't be New Col. I'm to young to be an *Old Col!*" Ma said.

The paramedics safely lifted Margi and New Col into the trolley and loaded them into the back of the ambulance.

"We'll see you at the hospital soon," Thomas said,

giving Margi and his new daughter a kiss.

"I think this calls for some plütz," Da said.

"None for me, thanks," Ondine said. She was feeling so weak now, one sniff of the stuff and she'd fall over.

"I meant me," Da said, giving her a wink.

"Come on lass, we've had a big day," Hamish said, drawing Ondine into a hug. "We've earned some time off."

~ Epilogue ~

Life had a way of falling into a happy pattern of regularity in the weeks that followed. Not normality of course, because nothing in Brugel is ever really normal.

Cybelle and Marguerite still treated Ondine as if she were a baby who told fibs to make herself important, but older sisters can be like that at times. Ma and Da had re-opened the restaurant, the public bar and hotel rooms again and the place was as busy as it usually was in spring. Weekends were booked out, and with the curfew gone, people enjoyed their dinners late into the evening.
The sun shone that little bit warmer every day. Figuratively speaking, the cold north wind got the memo and calmed right down for a while, letting the gentle, early summer breezes come out and play.

The Duchess, Anathea had come back from her exile. The Duchess was broke, of course, so she urged the Dentate to give her more money so that the Venzelemma palace would be restored for posterity.

Ma made Ondine promise that she would never, ever, *ever* get involved in political intrigues again and Ondine readily promised. When a letter arrived offering Ondine and Hamish a commendation for their actions in restoring Brugel they ticked the "Please deliver my award in the post" box instead of the "I would be delighted to attend the ceremony" box.

The Dentate, led by Interim First Minister Natalia Cebotari, called for fresh elections. As the voting age in Brugel was eighteen, Ondine, being only seventeen, was too young to vote. The rest of her family, however, were excited by the prospect, and dinner times became fuelled with friendly political speculation and intrigue. The rest of the family were so engrossed in their politics, it gave Ondine and Hamish time to slip away unnoticed and have a lovely time together.

They were so busy being in love, they didn't give a second thought to intrigues. Ondine would never, ever, *ever* get involved with them again.

Or help them.

Not in the slightest.

She'd much rather spend her beautiful summer evenings working in the family pub with Hamish, even if it meant spending hours each day elbow-deep in sudsy water, washing dish after dish.

Every morning for the next month, Melody, Alexei and Ondine would help restore Hamish to a little more of his earlier Hamishness. Being unable to replenish himself by sleeping as a ferret was everything Ondine had ever wanted. Of course, rapidly aging into an old man was not, so they relied on Melody's extensive knowledge of magic and witchcraft to restore him back to full health.

Not that Melody stayed at *The Duke and Ferret* the whole time. She had a whole new career opening up before her, taking over the running of the late Birgit Howser's

Psychic Summercamp.

In a classic example of, "It's not what you know but who you know," Ondine and Hamish scored the catering contract for Psychic Summercamp. There may have been more qualified caterers in Venzelemma, but there were certainly none more loyal.

One sunny morning in June, as Ondine and Hamish they were unloading their latest delivery, a fresh group of witches arrived for registration.

"This food might only last two days," Alexei said, wheeling a trolley around to help them out. "We have so many witches arriving now, all times of the day and night. Word sure is getting around. Might have to increase our order to three days a week at this rate."

"Are you getting any more cadets?" Ondine asked. They were the ones who needed the most help, in her opinion. They'd been turned into fighting machines by Mrs Howser, they needed help finding their way back to being normal.

"Heaps of them," Alexei said. "They keep turning up asking for help, and here they are. We don't have the heart to turn them away. Like lost souls, really."

"Of course Melody wouldn't be able to turn them away," Ondine said. "She has the biggest heart in the world."

"Aye, Melody took you in, eh lad?" Hamish said, winking at Alexei.

Alexei playfully batted Hamish on the arm and pointed to more boxes of food that needed shifting.

Hefting a box of lettuce and cabbage, Ondine strode towards the communal kitchen. She was pretending not to listen, but she couldn't help overhearing Hamish say to Alexei, "Yer a canny one for securing yer privacy out here instead of staying at the pub."

Alexei furiously coughed in reply.

Melody came into the kitchen with a clipboard under her arm. When she and Ondine saw each other, they both dropped what was in their hands onto the nearest bench and seized each other for a hug.

Hamish laughed. "Ye havnae seen each other for three days, but ye act like it's three months."

"Hugs are important," Ondine said as she broke away from the embrace and started sorting through their crates of goodies. "And anyway, it's not like Melody holds your youth and longevity in her hands. Oh, wait, she *does*!"

"Come 'ere," Hamish said, grabbing Melody in a bear hug and making her squawk under the pressure of it. "How's my favourite witch today?"

"I'm good, and you're good. We've been working on a health treatment for you that you're going to love."

On they chatted, unloading groceries and checking them off, enjoying the splendour of the mundane activity.

"Can I come in?" A voice said at the door. Raluca Pflugg came in, eyes downcast, arms clasped firmly together as if she were sure to be expelled any moment.

"Ah, Raluca, we were just thinking about you," Melody said, taking the girl under her arm and bringing her into the centre of the kitchen. "Are you sure about this?"

"Yes, we all are, and you've already done so much," Raluca said.

Intrigued by the spy-speak, Ondine's brow rose. "What are you up to?"

"We've got something for Hamish, if that's all right. We think we've come up with a way to give his health a boost."

"Aye, and what's in it?" Hamish asked.

"If you'd come this way," Raluca said, her expression nervous and timid.

Curious, Ondine followed, pulling Hamish by the hand

behind her. Melody and Alexei came along too, a little slower than Ondine. She suspected they were being deliberately slow to sneak in some kisses. Couldn't blame them really.

They followed Raluca outdoors, into a garden area filled with dappled light. Here, dozens of witches and former cadets were standing in a circle, holding hands, waiting for them.

"What's this?" Hamish asked.

"It's our way of helping," Raluca said. "You all did so much for us, it's the best way we could think of to return the favour. Please, won't you link hands with us?"

Hamish took Raluca's hand in his left, then Ondine's in his right. She in turn joined hands with a boy witch to her other side. Melody and Alexei joined in a little further along.

Raluca started humming. The rest of them followed. A warm sensation filled Ondine as an overwhelming sense of happiness and good health vibrated all around them. It was similar to the time Melody had helped them transfer a little of their youth into Hamish just before they headed into Savo Plaza, but this was on a much bigger scale. The world shimmered and glowed as positive energy flowed through everyone like a living, breathing thing.

When they stopped, her darling Hamish looked healthier than she'd ever seen him.

"Weil," he gave her a wink. "I'm all ticketyboo again."

"You've got that right." Ondine kissed him with all her heart. It was one of the best kisses they'd ever shared, and she never wanted it to end.

***

And that, dear readers, is where we must leave Ondine and Hamish.

In the coming years they will have more adventures and tribulations as they grow even more in love with each other.

Eventually they will grow terribly old and wrinkled.

Some of Hamish's hair will fall out, but that won't matter to Ondine, because she'll consistently forget to wear her glasses and won't notice.

I think everyone can agree they've generously shared their personal lives with the world over the past four books.

But now they deserve a little privacy.

Probably a lot of privacy.

Yes, lots.

–THE END–

For the fans

If you enjoyed reading the books in this series, please consider leaving a review on your book-buying website of choice, to share your opinions with others. Reviews are like oxygen for writers; they help spread word-of-mouth magic in an incredibly crowded marketplace.

To keep up to date with Ebony's book releases, events, and shenanigans, come and get distracted on social media with her.
www.ebonymckenna.com